Memoir of a Man

Memoir of a Man

―――――――

A Quest for Peace in a World of Struggle

H. M. Taylor
& Andrea H. Taylor

Published 2014
by H. M. & Young S. Taylor

Memoir of a Man is story based on real people.
Names have been changed and situations fictionalized.

Art & Design by Andrea H. Taylor

All Fotolia.com & Andrea H. Taylor images used by licensed permission

Copyright © 2014 H. M., Young & Andrea H. Taylor

This book is for your personal enjoyment only. It may not be re-sold or given away to other people. If you would like to share this book with another person, please purchase an additional copy for each recipient. If you're reading this book and did not purchase it, or it was not purchased for your enjoyment only, then please go to your favorite retailer and purchase your own copy. Thank you for respecting the hard work of the authors.

All rights reserved. Please do not reproduce any part of this book without written permission from the authors except for the use of brief quotations in a book review.

Printed in the United States of America

ISBN: 0-9834394-2-7
ISBN-13: 978-0-9834394-2-4

This book is dedicated to
My Wife & My Daughter
Bright stars shining in the darkness

Table of Contents

1 - The Train 2

The Life & Times of Old Man Conner 7
   2 - War 8
   3 - The Bombshell 17
   4 - Change of Life 29
   5 - Hit the Road 39
   6 - Kit & the Madman 48

The Sergeant 63
   7 - The Gift 64
   8 - Second Chances 73
   9 - Boot Camp 85
   10 - Mitch Meets Korea 103
   11 - The Missing 124
   12 - Chophouse of Destiny 130
   13 - Taking Chance 137
   14 - Fire 151
   15 - Lessons Learned 159
   16 - A Time to Die 175
   17 - Going Home 198

Keeping Young 205
   18 - Young in America 206
   19 - Running Young 219
   20 - Young Life 229

Things My Daughter Taught Me 239
   21 - Life on the Rocks 240
   22 - Up Close & Distant 245
   23 - Sandbox Love 252
   24 - The Move 261
   25 - Legacy of the Rose 269

Epilogue 279
   The Visit 280
   The Note 285
   About the Authors 286
   The Farewell 287

Acknowledgements

Very little in life comes from the efforts of one person.
This book is no different. I would like to extend my
heartfelt thanks to the people who helped me

Co-authored by Andrea H. Taylor
Graphics & Design by Andrea H. Taylor

Editing
Young Taylor, Marty Haas, Jerry Weber, and Clayton Smith
Final Editing by 'Rebecca@rjthesman.net

Reviews
Young Taylor, Al Gilbert, Raj and Lekha Kanungo, Kelly Haymes
Rick Dumm, Ron Devine, Ed & Mary Grow, Todd Pittman

Patience & encouragement provided by Young Taylor

Gma & Gpa Taylor

Mom & Dad

Author's Note

When my daughter was quite young, we would go camping. Arriving after dark requires the car headlights to set up the tent. When we finish, she jumps up and down with excitement.

"Can I turn off the lights now Daddy?"

She runs over to the car, climbs up in the driver's seat, grabs the steering wheel, and leans forward to push the headlight switch off. In the sudden darkness, she lets out a scream of fright, then runs over and clutches my leg.

"It's dark Daddy, save me from the dark!"

The silence is overcome by the sound of a thousand crickets, bugs, the wind in the trees, and stirring leaves. An owl hoots in the distance. We stand very still and my hand rests gently on her head for assurance. Our eyes gradually adjust to the darkness and we are able to see what was hidden just moments ago. It seems the darkness has lightened up all around us, but actually our eyes have adjusted to the lessened light.

So too with us. Darkness can seem all around, suffocating… depressing. Yet, sometimes in darkness it is possible to hear and glimpse the most amazing things.

Edward Teller was a famous theoretical physicist partly responsible for creating the atomic and hydrogen bombs. One of the other legacies he left us is this quote:

> *"When you get to the end of all the light you know and it's time to step into the darkness of the unknown, faith is knowing that one of two things shall happen: either you will be given something solid to stand on, or you will be taught how to fly."* - Edward Teller

My hope is that this story inspires you to know that, in the darkest night, you stand on solid rock, and it is possible to fly.

Memoir of a Man

A distant train is mournful over rusty, weed filled tracks
It's ever, never closer as it pulls the memory back
Slamming close beside with wind and waiting at the rail
Then crossing into darkness with a woeful whistle wail
Pulled aboard the cattle car to see another time
The happy life, the sad regrets, song along with rhyme
Yet all too soon the destination grabs the soul again
A quiet tombstone little known by family or by friend

Chapter One
The Train

Traffic is light as I pull my little car over to the curb. A blasting horn blare startles me as a black pickup truck barrels past. I can hear a muffled scream as it fades into the distance.

"You stupid old man, get off the road!"

Speeding down the road he turns to glare at me through the back of the truck's window, mouth going faster than the truck and arm pumping an all too familiar gesture. In a moment he is gone and I'm left to recover from the adrenaline surge of his madness.

"What's wrong with people these days? It's Sunday afternoon. Where can he possibly be going in such a hurry?"

Then I remember all the times when I was the one in a hurry. Rushing, panting, and slobbering to get no place fast; all irritated with everyone in front of me and no one in particular. Many times I would race ahead, only to be humiliated; stopped in my tracks at the next red light as all the cars I had passed by caught up to me. Drivers shaking their heads, Tsk, tsk, tsk, while thinking to themselves; He's going nowhere fast.

"Well, at least I'm not going around blasting my horn and yelling at people with rude gestures," I mutter, trying to comfort myself. "No sir, I just think it in my mind and get my blood pressure all up in a tizzy."

After calming down I think, "Am I relegated to live a life of bitterness and rage, taking my anger out on some undeserving poor soul? Will I end up like my dad; angry to the bitter end?"

Stepping around the car, I move to the safety of the sidewalk and out of the line of traffic to avoid further humiliation. The two story brick house with the white porch is a familiar view. This is the little town which could be any town. The place of tense high school football rivalry and the home of my youth.

Years have passed since I've seen this place and it hasn't changed much at all. Only I have changed and it's evident as I trudge up the steep incline of the driveway. This same driveway I used to run up and down all day long as a kid is now like part of a senior citizen's obstacle course and I'm out of shape and out of breath.

The storm door on the porch is still loose, and it bangs against the peeling wooden frame in the pre-winter November wind. My knees are creaking as I slowly make my way up the reddish colored concrete steps. No bounding up those stairs like I used to do; all in a hurry to go nowhere fast. Now I'm a little slower... Okay, I'm a lot slower. As I struggle up those few steps, my diminished speed reminds me of my grandpa. Back in the day I was a young whippersnapper wondering why he took so much time to get where he was going.

"Hurry up, Grandpa!"

I pull at his sleeve to get him to move faster cause we just need to get where we are going! This particular day it is up the steps of his house where there are marbles to play with, and little glass animals, and all kinds of knick knacks on the shelves. But my most favorite of all is a small model train engine made out of thin tin and painted up real nice. Load two D size batteries in it, flip a small switch, and it chugs around on the carpet. As I tow Grandpa he just smiles.

"Hold your horses, babe. There's no sense in rushin' cause the train ain't leavin' for a good long while," even though the only train to leave is in his mind.

Grandpa really loves trains. We often go to the old Union Station on Market Street and watch them go in and out. He knows all the different engines and their history and the cars they pull and where they go. Then one day, as the golden days of railroad decline, they close that train station down. He suddenly seems to become old, brittle, and I can't find the fire in his eyes any more. That old station remains empty, unused, and untouched until after he passes on; almost as if in tribute to his love for her. Eventually a hotel and shopping mall go into the space but they are never really successful. It is meant to be a train station and nothing else will do.

Years later, when I am a young teen, a friend of mine is selling his model train that is all set up on a big board. My dad and I buy it for Grandpa (though I'm sure I probably want it more for myself), and we set it up in his basement. It had a tunnel and multiple tracks, little people and houses, and switches and everything — it is so awesome!! After I go in the army I hear that my grandma made him give it away. Took up too much space or some such nonsense, but then Grandma didn't really put up with any nonsense and didn't expect anyone else to either.

In spite of Grandma, my grandpa just loves everyone. He is the kind of guy who would give you the shirt off of his own back. My grandma is a different story. They lived through the depression era of the 1930's and she is pretty frugal with a dollar. Somehow they manage to pay cash for their house, their car, and help my mom and dad buy their first house. Even though they are frugal, they are pretty giving and always help us out a lot. There is no way to do anything for them but they would have to pay you for it. No sense in saying "no" either, because they just make your life miserable until you take the money. In spite of their differences (or because of), they always come out on top no matter what the situation; a blessing they seemed to pass on to my dad.

Climbing the steps to the front porch, I think back again on my grandpa's wise advice: There's no sense in rushin' cause the train ain't leavin' for a good long while. Grandpa always seemed so old to me and now it seems I've become him; old and slow of step. Now that I'm the one with the creaking joints, I begin to understand his slow 'patience born of pain' a little better. Funny how it takes us a lifetime to learn and truly understand. I was once a young man, thought I knew everything, yet understood very little. Now I'm an old man, realize I know nothing, yet understand so much more. I desperately needed that wisdom when I was young and wouldn't listen. Now that I'm old, what good does it do me? Before my mind starts to spin down that path, I shake myself back to reality.

Pushing through the porch door I latch it behind me and turn towards the heavy wooden front door. Rummaging around for my key gives me time to think that I really don't want to go in here. When I open this door, I'm not sure what I'm going to find. Just as well to leave it unopened and be done. But I didn't come here to not carry through.

I twist my arm at an odd angle to turn the key in the lock and it sticks a bit as I jiggle the key up and down. My breathing seems strangely labored as I manage to give the key a complete turn, and the tumblers clink into place. A wave of dizziness washes over me. I pause to catch my breath and rub at the stabbing pain in my chest.

Suddenly the door opens and I half fall through it. As I look down to regain my step, I freeze. In front of me are a familiar pair of old, dusty hunting boots with a single blade of bright, green grass stuck to one of the laces. I look up and gasp. It's a younger version of… me? He looks at me in his typical, all knowing, way. His voice is the same as it was so many years ago.

"Mitch, there isn't much time. Follow me."

A long time ago I would balk at my automatic compliance, would silently question his unexplained command. A feeling of irritation would rise in my heart and mouth. But now I'm so overwhelmed to see him... yet I hesitate. My heart and mind fill with emotion and questions never asked.

I think of all the regrets. The inability to break out of my own behavior to make a better relationship. All I want is to sit down with him and talk about things I can't remember. What made him do the things he did? What secrets does he see in me?

Am I simply a product of his madness? If I could understand him could I perhaps understand me? Before the thought has time to float away, I know it isn't true. I'm locked in a painting, unable to step out and see life from a different perspective than my own. He disappears into the hallway and I want to follow but my mind is in a dream and my legs are stuck in molasses. Everything begins to vibrate from the passing of a nearby train.

The sun slants through a couple of windows on either side of the fireplace, dances around on the polished wood floors, then cartwheels off of the floor onto the plaster walls. My mind begins to spin away as well. Leaping up with outstretched arms I grab at my thoughts but they are lighter than air. They fly away like a broken kite torn from its string and I can only watch as it flutters out of sight far beyond my grasp. Gasping for breath I feel myself falling as my memories carry me far away to another life I never knew.

*The Life and Times
of Old Man Connor*

Chapter Two
War

Little Kay! Skinny Kay!

The pungent, freshly mown grass presses against Kit's face. A sharp pain rattles his bones as a foot kicks him in the ribs and a stomp to the back grabs his breath away. He struggles, gasps a bit of air, as their taunts circle around him.

"Come on, get up! Get up and fight, you little baby!"

A band of kids watch the bullies attack. A girl laughs.

She's the one I kind of like, thinks Kit. Her laughter floats around him, so he is not sure he really likes her anymore. A burst of stars draws him back to reality as another shoe slams down on his head.

"Kick him! Kick him again! He's just a baby. Big Baby Kay with a stupid name."

Finally growing tired of their game, they leave their prey lying on the grass and run across the school's baseball field. A hot summer silence replaces the laughter, shouts, and taunts.

Just play dead. They always get tired sooner or later. It's just a matter of waiting them out.

Daring to slightly lift his head off the cool grass, Kit sees them running, jumping, and kicking up dust like wild animals in search of other sport. Kit lies still for a long time, to make sure they are really gone. Somewhere in the distance, a door slams and he finally raises his head to look around. At the edge of the field where the woods start, a deer stands and stares at him curiously with big brown eyes. It returns to grazing, then meanders back into the tree line and fades into the autumn leaves.

One final look around and Kit staggers toward the edge of the woods, to safety. Once he pauses, leans against a tree, pants. He looks around to make sure he's alone, then runs deeper into the protection of the woods. The other kids are afraid of the woods, but for Kit – the woods and trees are his only friends.

At home, he quietly opens the back door and slips inside as silently as possible, but his wheezing breath betrays him. Mom Conner's hearing is as sharp as a tack and she calls out from the kitchen.

"Kit come on in and I'll fix you something good to eat. You need to get some meat on those bones."

As he tries to slip past the kitchen, she grabs him to give him a hug. Then she sees his bruised face and eye, along with the dried blood from his nose. Holding him at arm's length, she leans her face in real close.

"Who did this to you, baby?" she coddles. "You give me their names and we'll put a stop to this nonsense!"

She lifts a freshly-washed towel out of the drawer, throws it into the sink and works the hand pump until the towel is wet. A dab at the face and Kit jerks away.

"Ow! You're hurting me!"

Lunging into the other room he yells, "Leave me alone, I don't need your help!"

Even as the words tumble out, he is sorry and hot tears trail down his thin cheeks. Later, Dad Conner comes home from his sales at the furniture store. Mom fills him in on the sordid situation.

"Babe, come in here and let me see what those kids did to you. You've got to learn to fight back and give them a good uppance. I'll go up there and give them a whupping they won't soon forget."

Mom and Dad Conner make a fuss over their only child, but Kit only feels humiliated by their love.

As the prosperity of the 1920's roar to a close, President Calvin Coolidge is about to turn over his reign to Herbert Hoover. In China, Chiang Kai-shek leads the Nationalists against the Communists in a nationwide civil war. That same year on a chilly March day in 1927, the wind rattles the the thin glass windows of the Conner homestead and their only child is born. He is named Howard after Dad Conner and Kay after Dad's brother, Uncle Harry Kay, but everyone calls him Kit. However, that doesn't stop the kids at school from discovering his legal name of Kay and teasing him unmercifully. They make fun of him, because he cries easily. So he vows to never 'wear his heart on his sleeve.' His schoolmates are all the more determined to tear down Kit's dam and witness his betraying tears.

The Great Depression of the 1930's leaves its scar on families across America as they learn to live with much less, while many have nothing at all. Although Dad Conner does well selling furniture to high profile clientele, the family is frugal and manages to help others who have nothing. Kit's love of hunting and fishing grows along with him, and he always gives whatever he bags to help feed poorer families. He loves riding to grandma's country home and spends days in the woods, away from the taunts of kids and the coddling of adults.

In 1939, Adolph Hitler invades Poland, and World War II pushes its way to the forefront of thought, eclipsing, to some degree, the ravages of the Depression. On Sunday, December 7, 1941, Kit is fourteen years old. He and Dad Conner listen to the Philco tube radio as it broadcasts the scratchy sound of a radio program. In the small living room, Dad Conner relaxes in his favorite overstuffed chair next to several shelves full of Mom Conner's knick-knacks; little glass dogs and cats and other who-knows-whats. Kit sits cross-legged on the floor, cleaning a rifle that lies across his knees. Mom Conner is on the couch, reading the newspaper. Suddenly, a news flash breaks into the radio program.

"We interrupt this broadcast to bring you this important bulletin from the United Press. Flash, Washington. The White House announces a Japanese attack on Pearl Harbor."

Mom gasps and Dad bangs his fist on the cloth armchair. A cloud of dust poofs out. Dad Conner jumps to his feet.

"That's it!" he bellows. "Tomorrow I'm going down to the draft board and sign up."

Kit grabs his rifle and jumps up as well, "Me too, Dad!"

Later that night from his bedroom, Kit hears his parents' lively discussion.

"Now look what you've up and done. He's our only child and you've put some hair-brained idea in his head to join up and fight. We could lose him forever."

Mom's just as steamed about Japan's attack on Pearl Harbor, but she's not about to back down on this. Dad's familiar refrain only incites her more.

"Aw, Mom, quit your yackin'. He's old enough to fight for his country."

Dad Conner always called his wife 'Mom' because his father addressed his wife that way. The next day is cold and clear as Dad, in a rare act of rebellion, pulls the black 1933 Buick onto the road as he and Kit drive down to the draft board. The nation is outraged and it is never good to outrage an American. The building is packed as both young and old men pour in, ready to serve their country. As they anxiously wait in line and then fill out the paperwork, disappointment is around the corner. Dad Conner is more than a bit overweight and past the age cutoff. Kit is three years below the legal age. Later, Kit heads for the woods to comfort himself.

Throughout the next year, the subject of Kit joining the service becomes a source of contention at home. Arguments fly on a weekly basis. Mom Conner can't bear to let go of her baby boy.

Almost four long years pass as Mom Conner maintains her impasse. Then, two months before his eighteenth birthday, Kit stands in line at the draft board building. His sweaty palms clasp the signed parental authorization form. Fewer men stand in line now, different from that December day in 1941, but plenty are still eager to enlist.

"Howard Conner," the brusque voice of the Navy Petty officer shouts.

Kit stands at attention in front of the highly polished, heavy wood desk. He tries to hide a cough as a cloud of cigar smoke spreads out and assaults his face. The large petty officer looks like a walking fire hydrant with a heavy steel, square head. Kit can't see an inch of fat anywhere. The petty officer shifts his weight. The chair creaks to one side and leans dangerously close to breaking. He blows out another cloud of smoke and taps his large cigar on the edge of the paper he holds. Ashes swirl around, caught in a sudden, warm breeze from the open window. Kit jerks his head away as the ashes blow across his eyes and face.

"Well, Conner, you scored very high on the typing test. We're going to train you as a radio operator."

Slamming the paper down on the desk, the chief petty officer grabs a stubby pencil and makes a few notes on it, then tosses it into a bin. Looking up at Kit like he's not supposed to be there, the chief motions with the cigar.

"Dismissed, Sailor!"

Finally able to join in the war effort, Kit leaves happy. He would have been thrilled to clean latrines. Kit's one friend, Shorty, has signed up as well. They meet outside and thump each other heartily on their backs and arms. With similar assignments, they are headed to the same Naval base near New Orleans. They celebrate at the local five and dime with a couple of cherry soda waters.

The staccato clacking of fifty typewriters fills the classroom as the Chief Petty officer paces across the front of the room. He looks at his new pocket watch, a recent birthday gift from his wife.

The room consists of double rows of tables with alternating bays just big enough for a typewriter. The surface of the table is waist high. Each typewriter bay is six inches lower than the surface, allowing the top of the typewriter to extend above the tabletop just high enough for the carriage to travel back and forth.

The recruits sit at their stations facing each other on either side down the length of the table. Each recruit is dressed in the standard white Seabee Navy uniform. The students wear small headphones with the associated thin wires trailing down the front of their shirts and plugged into a mass of cables on the floor. They have learned Morse code and the art of touch-typing without looking at the small round typewriter keys. The Chief no longer walks around with his long stick, to pop them under the chin with "Look up; not down!"

As their hands fly across the keys, most look straight ahead. Some close their eyes. Others stare off into the distance as though hypnotized. They sit for hours, translating the sound of code into key strokes. Each press of one typewriter key slams a lettered arm against an inked ribbon, creating a black ink character on the white paper.

The fingers of these soon to be 'radiomen operators' fly across the keys in a blur, most typing over one hundred words per minute. A few reach one hundred and fifty. The carriage is loaded with a single sheet of white paper that moves steadily to the left as characters become coded words and words become sentences. Upon reaching the page right margin, left hands leave the keyboard in a poetry of motion to slam the carriage back to the left side of the page. Hands and fingers quickly return to their entry task without missing a character.

"Time! Hands off the keys, all hands down, all hands down," the chief intones. He looks around the room for any violators who attempt that last illegal keystroke. This is the day of their final test, and the room is suddenly quiet. All students sit at attention as another Seabee moves around the room to collect the completed typewritten sheets for evaluation.

Later, in the Chief's office, three new Seabees stand at attention as the Chief examines their scored tests. "You three men scored amazingly high on the test with sustained typing rates of over one hundred and fifty words per minute. You will graduate at the top of your class." The Chief pulls out one particular sheet, and looks up.

"Conner… your rate was one hundred and eighty which would be unbelievable if I hadn't seen it myself. That's about the limit of those machines. Congratulations to all three of you."

The Chief stands at attention and pipes, "Dismissed!"

Afterwards, Shorty catches up with Kit at the barracks.

"Hey Kit, congratulations. I heard you're at the top of your class."

The white, wooden barracks consists of a long open area with double-decker bunks arranged across from each other in military fashion. Wooden footlockers at the end of each bunk complete the simple but stark layout. About halfway down the aisle, Kit sits on his tightly made lower bunk. He looks up from cleaning his rifle.

"I guess I just have a knack for it or something. I wasn't trying to type faster than anyone else."

Shorty snorts. "Yeah, yeah, whatever. Listen, you're the only one left here. It's Friday and everybody is taking leave for the weekend. Sam's dad has a place in New Orleans right down on Bourbon Street, and he's invited us to tag along. Come on, if you clean that rifle any more you'll have nothing but dust left. We can't be this close to New Orleans and all those dames and let opportunity pass us by, can we?"

Kit grins and nods, "Yeah, I guess not."

Sam is also a radioman. Since he arrived at the barracks a month before Shorty and Kit, he took them under his tutelage and showed them the ropes. Sam's father owns an apartment as a vacation place and allows Sam to use it whenever he wants.

Sam is one of the very few people on base who owns an automobile, also courtesy of his father. His car is a gleaming maroon 1940 Ford Coupe convertible with a peppy v8 engine. The move of the manual shift lever from the floor to the steering column provides more leg room and makes it a bit more comfortable for Sam, Kit, and Shorty to share the bench seat during the two and a half hour trek to New Orleans. They lower the convertible's top and enjoy the sunshine and breeze.

Sam parks a couple of blocks away from the apartment. It's impossible to navigate the car any closer as people fill the streets. Walking with the massive crowd, they manage to squeeze into a current of people headed in the right direction, then move into a large stream turning left onto Bourbon Street. They gradually drift to the right toward the apartment entrance.

If New Orleans was dubbed 'The most interesting city in America,' then Bourbon Street is the epicenter of its activity. Within this particular five-block stretch in the ill-reputed French Quarter, there is plenty to see. Shorty, Kit, and Sam stand on the second story balcony of the tiny apartment overlooking the busiest part of Bourbon Street.

Sam yells at some dame to come up and join them. Waving his beer in the air, he unknowingly sloshes it on bystanders below. They duck and yell back up at him. Kit and Shorty lean on the railing above the cacophony of activity below. Men and women hawk various wares all the way from popcorn stands to houses of ill repute.

Masses of people stream through the narrow streets in every direction. Some are quite scantily clothed, while others are well dressed. One gentleman passes by with a black top hat and tux. Shorty points and says, "Wow, look at that dame with the guy in the top hat." With the mass of people, Kit has to strain to spot the girl in the crowd. Then he sees her pass by a guy in a brown suit who holds up a poster of a girl with a gigantic snake wrapped around her. The top of the poster proclaims, 'Contortionist Girl,' in large, bold letters. The 'dame' turns out to be a lovely lady wearing a sparkling, white-laced gown. To Shorty, every female is just a 'dame'.

Shorty suddenly gestures in another direction and almost knocks Kit off the balcony. "Oh, no, that guy over there is throwing up on the side of the street! Hey look, over there…."

Kit ducks as Shorty's arm swings around again. "Those dames are waving at us. Come on, let's get down there and meet them!"

The two-day weekend passes quickly.

On Monday morning, Shorty leans over the gunwales of the small PT cruiser. The water is calm as they maneuver about a mile from shore. But the calm waters of the gulf don't keep Shorty from throwing up over the side of the craft. Kit looks over at him in sympathy.

"I told you not to eat all those eggs this morning at the mess hall. Especially since you were so drunk last night I had to carry you back to base. I saved your life from all those dames, you know."

Shorty moans and leans farther over the side. "Oh, my aching head."

The boat bounces, then sluices sideways as it hits the large wake from a passing ship. Then a harder bounce as the pilot reaches for his cup of coffee. He loses his grip on the wheel and the PT cruiser slams in a tight turn starboard. Kit feels himself pitched through the air and braces for a fall into the water. But the only impact is something that slams against his head. Darkness envelopes him.

Chapter Three
The Bombshell

An out-of-focus overhead light spins around, first to the right, then to the left as Kit becomes aware of his surroundings. Sunshine pours through the open window, heating the white, light cotton blanket that covers Kit's body. A slight breeze ruffles the short, white curtains and causes the window screen to shake ever so slightly as a bee bangs against it over and over in its quest to escape. The stark light fixture comes into focus as Kit slowly wakes. Hot and sweaty, he throws back the covers and makes a feeble attempt to get up, but he can barely move.

"Oh ho there. So Sailor Conner is finally coming back to the land of the living, is he?"

With great effort, Kit turns his head toward the door. A large woman in a white nurse's uniform comes into view. She sizes him up while nodding and tapping a clipboard against her chest. With each movement, the papers flap back and forth. Tap, flap, tap, flap — the slow methodical rhythm captures his full attention. As though time suddenly surges and catches up with itself, she bustles around and removes the knotted sheets that restrain Kit.

"Let's see if you can sit up a bit, eh?"

With no more effort than lifting a pillow, the nurse picks him up and places him in a sitting position. The world once again disappears as Kit loses consciousness.

"Ah, Kit da derereduiman ya wowa. Didn't you see de yaca do somma? Ha, ha, ha."

Muffled laughter and voices in the hall. The creaking of the door hinge, then click. Kit opens his eyes again which brings Shorty into view. This time he feels a bit stronger. The screen flaps with the breeze, but the bee, the nurse, and the sunshine are gone. Shorty peers out the window into darkness.

"Ugh, I neewata."

Kit moves his lips but the words only whisper through his swollen, dry mouth.

Shorty turns, then grins. "It's about time, Buddy. I didn't know if you were going to make it or not."

Blinking against the grit in his eyes, Kit struggles to prop himself up on one arm. He tries to speak again.

"Can a gisawala?"

Shorty snorts. "Take it easy, Kit."

Reaching over to a small table, he grabs a glass of water and helps Kit hold it to his mouth. A couple of swallows exhaust him, and he falls back in the bed. Kit tries his voice again which is now understandable though still a whisper.

"Wha happen?"

Shorty pulls up a chair and straddles it backwards. The screech shoots through Kit's nerves like a knife.

"I guess we're even now. You saved me from certain death in New Orleans, so I saved you from certain death in the Gulf. Didn't know if you were going to make it there for a while."

Shorty laughs full out then turns serious.

"What do you remember?"

Kit closes his eyes, thinking back, "You were sick."

Shorty nods.

"Our boat took a dump and you got a knock on the noggin'. I hit the water hard, then I surfaced. You were floating face down. We were only a mile out from shore, so I swam you in. Somewhere along the way you got hit by a swarm of stingrays. The sting from one could have killed you. Funny thing, they didn't bother me at all, not a one of them. In the base hospital, you got a bad case of scarlet fever. You're lucky to be alive."

Shorty shakes his head in amazement. Never one to sit still for long, he stands up and moves the chair back, producing another long screech. Looking down at his friend, he slowly shakes his head. "The amazing Kit Conner triumphs again."

Shorty has been around Kit long enough to know he always pulls out with flying colors. Kit tries to raise himself again and this time manages to prop himself up on a pillow. Another drink of water clears some of the gravel from his voice.

"How long?"

Shorty smiles again.

"You've been out for about a week. But I'm sure the duty officer will want you to report as soon as possible. There is one small thing you should know."

Shorty grabs a mirror out of the drawer and holds it up to reveal Kit's shiny bald head.

"Oh no!" Kit grabs the mirror with one hand and his head with the other. "What happened to my hair?"

In spite of his friend's obvious shock, Shorty can't keep from laughing.

"Don't worry. The nurse says it will 'probably' grow back. Your fever was so high, all your hair fell out. Who knows, the dames might really love your new look."

Within a few days, Kit recovers enough strength to return to duty. As a Radioman, his job is to listen to code that comes across the wire and translate that code into typewritten pages. His speed has gained him prime real estate on the commander's team which causes some longer-term radiomen to grumble at Kit's good fortune.

In June of 1944, a massive invasion of Europe by 156,000 British, Canadian, and American soldiers at the beach of Normandy, France, began the defeat of Hitler's armies. The Battle of the Bulge from December to January was the last major battle effort of the dying Reich, or the German Empire as it was called. On May 8th, Germany officially surrendered.

However, this did nothing to calm the threat of the Japanese. The battle at Iwo Jima in February, and the two-month battle at Okinawa left the Allied forces with large casualties. The Potsdam Declaration of July 26th called for Japan to surrender, but it was largely ignored and formally rejected two days later. President Truman is concerned that a land invasion of Japan will end up worse than the battles at Iwo Jima and Okinawa, so he makes a decision to authorize the use of a new type of weapon.

On Monday, August 5th, 1945, top secret operations are already underway for an earth shattering event of historical significance. Kit realizes he's only been in the Navy since January. He completed basic training at the Recruit Training Command in North Chicago, and was then transferred to his current duty station in Gulfport, Mississippi. Every few weeks he receives a letter from Mom Conner detailing how she isn't doing all that well and no telling if she'll still be alive when he returns. After reading another such letter, he crumples it and pitches it in the large trash can by the door as he heads out of the barracks for some chow.

Kit looks up from his scant Navy mess hall dinner of hot dog and beans as Shorty rambles up to the table. Shorty leans over a chair and rests both of his well-shaped muscular forearms on the table.

"Kit, Kit…."

Keeping his voice low, he looks around to see if anyone is listening. "I need a favor. I gotta' go and see this dame in an hour. How about you take my shift tonight?"

Kit purses his lips and manages his best frown.

"I don't know. What if the commander finds out we've switched?"

Shorty studies a crumb of bread on the table, then coughs. "Uh, well, I uh… I kind of already put your name on the duty roster."

Kit laughs. "Shorty, these dames are going to be the death of you, or at least cause you to wind you up in the brig. Give her a kiss for me."

But Shorty is already halfway to the door. "Thanks, Kit!"

On shift for his friend Shorty, the time rolls by quickly. As the fast audible code beeps sound into the earphones, Kit's hands fly over the typewriter, which is referred to as a 'mill.' He translates the code into line after line of military communications. Kit sits for hours, automatically translating and typing, not consciously aware of what he is translating. Suddenly the end of the page arrives, surprising him.

A little after 1830 hours, Kit is on full cruise control when the end of the page flips out of the typewriter carriage. Shaking himself back to awareness, he hands the page to one of the strikers, then inserts another blank sheet into the carriage.

Strikers are apprentice radiomen and part of their responsibility is to hand off the finished pages to the Chief. Several other radiomen are on duty as well, listening on different radio frequencies. If one of the radiomen misses part of the code, the others will probably pick it up.

The other member of the team consists of the Chief Radioman who serves as a supervisor and passes the typewritten sheets to the Code Room for decoding and distribution. Messages come in as five character groups of letters and numbers, thus the radioman typing out the code has no idea what message he is receiving. The Chief passes the finished typewritten code to the Code Room where the message is decoded into something meaningful.

Kit is almost finished with his next page when the door to the Code Room bursts open. One of the coders runs out, and after a quick conversation with the Chief, he hurries out the door with a large brown envelope. The chief turns to the men in the room. It's obvious that something big has happened.

"Gentlemen, I think we are a part of history. The United States has just dropped a single bomb on Hiroshima, Japan."

The radiomen look at one another. Allied forces, including the United States are still at war with Japan, so it isn't earth-shattering to bomb Japan. But only one bomb? That hardly seems noteworthy until the Chief continues.

"That single bomb is the first atomic bomb used in war, and the city of Hiroshima has been destroyed."

Kit will always remember one of the strikers, about to hand the Chief his coffee. The striker's eyes widen, his mouth drops open so far his teeth should fall out, and the coffee cup does a slow motion crash onto the floor. Coffee sprays across the floor and onto the Chief's starched pants. Yet, no one moves or reacts. The room grows silent.

Finally, the Chief speaks, "Okay, let's get back at it. Get that mess cleaned up and get me a fresh cup of coffee!"

"Aye, aye, Chief," is the only sound as operations return to normal.

Later that night, Kit lies on his bunk and reads one of his favorite gun magazines. Shorty plops himself on Kit's bed, snatches the gun magazine out of his hand, and throws it against the wall.

"Hey!" Kit sits up abruptly. "What's wrong with you? Didn't your 'dame' work out?"

Shorty just shakes his head. "This ain't about no dame, Kit. How in the world can you always be so doggoned lucky every single time something happens?"

At Kit's confused look, Shorty continues.

"The one night… The one night you replace me… that's exactly the time the message comes in that we've dropped an atomic bomb on Japan, and you took that message, Kit. Do you know how important this is in all of history? It should have been me taking that code."

Shorty walks back to his bunk and falls across it in defeat, muttering about the luck of it all. Suddenly the gun magazine smacks him on the back of the head, and he looks up to see Kit still lying on his bunk, pleased with his aim.

"I'm not that sure it's such a big deal," Kit says. "No one is offering me a medal. And, by the way, it is not the only time I have replaced you so that you could run after dames."

Kit ducks as the magazine comes flying back.

During the next few weeks, Japan officially surrendered to the Allied forces, and over the course of the following months, World War II came to a grinding halt. Over its six year duration, from 1939 through 1945, an estimated fifty to seventy million people from almost every nation died, and the entire course of history was altered. Once the war officially ended, the military services began releasing service men and women back into civilian life.

Shorty and Kit are transferred to the Naval Station at Millington, Tennessee, to assist with out-briefings for military personnel exiting the service. Kit operates the film projector in the out-brief classes and Shorty's favorite pastime is still chasing dames.

February 6th, 1946, dawns cold. By mid-day the temperature has risen into the sixties. Kit blinks in the sudden sunlight as he comes out of the makeshift theater where he has run the projector for an out-brief class. Shorty waves him over, and they walk towards the mess hall for some lunch. Kit yawns several times.

Shorty looks over at him with a grin.

"You were snoring pretty good last night, so don't tell me you didn't get any sleep."

Kit yawns again and nearly trips himself.

"It's those boring movies we run over and over. I think I can recite every word."

"How about we go see a movie tonight then?" Shorty jokes, but Kit takes him seriously.

"Yeah, let's do that. We can go into Memphis and get something decent to eat, too. Maybe you'll spot a dame or two, huh?"

Shorty looks forlorn. "We haven't been very successful with the dames lately, have we?"

Kit pulls open the door to the mess hall and holds it so a couple of WAVES can pass through. Shorty follows close behind. Kit smiles at these Women Accepted for Voluntary Emergency Service and follows behind.

"Who knows? Maybe tonight is our lucky night."

The two-hour bus ride from Millington to Memphis is fairly empty. Kit jabs Shorty in the ribs.

"Hey, go ask that elderly nurse sitting up there if she wants to go with us to the Malco."

Shorty returns the jab but a bit harder.

"Ha! Take her to the Theater? You go ask her. It's your idea."

As they punch each other, the older lady turns and smiles at them. Kit pushes Shorty out of the bus seat.

"See? She just smiled at you. I would never take your dame, Shorty. Trust me on that one."

The bus pulls up a couple of blocks short of the theater and they jump off, grateful to stretch.

Shorty starts out at a trot.

"Come on. The movie starts pretty soon."

Kit runs to catch up. "I'll bet you're really interested in the 'movie,' huh?"

Shorty shakes his head. "Might as well. Who's going to be there on a Wednesday night, anyway?"

A nickel bag of popcorn later, they are seated in the balcony. Shorty leans over to Kit. "You see what I see?"

Kit glares at him.

"Are you going to talk all the way through this? This is that 'Anchor's Away' movie and I've never seen it. Shh!"

Shorty ignores his rebuke.

"What do you mean, 'Shh?' There's nobody else in here except us... and those two dames that just sat down in front. Huh? Huh?"

Shorty jabs Kit as he cranes his head to see over the balcony.

"Ok, but I really want to see this movie."

Shorty plucks the popcorn bag from Kit's hands and stands up.

"Hey, quit whispering. You can see there's no one here, except us… and those dames."

Kit shakes his head and throws his hands in the air in resignation. Standing up, he smoothes his Navy uniform and straightens his sailor's hat.

"Oh, okay. Attack formation from either side?"

Shorty nods as they move towards the stairs.

"Implement the formation, Sailor."

The girls sit in the middle of the second row from the front, giggling over something as Shorty comes into the row from the right and Kit comes in from the left. The two girls are schoolmates from high school and just past their eighteenth birthday. Jo, the girl on the right and closest to Shorty has curly auburn hair, laughing blue eyes and a stunning smile. On the left, closest to Kit, is Marti, a fiery redhead with hair down to her shoulders and piercing green eyes. Both girls wear similar brown blouses with matching skirts and black flat shoes. Somewhat nervous, Kit trips and almost falls into Marti's lap before catching himself and stumbling into the seat next to her. Luckily, Shorty carries the popcorn. Still standing, he quotes his line.

"Hi, girls. Would you like to share some popcorn?" Shorty holds out the bag as if luring a mouse into a trap. The girls look at each other and giggle again.

Kit pipes up with his memorized line.

"Mind if we sit down?"

Marti looks down her nose at him with a sly grin.

"Looks to me like you already have, Sailor."

Jo, seated closest to Shorty, laughs then smacks her friend on the arm.

"Oh Marti, give it a rest, will ya'?"

She speaks with a pure Southern drawl. Reaching across Marti, she holds out her hand to Kit.

"Hi, I'm Jo, and this is my friend Marti."

Not to be outdone, Marti reaches across Jo and holds out her hand to Shorty.

"I'm Marti and this is my friend, Jo. Are you going to sit down or just stand there looking dumb?"

Marti has a tendency to say whatever comes to her mind while Jo remains quiet most of the time. In fact, she has just won a city-wide contest where she named Memphis the 'Quietest City.' She also won fifty dollars, which is pretty good money in 1944 — more than enough to celebrate with a movie.

Shorty seats himself next to Jo, Marti leans across her friend to talk to Shorty. Jo, on the other hand, wants to watch the movie.

"Marti, Shh. Will you sit down? I want to actually see the movie we paid for."

Shorty leans back and looks over at Kit, and Kit leans back to look at Shorty. Both nod, and at the same time, stand up, walk to opposite ends of the row, then cross each other in front of the theater, saluting as they pass. Walking back down the row, they take each other's seat. Kit now sits next to Jo, and Shorty sits next to Marti who sniffs and gives a toss of her blazing red hair.

"Huh, will you look at that? I've been spurned. We got ourselves a couple of wise guys."

While Kit and Jo watch the movie, Marti and Shorty talk the whole time and throw popcorn at each other. After the movie, Kit turns to Shorty. "I'll catch up with you back at the base, eh?"

Shorty grins and pulls an imaginary train whistle cord.

"Woo, woo, Kit. Moving kind of fast there aren't you?"

Then he slaps his good friend on the back. "You two have fun."

With his arm around Marti, Shorty escorts her down the street in the opposite direction. Kit and Jo start walking toward a nearby bus stop. The temperature has fallen into the 40's and she shivers a bit as the wind picks up. Bits of old newspapers blow around. Kit takes off his gray, woolen Navy pea coat and places it around her shoulders just as the bus pulls up to the stop. Jo takes the bus step first and Kit follows, reaching around her to drop a fare for both of them into the coin container. Before they sit down, the bus jerks into motion and Kit quickly puts his arm around her waist to keep her from falling.

The bus driver grins as they drop into a seat.

"Thank you Kit. I guess you saved me from taking a fall."

Jo smiles as Kit quickly looks away, a bit embarrassed.

"Kit seems like an unusual name."

Kit, glad to change the subject, explains.

"Well, I was born Howard Kay Conner; Howard after my dad, and Kay after my Uncle Harry Kay. But when I was a little tyke, my mom says I used to purr like a kitten, so they took to calling me Kit, short for kitten. What about you? Jo seems like an interesting name for a girl, if you don't mind me saying so?"

Jo giggles a bit, "Yeah, but it's 'jay, oh', not 'jay, oh, eee'. It's short for Josephine and everybody is too lazy to say 'Josephine', so they just call me Jo."

Their conversation is cut short as Jo stands up and jerks on the stop cord. "This is my stop."

Kit stands up and follows her off the bus.

"You don't live very far from the theater. That was a fast ride."

Jo is surprised that he has gotten off of the bus with her.

"Don't you have to go back to the base?"

"Oh, shoot!"

Kit turns around and runs a few steps after the retreating bus but is met with a blast of exhaust. He frowns and turns back.

"Well… how about if I walk you home? Then I can catch the next bus for the base."

She points to the house in front of them.

"I live right there so it isn't going to be a very long walk. The next bus doesn't come by for an hour."

Kit laughs, then pulls up his pants leg with one hand and sticks the other thumb out. He strikes a pose.

"Maybe I'll just hitchhike. I want to walk anyway."

Laughing, she pulls his arm down,

"Stop that, the neighbors will see you."

They stand in awkward silence for a moment.

"Well, I, um… I guess you can come inside till the next bus. Mom probably won't mind."

Kit sticks out his arm in a gentlemanly fashion.

"In that case, you can wear my pea coat to the door."

Taking his arm, they walk to the door, and Jo smiles. "What a proper sailor you are."

She suddenly gives him a quick peck on the cheek but before he can react she's through the door, and he has no choice but to follow her in. After meeting Jo's family, Kit catches a bus back to base. Jo stands on the sidewalk, watching him wave through the back window until the bus is far out of sight.

She doesn't remember re-entering the house or going to her bedroom. After a while of lying in bed, she jumps up and grabs a sheet of notepaper and a pencil. Then, stretched out on her bed, she begins to write a letter, "Dear Kit…"

Chapter Four
Change of Life

Mail Call! Another chilly morning and The sailors stand at attention while the mail orderly calls out the names of the lucky ones who receive mail.

"Carney, Dimons, Gantry…"

It has been several weeks since Kit missed the bus at Jo's house.

"Smith, Conner, Conner… another one for Conner."

The clerk looks up as Kit comes forward to retrieve his mail.

"Are you sure you aren't sending yourself letters, Sailor?"

Muted laughter echoes from the formation of sailors.

"That's all. Dismissed."

Shorty catches up with Kit as he walks back to the barracks with his stash of letters. He is already reading one of them. Suddenly, Shorty snatches it out of his hand and takes off running like a mad man, waving the letter in the air. Kit runs after him with a yell.

"Hey, give me that back right now!"

Shorty reaches the barracks and slams into the door so hard that he is momentarily stunned. He barely jerks it open and jumps inside before Kit catches up. Then he leaps from bunk to bunk as Kit races down the middle aisle to catch him.

Shorty pretends to read as he dodges a swipe by Kit's hand.

"Dear Kit…"

"I love you and I want you to know I love you, and by the way I love you. Love from Jo."

Kit pins him against the wall and snatches the letter out of Shorty's hand.

"You're just jealous that Marti dumped you after a single date."

Shorty leans over with a hand on each knee as he pants from his mad-dash run.

"Nah, Marti isn't really my type anyway. You've been seeing Jo every chance you get. You're not really serious about this dame are you, Kit?"

Kit falls into his bunk, still reading Jo's letter. "She's more than just another dame, Shorty. I'm saving up for a ring."

Shorty sits on his bunk and faces Kit. "Come on, Kit. You hardly know this dame… uh, I mean girl,

Kit glares at Shorty's use of the word, 'dame.'

"You've known her for what… three weeks now?"

At Kit's silence, he continues. "I'm serious. Take a lesson from me, Bub; dames is, dames is, dames. You're better off with a date or two and then moving on."

Kit nods vaguely, still lost in the letter as he lies on top of his bunk. After a few minutes of silence, Shorty gives up, stands, then walks out muttering to himself about Kit completely losing his mind.

Melting ice cream runs down the side of the cone and drips off Jo's hand. She licks at it but misses and it drips onto the dark green grass. Sitting side by side on a field across from the airport, Kit and Jo watch the planes take off and land. Kit calculates how much longer it is going to take to buy a ring. Their typical date is cheap enough. Walk to the airport, pick up an ice cream cone, then walk home. Other than the cost of the bus and a few personal items per month, Kit saves most of the fifty four dollars a month he receives from the Navy. By August, he should be able to buy that ring, and they can get married.

The sound of Jo's laughter snaps him back to the present. Her soft southern twang is like music to his ears. "I'll bet you didn't hear a word I said, did you, off dreaming and all?"

She leans over as if to kiss him on the cheek, then jumps up and runs away before he can respond.

"I heard every word," he lies as he jumps up to run after her.

A few hundred feet later, they join hands, breathless, for the walk back home. In the warm breeze, a Douglas C-47 Skytrain with its dual prop engines drones overhead on its approach to the single runway of the Memphis Airport.

As they approach Jo's house, Kit falls into a more somber mood. It's time to have that talk with her father. Jo's older sister has been married for several years now, and her younger sister will still be around for her mother and father to fuss over. Kit hopes Jo's father won't make a big deal about Kit's proposal. Still, he is an intimidating figure, and Kit respects him. He owns a sawmill, but before that, he and his construction business built some of the neighborhoods in Memphis. He even named two of the streets after his two eldest daughters, Louise and Josephine. Kit doesn't know much about Mother Hanley. She's is a quiet woman.

Lew Wallace Hanley, however, is an imposing man, who stands about six foot two, lean and muscular. His snow white hair is trimmed at three eighths of an inch and sticks straight up like closely-mown grass. His piercing dark eyes could drill a hole right through you, and his straight white mustache matches his hair: white and shortly cropped. Lew Wallace never cottons to any nonsense and sometimes entertains himself by making people uncomfortable. His daughters and wife referred to him as 'daddy,' but other people call him 'sir'. Only one other person ever dared to call him 'Mister Hanley' and that happened only once. On this Sunday, Lew sits in the living room on a burgundy custom leather chair reading a newspaper. Mother Hanley is nowhere to be seen. After Jo and Kit walk in, Jo gives her daddy a kiss on the head. Then with a nod to Kit, she leaves the room.

Daddy calls after her. "Hello, baby."

Without glancing at Kit, he speaks from behind the newspaper. "Shut the door. You're lettin' the bugs in."

Kit dutifully closes the door, then sits on the couch, directly across from the handmade chair. He stares at the back of the newspaper, then swallows hard.

"Sir, I was wondering if I could talk to you."

The newspaper doesn't move.

"You are."

"Uh, well, I…"

Kit struggles as his memorized script flies out of his mind. This is not going according to plan.

"Spit out what you want to say. I don't like a man who can't make up his mind."

The newspaper still hasn't wavered.

Gathering his courage, Kit manages to blurt out,

"Sir, I would like to ask to marry your daughter."

Inside her bedroom, Jo and her younger sister Jeri plaster their ears against the door. Daddy Hanley takes his time turning a page of the newspaper. The silence stretches on for several minutes until Kit nervously speaks up again.

"Sir, if you don't mind, I'm asking for permission to marry your daughter."

"I heard you the first time."

Daddy Hanley lowers the paper and squints at Kit as if sizing him up. Several minutes crawl by. "Once you up and marry her and take her home, you can't bring her back."

Kit slowly nods and tries to comprehend what was just said. Daddy Hanley brings the paper back to eye level to hide his grin from Kit. In her room, Jo and Jeri grab hands and jump up and down. Daddy Hanley's stern order to "Stop that jumping in the house" does nothing to dampen their enthusiasm. Jo never doubted Kit's intentions, but she wasn't sure if her daddy would scare him away. Jeri is thrilled to finally get a room all to herself.

The next weekend, Kit and Jo bump along in the back of the chaplain's green 1939 Studebaker Champion. One of the local Southern Baptist congregations offered it to the chaplain for a good price. With low mileage, it's in mint condition. One of their elderly members donated the car to the church, and the board members voted to sell it to the Navy chaplain. They considered giving it to him, but it proved to be too much government paperwork. After purchasing the car, the chaplain visits his family in Saint Louis whenever he can. Kit often rides along with him to visit his own family.

On this particular trip, the chaplain, a staunch Baptist, allows both Kit and Jo to ride along with him since they are now engaged. Jo is nervous about meeting Kit's parents and doesn't quite know what to expect. Kit hasn't talked a lot about his parents except to say his dad would love her to death. The absence of any comments about his mom concerns Jo.

As they motor through small town after small town, Kit thinks about how his mom wanted him to marry a local girl. Mom was crazy about one girl down the street, Mildred. She was one of the girls Kit grew up with and Mom made comments about their 'eventual wedding' as if it was already planned and a done deal. At the moment Kit's only memory of Mildred is when they were eight years old at school. He put a bunch of worms on her desk as a gift. Her reaction was not appreciative. For some reason his mom liked Mildred. Kit could only hope his mom would like Jo just as much.

As the chaplain brings the car to a stop in front of Kit's house, Kit scoots across the bench seat and reaches forward to pop open the passenger door of the two-door coupe. Mom Conner is in the front yard, building a decorative well out of stone. She wears a long dusty skirt with faded flowers on it. As the car pulls up, she stands and shades her eyes to see who it is. Kit waves and starts up the driveway, completely forgetting to help Jo out of the car.

"Hi, Mom."

The chaplain walks to the passenger side, helps Jo out of the car and unloads Kit's duffel bag and Jo's small suitcase. Then he motors off leaving Jo standing by herself with the bag and suitcase. Mom Conner meets Kit about half way down the gravel drive and gives him a big hug.

"Ah, my little kitten has come home to roost."

She starts to fuss over him and drag him toward the house. Kit wriggles out of her grasp and points at Jo, who has grabbed the luggage and started walking up the drive.

"Ma, stop it. Kittens don't roost and I want you to meet someone."

Mom steps back and places her hands on her ample hips. Her eyes narrow and she cocks her head to one side, frowning.

"What is this supposed to be, your servant girl?"

Jo sets the luggage down on the gravel and extends her hand.

"Hi, I'm Jo…."

Mom cuts her off. "That's a terrible name for a girl." Turning back to Kit, she grabs him again and tows him toward the house. "Dad will be thrilled to see you, Babe."

Jo swallows her disappointment, picks up the luggage, and follows as Kit looks helplessly over his shoulder.

A breeze rattles through the window, stirring the dust as they sit in the living room. The silence is deafening. Dad Conner pipes up from his favorite armchair, attempting to make Jo feel comfortable.

"How was the ride up from Memphis?"

Kit and Jo sit together on the couch like a couple of school kids in the principal's office, hands folded in their laps. Jo smiles.

"Oh, the drive was long and hot but it was okay."

Dad Conner nods and smiles back. Mom Conner pulls up one of the oak dining room chairs and sits with her arms folded across her chest.

"It's a darn shame they don't teach you to speak properly down there. That accent is atrocious," referring to Jo's heavy Southern drawl.

"Aw, Mom, give it a rest, will ya'? Why don't you go fix something for us to eat?"

It is not really a question. As Mom Conner drags the chair back into the dining room, Jo stands up and starts to follow her into the kitchen. Both Kit and Dad Conner quickly stand up, and Dad Conner grabs her by the arm.

"Kit, bring Jo out in the yard and let's have a little air."

Jo begins to protest, looking to the kitchen. "I should help her with the food."

"Oh no, no, we wouldn't hear of it. You're our guest for this visit."

Dad, still holding her arm, guides her towards the front door.

Later, sitting around the dinner table, the only sound is the occasional clink of a fork or knife against one of the dishes. Jo finally breaks the silence. "Your yard and home are very beautiful."

Ma Conner, sitting across from Kit, doesn't look up from her food as she says, "Kit, how much longer till you come home and marry Mildred, that nice girl down the street that you like so much? I've always said what a good wife she would make."

Kit slams his fork on the table.

"Mom, I'm marrying Jo!"

Dad Conner quickly grabs his beer bottle and drains it, choking himself in the process and spewing beer across his plate. Ma Conner turns to him and wags her finger in his face.

"I told you nothing good would come out of our babe enlisting in the service."

Dad Conner tries to respond but he coughs again and can't get any words out.

Kit, face beet red, interjects. "I make my own decisions and I'm not your 'babe'!"

Mom Conner jerks her head around as if slapped.

"You will always be my babe, and I warned you don't be bringing no low class Southern girls back here. They only make you miserable."

Kit jumps up and plants both hands on the table, leans over and screams back.

"I've never been happier than I am right now!"

Mom Conner stands up, throws her napkin onto the table, then stalks into the kitchen. The banging of pots rattle from the kitchen. Kit turns from the table and slams out the back door, heading towards the woods. Dad Conner finally recovers, coughs and squeaks, "Jo, can you please pass those mashed potatoes?"

Horrified, Jo complies as tears form in her eyes and splash onto the china plate.

On Sunday, August 18th, 1946, the weather is clear and fair. A few clouds scud overhead and a slow breeze blows in from the South. Air traffic is slow at the base as Kit and Shorty arrive at the chapel, in their full Navy dress uniforms. As Kit's last day on active duty with the Navy, this is also the day he will marry Lois Josephine Hanley, soon to become Josephine Hanley Conner. Jo determined to drop 'Lois,' a name she disliked, and retain the family name of Hanley for her middle name. Kit and Shorty speak with the chaplain for a few minutes, then Shorty turns to Kit and puts out his hand.

"Well Kit, it's been a good run with you the past few years. You're about the luckiest guy I've ever come across. Jo's a great catch, I have to admit."

Kit smiles and gives him a hearty handshake. "Thanks Shorty, but it's not like we won't see each other again."

Shorty nods and then breaks the news.

"Well, it may be. I've re-enlisted and I'm being shipped out next week for parts and dames unknown."

This time it is Kit's turn to nod, with his ever-present quip.

"Just remember, Shorty, those dames are going to be the death of you yet."

Jo and her sisters are sequestered in the small room that serves as the chaplain's office. Louise is already married and takes charge, experienced at weddings. Jeri, Jo's fourteen year-old sister assists. Jeri applies a couple of bobby pins to Jo's hair while Louise adjusts her dress.

"Is mom here yet?" Jo asks nervously.

The Hanley family communicates poorly with each other. Only a couple of weeks ago, everyone discovered Mom Hanley was upset because she wasn't the first to know of Jo's engagement. No one was sure if she would come to the wedding.

Louise adjusts the bow on Jo's long wedding gown.

"Mom's not here yet, but I'm sure she will be."

Jeri tries to be helpful. "Kit's mom has been here all morning, fussing over him."

Jo frowns, and Louise pats her on the cheek. "Don't frown on your wedding day. You're making lines. Things will be okay."

The door opens and Marti sticks her head in.

"Hurry up. You don't want to be late for your own wedding."

The chapel is a square white clapboard building just large enough for eight bench pews and a podium. Off to the right is a small office for the chaplain with an extra door to the outside. The office is just large enough for the small wood desk and two folding chairs. Jo and her sisters bring it to capacity and Marti has to wait outside.

The main entrance consists of a double door which leads directly into the back of the seating area. In order to walk down the short aisle, Jo will need to exit the chaplain's office through the door leading to the outside and walk a short distance to the front entrance. As Jo, Louise, and Jeri come through the door into the bright sunshine, they see Daddy Hanley walking up in his best white suit… alone. Jo stops short and bursts into tears as Louise and Jeri try to comfort her.

Her father stands for a minute, unsure of what to do. Then placing a hand on her shoulder, he begins walking her toward the front of the chapel. Louise and Jeri follow a short distance behind. Daddy Hanley stops just short of the closed chapel doors and turns to face her. In a rare moment of compassion, he takes his daughter's face in his large, calloused hands, tilts her eyes up to look into his, and speaks softly.

"Josephine Hanley, there's a fine young man in there who is crazy about you. Just keep your eyes on him and don't pay any attention to who is or who isn't sitting in that chapel. Do you hear what I'm saying to you?"

Jo nods. Pulling out his monogrammed silk handkerchief, he carefully blots the last tears from her face. Then offering his arm, he looks down at her once again.

"Are you ready, baby?"

Taking a deep breath, she takes his arm. "Yes, Daddy."

The doors open and they enter the chapel.

Chapter Five
Hit the Road

After living in Memphis a few years, Kit pines for Saint Louis and his parents. Every few weeks Mom Conner crafts a carefully designed letter to create maximum guilt. She explains how elderly they are, and how she is sure she is dying and won't make it through the week. She mails these letters after Dad Conner goes to work so he cannot intercept them and pitch them in the trash, which he has done a couple of times. Jo has been raised to respect and follow her husband. Even though she knows it will be difficult for her to live near a mother-in-law who hates her, she encourages him to move back to the Midwest.

They sell their house and live for a while with Jo's mom and dad. On a rainy Saturday morning, they pack up the last of their few belongings and put them in the back of the 1939 Model A Ford for the trek to Saint Louis. The weather is chilly with temperatures in the low thirties.

Father Hanley drinks his early morning cup of hot Earl Grey tea when Kit comes into the living room, grabs a small stack of old newspapers and heads out the front door. Intrigued, Father Hanley watches from the front window as Kit stuffs the papers under the front of the car and lights it with a wooden kitchen match.

"What in the world is that boy up to now?" he muses to no one in particular as he rubs his chin.

All three women in the house, Jo, sister Jeri, and Mother Hanley chorus, "What?" at the same time.

"Nothin'. I'm just saying… I wonder what Josephine's husband is up to putting a fire under that automobile, is all."

Jo walks into the room, still working on her hair which is full of curlers. "Oh, he's just warming up the oil so it will start."

Father Hanley turns around and cocks his head at an angle.

"Huh? What do you mean he's 'warming up the oil'?"

Jo shrugs her shoulders.

"When the weather is cold, the car won't start so Kit lights a fire under it."

Smacking his palm on his forehead in disbelief, Father Hanley slowly shakes his head. He walks outside where Kit is wedged slightly under the car, tending his small fire. Father Hanley approaches quietly, then stoops down and shouts, "What are ya doin' under there, son?"

Kit's head jerks up, and he smacks it on the underside of the vehicle. Then he slides out and steadies himself against the front of the car as beads of rain run down his head and neck.

"I didn't hear you walk up, Sir. I'm thinning out the oil so I can get old Mable started."

Every car Kit owned was for some reason christened 'Mable.'

Father Hanley nods, so Kit does, too.

"Thinning out the oil, huh?"

"Yes sir. Gotta' thin that oil before she'll start."

Kit continues to nod and grins a little, pleased with his technical knowledge of how the car works.

Father Hanley frowns, his voice sharp and icy. "Anybody ever tell you to change the oil in that there automobile?"

Kit feels his neck and face flush hot red.

"Change the oil? Why would I do that?"

"That's about the answer I expected."

Oblivious to the cold and the rain glistening in his white hair and mustache, Father Hanley puts his hands on his hips. "Have you completely lost your mind? You don't build a fire under an automobile. There's gasoline in there. Are you crazy or something?"

Kit starts to explain, "Well I thought…"

"That's exactly the problem here, too much thinking and not enough asking. Now put that silly fire out before you burn the whole thing up and my house with it."

Father Hanley runs his hand over his hair, brushes the water from it and walks back to the house. "And don't leave the ashes in the drive, either."

Kit stares after him. "But I have to get the car started so we can leave, sir."

Father Hanley stops and without turning around takes a deep breath, straightening up to his full height. "I said put that fire out and clean that mess up. There won't be no leavin' till that oil is changed."

He strides into the house, then closes the door just firm enough for emphasis. Kit takes in a breath and blows it out in frustration, then mumbles to himself, "Change the oil… nobody ever said to change it."

Later that day Kit, with Jo by his side, guide their happy Model A, with brand new oil and a purring engine, onto U.S. Route 61 to begin the seven hour journey to their new home.

When they arrive, Kit's mom immediately embarks upon a journey to make life as difficult as possible for Jo. Either silence or an insulting comment. Jo tries to make the best of it, but after a few weeks, Kit decides they need time away.

With permission from his dad, they motor out to the country house and stay there for a week. However, with the water supply limited to whatever they bring with them and the only heat provided by a small fireplace, living there is a challenge. In the middle of March, the weather is still cold at night and by morning the fire is always out. Kit figures Jo should get up at night and put more logs on. This becomes a source of contention, because Jo wants to stay in bed where it is warm. While Kit has a great time roaming the woods hunting and fishing, Jo can only clean the house so many times before boredom sets in.

In the outhouse she finds an old, beat up, copy of Jekyll and Hyde and relegates herself to read it. She manages to entertain herself for a couple of days despite the absence of several torn out pages. Kit expects her to keep the fire going and clean, dress, and cook what he manages to hunt every day. Life isn't turning out to be as much fun as it originally sounded. Jo doesn't know which is worse, the country house or living with Kit's mom, but after a week, she convinces Kit to go back to his parent's house.

It's difficult to find a job, and Kit is still unemployed after several months. No one seems to have any particular need for the services of a Navy Radioman. Then one day, the Conner household receives a visit from an FBI agent. Mom Conner answers the door then yells back into the house for Kit, "Some government man is here. Come and talk to him."

Although Mom invites him in, she does not offer him anything to drink so he won't be tempted to stay longer than necessary. Sitting on one end of the couch, he places his fedora on his knee. Kit and Jo sit on the other side, and Mom Conner listens from the dining room.

"I'm investigating a man by the name of Big Joe Cannon. Ever heard of him?"

Kit nods, "If you're talking about the same Joe Cannon I'm thinking about, I worked with him in Memphis last year."

The agent scribbles notes in a leather-covered note pad that he pulls out of his inside black suit coat pocket.

"Tell me what you know about him."

Kit purses his lips in thought. "Not much to tell. Is he in some kind of trouble?"

"Maybe. Best you tell me what you know."

"Well, I was in need of work, and he hired me right off. We sold musical instruments to families with kids so they could learn to play. Then we sold them lessons to go along with whatever instrument they bought. I guess I followed him around and helped out for about six months. Then he suddenly disappeared and didn't even give me my final pay."

"So you never saw him again?"

"No, never did. Always kind of wondered what happened to him, especially since he owes me a hundred dollars."

"What did you do after that?"

"Worked for my father-in-law for a year, then Jo and I came up here a couple of months ago. I've been looking for work, but not much around. What got your attention about Joe Cannon?"

Putting his notes away, the agent stands and places his hat back on his head.

"Seems as though he made a lot of sales but never delivered anything. His mode of operandi is to go into a major city, get someone like you to help him, then hit the smaller surrounding towns, collecting money from families that can ill afford it. When things start to get hot, he's off to a different part of the country. I'm thinking you were as much in the dark as the families he cheated. But don't be leaving the country anytime soon."

The agent winks and in one deft move, flips a card out of his pocket. He holds it out to Kit between two fingers.

"This is a friend of mine at the American Service Bureau downtown. It's also known as the ASB for short. They're looking for an investigator, somebody to start out. Tell them Thin Eddie sent you down."

"No kidding? Thank you very much."

Kit pumps his hand with gratitude.

Just as Thin Eddie turns to leave, he glimpses a rifle above the hewn stone fireplace. "Oh wow, now thats a real beaut. Where'd you get that muzzleloader?"

Kit walks over to the heavy oak mantel and lifts it from the wood pegs holding it on the wall.

"This is an early 1900's hammerless long rifle. It's a muzzleloader, typical of that time period. This one has been in our family for the past forty five years."

Thin Eddie blows out a low whistle. "Wow, mind if I hold it?"

Kit checks to make sure there is no load in it, then hands it over to Thin Eddie. He examines it like a delicate baby, turns it left, then right, then sights down the barrel.

"You know, we have a muzzle loading club just Southwest of here if you're ever interesting in coming out."

Kit's eyes light up and Jo smiles as she leaves the boys to their toys. Kit and Thin Eddie spend the rest of the morning talking about guns and hunting.

Several months pass by as Kit and Jo expect their first baby. Although Kit has sent out a multitude of work applications, no one seems interested in hiring him. Despite the recommendation from Thin Eddie, there has been no word from the ASB. For the last few weeks, Kit has accompanied Dad to the furniture store to help out with odds and ends and assist with deliveries.

Dad Conner sees the constant conflict between Jo and Mom, and he has convinced Mom to help Kit and Jo find a house of their own. Mom Conner lives frugally and counts every last cent. To save electricity during hot summer months, she won't let Jo turn on the stove. But once she makes a decision to help someone, it is all or nothing. She doesn't believe in loans, neither taking nor giving. It is either a gift or nothing, and she hates receiving gifts. Even when Jo helps clean the house, Mom insists that Jo be paid lest it feel too much like a gift. No one argues with her. She wears you down until you end up taking the money just to shut her up.

Once Dad Conner manages to convince her that Kit and Jo need a home of their own, she pays for it up front. A neighborhood is built not far from their present house, and Dad Conner, a great salesman, manages to talk the contractor into giving them the property at his cost. Construction is due to be complete in another month. Kit and Jo prepare to move out of his parent's home, but two life-altering events occur on the same day.

One afternoon, Dad Conner and Kit leave for the furniture store. Mom Conner grooms her yard: a picture of perfection. The short freshly-mown lawn and carefully primped flowers frame the hand-built decorative well, complete with Mom Conner's own handcrafted wooden bucket. White lilies surround the base, and the bucket sits on the top edge with roses growing in it. Mom Conner bends over and edges the grass with a large pair of scissors.

Inside the house, Jo runs the carpet sweeper back and forth over the thin living room rug. Then, with a broom, she brushes under the couch and retrieves a clump of dust. "Oh, yuck. I don't think we've cleaned under this couch forever." Grabbing one end of the heavy couch, Jo pulls it out from the wall so she can sweep behind it. As she sweeps, a mass of dust comes out, along with a dirty, white envelope. Jo gets down on her knees to pick it up, shakes and blows on it a couple of times which elicits a cloud of dust. Turning it over it is addressed to Howard Kit Conner.

Suddenly a demanding voice behind Jo asks, "What are you looking for back there?"

Caught by surprise, Jo jumps up, hits her shoulder on the couch and loses her balance. As she sprawls backward onto the floor, she hits her head on a nearby table leg. Mom Conner reaches down to snatch the letter, but Jo jerks it back and manages to jump up.

Mom Conner faces off. "What have you got there? Give me that letter right now."

Jo puts the letter behind her back.

"No. It's addressed to Kit."

"Kit is my concern. Now give it to me."

"Kit is *my* husband. He's not your 'babe' anymore!"

Jo rips the envelope open, pulls the letter out, and throws the empty envelope at Mom. Then she dodges past her, runs into their bedroom and locks the door, collapsing on the bed in tears.

In a moment Mom's voice is outside. "You've ruined this house. Do you hear me? You've never belonged here, why don't you go back where you came from?" She bangs on the door. "Open this door right now."

Suddenly Jo's stomach knots with cramps as she goes into premature labor. Gasping and stumbling towards the door, she falls onto the floor in pain, holding her stomach.

Mom Conner continues her assault on the door with her large leathery hands. "I said open this door right now. This isn't your house. Open it before I break it down!"

Jo manages to drag herself to the door, reaches up and unlocks it. Mom Conner shoves the door open, sending Jo sprawling across the floor in a pool of blood.

"Now look what you've done. This is a fine mess you've made. Where is that letter?"

Looking around the room, she sees it on the bed and snatches it up. Then, grabbing Jo by the arm, Mom Conner half drags her across the floor, into the hall and to the nearby bathroom.

"Come on. Get cleaned up while I mop the floor, if it isn't ruined already."

Then she marches out leaving Jo on the floor, crying.

Later, Jo hears the sound of Dad Conner and Kit laughing over some event of the day as they approach the house. The front door slams shut and Dad Conner notices Mom Conner sitting on the couch which is very atypical for her.

"What's wrong with you? Are you sick? How come you're not out in the yard?"

"Where is Jo?" Kit asks.

"Your lazy wife is lying in bed, resting. She's had a bit of a day today and I've had to take care of her. And by the way, this letter came for you, but she already opened it."

Mom sits on the couch and holds out the letter.

Kit walks over and takes the letter, unfolds it and starts to read.

"Oh, this is from the American Service Bureau. Oh, wow! They accepted my application as of… what?"

Kit holds the letter closer to make sure the date is correct.

"Wait a minute… this is dated almost two months ago." He looks up in confusion.

"Your wife was cleaning behind the couch this afternoon and found an envelope with that in it."

Kit tries to figure out what is really going on.

Mom Conner continues. "I told her not to be cleaning in her condition, but you know she never listens. I warned you that marrying a Southern girl was going to lead to disaster."

"Mom! What are you saying? What happened?"

"She lost the baby, pure and simple. I warned…."

Kit runs out of the room as he yells, "Jo!"

Chapter Six
Kit and the Madman

For a few days after the loss of the baby, Mom Conner manages to constrain her mouth. The Conner household is eerily quiet. Jo wanders from one room to the next while Kit and Dad Conner, oblivious to Jo's pain, enjoy the unusual calm. Fairly soon, however, the normal tension returns.

Kit and Jo move into their new home over the protests of Mom Conner. Even though she paid for the house, she accuses Dad Conner of 'tricking her into it,' but it is already a done deal. Doing her best to be a good wife, Jo takes care of the house and the yard work, makes sure dinner is on the table, and generally takes good care of her husband.

Kit goes down to the ASB office and is hired on the spot. He is responsible to investigate health insurance claims, looking for any possible fraud. Some people apply under different names for multiple insurance policies for the same injury, or they claim to be more disabled than they really are. By investigating and refusing to pay on these types of fraudulent claims, the insurance companies save quite a bit of money.

Part of the investigator's job involves typing reports to submit back to the companies. This is where Kit excels. His one hundred and eighty words-per-minute typing speed has slowed a bit, but is still well over one hundred. This enables him to quickly pound out the reports with almost no errors. During the day, he searches police and hospital records, then talks to any number of people, including the insured themselves. People seem to inherently trust him and tell him anything he asks, an art passed to him by his father. A number of people actually admit to cheating the insurance companies in one way or another.

One of Kit's first investigations nearly stops the Conner family in their tracks. The weather is muggy with a high temperature and an even higher humidity. It's the kind of day Kit wants to dive fully dressed into a pool of water because his clothes are soaked through anyway. Stopping by the office, Kit picks up his caseload for the day. Art, the case manager, calls him over. "Let's go in my office."

Kit follows him in and sits down.

After lighting up a cigarette, Art pitches the heavy brass flip lighter onto the desk and picks up a file folder that lies on a heap of other papers. Opening the folder, he takes a draw on the cigarette and exhales a stream of smoke onto the forms. The smoke hits the paper and clouds across the dark oak desktop. He pokes at the form in his hand.

"Here it is. Yesterday you interviewed a Mr. Solomon. Your report looks fairly complete."

Art begins to read through the report.

"Mr. Solomon is a fifty year-old male, living in the twenty two hundred block of Oleosee and so forth. Then you provide some previous medical history, a description of his recent injury at work and information from interviewing the neighbors. Can you think of anything you may have overlooked?"

Kit rubs his chin and then shakes his head.

"No, that's about it."

"How about the small detail that Mr. Solomon has been confined to a wheelchair for the last ten years because he lost both of his legs during the war? Did that seem unnoticeable to you?"

Kit's face turns red and, always honest, blurts out, "He didn't have any legs? I had no idea."

Art starts laughing.

"Yes, that's pretty evident. As an investigator, you have to be aware of every little detail."

"Well, come to think of it, I did notice he had a blanket over what I thought were his legs."

Art nods, still chuckling and throws another manila folder across the desk to him.

"You're new at this, but you'll pick it up. Just remember to take good notes, pay attention to your surroundings, and include 'everything' in your reports. Otherwise we are losing money."

Art points at the new folder. "This is a case no one else wants to take. You want to look into it?"

It's a lame question. Kit is thrilled to be working as an investigator and would happily even mop the floors.

"Sure, I'll take it."

"Well, be careful. This guy is claiming he's disabled, but his wife says he's a nutcase, a real crackerjack. Find out what's going on."

Kit parks his company provided dark grey sedan on the city street next to a crumbling concrete curb. There is no parking meter to fool with and several nearby buildings are boarded up. Once thriving businesses were unable to survive the deteriorating economy in this part of town. The street is deserted as Kit climbs out of the car and walks toward an old brick apartment building. The entrance door has several sheets of peeling plywood nailed over broken out glass. Stepping into the gloomy hallway brings a feeling of suffocation and a foul odor. Apartment 101. Kit raps on the door but there is no response. After waiting a few seconds, he knocks harder.

"I hear ya'. Get out of here, I'm not talking to anyone." Kit frowns, unsure how to proceed. He leans close to the door.

"My name is Kit Conner. I'm here about your insurance claim."

"Go away or you'll be sorry."

Kit thinks he can't be much sorrier than he already is.

"This will only take a few minutes, sir."

"Alright then, come on in but don't say I didn't warn you."

Kit waits but no one opens the door.

"Hello, should I just come in?"

Silence. After a few more minutes, Kit gingerly turns the knob and the door creaks open.

"Hello, okay to come in?"

No sound. Kit steps into the apartment, then pushes the door shut behind him. As he turns around, he instantly freezes. Across the tiny room, a middle-aged man sits on a couch. He holds a double-barreled shotgun and aims square at Kit's chest. Both barrels are cocked, and the man's finger nervously twitches on the trigger. One tiny jerk of his finger and Kit will be dead.

Kit's mind races. There seems only one conclusion — just try to ignore the shotgun.

"How are you doing today?"

His voice comes out high and squeaky. Clearing his throat he tries again. "I guess that was a stupid question. You want to tell me why you want to shoot me?"

Kit stands motionless and tries not to stare at the trigger. The man's finger continues to twitch.

"I told you to stay out. I warned you."

Kit slowly nods.

"You did that all right. But it looks to me like you could use somebody to talk to."

"Why should I talk to you? You don't care about me!"

"Maybe I do, and maybe I don't. But at least I'll listen to what you have to say. I'm going to sit down in this chair right here, okay."

The man slowly nods. "Go ahead then. Funny how a loaded gun

makes a person real polite and careful, ain't it?"

Kit sits down with his note binder across his lap.

"I have a respect for guns. That looks like a Savage/Fox Model B."

"Yeah, what if it is? You a cop or something?"

"No, I'm an insurance investigator, but I like hunting and guns are a hobby of mine."

"Yeah? What do you hunt?"

"Mainly deer, up around Northeastern Missouri."

Shotgun man takes his hand off the trigger and places both hands on top of the gun as he leans forward, suddenly interested.

"Up around Lewistown?"

"Yes, sir. Lot of big bucks up in that area."

Kit watches closely to see how careless the man might be.

"Sure are! I really used to love hunting up there."

Kit reaches into his shirt pocket for a cigarette.

In an instant, the shotgun muzzle is pointed in Kit's face again. "Don't move that hand any farther. What do you think you're trying to pull?"

Kit slowly pulls a crumbled pack of cigarettes out of his pocket and shows the man.

"You seem like a reasonable man. I'm kind of nervous. Mind if I have a last smoke?"

Lowering the gun, the man relaxes his grip a little and slightly nods. "Yeah, go ahead."

Kit can tell this guy is on the edge so he tries to keep him talking. "So what's your name?"

Pulling out a silver flip lighter from between the pack and cellophane, Kit lights his cigarette, then holds the pack out to the man who simply stares at him.

"Cigarettes will kill you."

Putting the pack back in his pocket, Kit continues. "Folks call me Kit even though my real name is Kay."

"Yeah? Kay's a funny name."

"I get that a lot. I was named after my uncle, Harry Kay."

"Well, my name is Harvey."

"Nice to meet you, Harvey. I don't have to be a detective to see there's something on your mind."

"Do you have a wife, Kit?"

Kit swallows hard.

"That I do, Harvey."

"I did, too, until last week."

Breaking into a cold sweat, Kit stares at the gun and then he asks, "You did?"

"Sure did… until she ran off with my best friend! You work hard your whole life so she can have the best of everything, then she runs off with your best friend. But you know what I'm talking about."

Relieved, Kit nods vigorously and says, "Oh yeah," even though he hasn't a clue.

Harvey continues. "My best friend, can you believe it? Can't trust nobody nowadays. I thought she really loved me. I got nothin' to live for no more."

"Do you have any kids?"

"Norma never wanted kids. I always wanted four kids."

Not knowing what else to say Kit asks, "Do you have a dog?"

"She took the doggoned dog."

Harvey starts crying.

"Harley was the best bird dog this side of the Mississippi."

Kit tries to get Harvey's mind elsewhere.

"What kind of bird do you hunt, Harvey?"

Harvey wipes his eyes and perks up a little.

"Dove. Lots of dove up in those bean fields."

"Never hunted dove much. Was more of a pheasant man myself. Be about the same process, I wager."

"Oh no, no. Not at all."

Harvey lays the gun across his lap so he can gesture freely. He talks on and on about hunting and fishing for about an hour until he's pretty much talked out. As he lapses into silence, he stares halfheartedly at the gun.

Kit speaks softly, "So, are you gonna let her win?"

"Huh? You mean my wife? It's like I told you, she took everything I had; my house, my money…"

"Well, if you shoot me and yourself, she's the one who wins in the end, doesn't she?"

"Wins? Wins what?"

"You said it yourself. She has the house, the money, a new man, and you're completely out of the picture. If it were me, I wouldn't just give up without a fight. Then there's the insurance…"

Jumping up from the couch, he gestures with the shotgun.

"Doggone it boy, you're absolutely right! She's trying to trick me so's she can get even more out of me. I never even thought about the life insurance policy. That old hag. If it wasn't for you, I would have fallen right into her trap."

Kit knows that no policy would pay out if this guy murdered someone and then killed himself. But he is counting on the fact that Harvey won't know that.

Kit takes another chance and stands up. "Well, I'm only trying to help out."

Setting the shotgun against the couch, Harvey comes over, grabs Kit's hand and pumps it vigorously.

"Well, I sure do thank you for stopping by. I think you surely saved my life, you did."

Harvey continues to babble about how grateful he is as he escorts Kit the few steps to the door and bids him farewell.

Once out of the building Kit jogs to his car and jumps in, looking back to make sure Harvey didn't suddenly change his mind. Pulling his keys from his jacket pocket, he drops them twice and shakes so badly that it's hard to shove the keys into the ignition. A couple of hours later, Harvey is taken into custody without a fight. Kit answers questions at the police station. The burly detective looks up from his stack of paperwork.

"Anything else you want to add to this?"

Kit takes a long draw on his fifth cigarette. "I think that's all."

The detective nods and chuckles as he throws the forms to the side of his desk.

"Still a little nervous? I don't blame you a bit. You know those cigarettes will kill you some day."

Pulling out a pack, the detective lights up one for himself.

"You'll get over it soon enough. I have to say you're a lucky guy, Conner. You talked the guy down and that takes a lot of guts. When we arrived, he was as cooperative as can be."

"What was I going to do? He had the gun, not me."

The detective nods.

"Still, you did the right thing. If you tried to rush him, it could have ended differently. Being an investigator, you may want to get yourself some protection, you know."

He pats his shoulder holster, but Kit shakes his head.

"I don't know. Hunting is one thing, but shooting a person is something else. I don't know if I could do that."

As the detective walks out with Kit, they discuss guns and hunting. Kit makes several friends at the station.

A couple of weeks later Kit walks into the office. Everyone jumps up and yells, "Surprise!" Kit, never one for attention, tries to duck out the door. But Art catches him by the arm and leads him over to his desk where he is presented with an embroidered cloth wall hanging. It reads

'LIKE A ROSE AWARD,'
'PRESENTED TO KIT CONNER'.

Kit feels his face turn red as he mumbles, "What's this for?"

Art explains, "After that guy almost killed you, we figured the least we could do is get something to celebrate the fact that you're still alive. Sal mentioned that you came out 'smelling like a rose,' so she sewed this for you."

Sally, the secretary, has been a fixture around the office for many years, so everyone just calls her Sal.

Sal pats Kit on the back. "Oh Art, you don't know anything. That's not sewing; it's embroidery."

"Kit, we're just glad you came out of it okay."

Kit smiles broadly.

"No more than I, Sal, no more than I."

A few months later Jo becomes pregnant again, but it ends in horrible disappointment. She loses the baby within six months. Whenever they visit Kit's parents, Mom Conner takes every opportunity to remind her about these losses, especially that first time in her house. Finally, Kit has had enough, and their visits are reduced to major holidays and their birthdays.

Not seeing her babe for most of the year leaves Mom Conner lonely and miserable, but Dad Conner carries the brunt of it. Many times he's tried to reason with her to 'stop complaining and criticizing Jo' so they can visit together in harmony. But Mom just can't seem to do it. No matter how hard she tries, eventually she ends up saying the wrong thing. Being around 'Little Miss Southern Perfect' rubs her the wrong way, and Mom's mouth doesn't seem to have an 'off' switch. Whatever comes to her mind just pops out.

Dad Conner is gentle and has an easy going style and personality that calms the soul. He has learned long ago to just leave her be and go with the flow. Still, he misses his son and daughter-in-law, especially when they live so close. But even though he seldom agrees with Mom, he always stands by her. He isn't shy about letting her know what he thinks on any subject, including her behavior, and he often acts as a shield between her razor sharp personality and other people. But he would never betray her, or do something behind her back — including visit Kit and Jo without her.

Those same qualities of honesty, integrity, and loyalty make Howard Raymond Conner a successful salesman. People immediately like his humble, honest, yet direct personality, and he never attempts to make a dishonest penny. He has quite a loyal following of customers who refuse to do business with anyone else. They tell all their friends to buy from Howard. His success in sales, even during the depression, and Mom's careful frugality, enables them to save enough money to pay cash for everything. This includes big-ticket items like automobiles and homes. It also enables them to help other people who are less fortunate. Even though they do have a small amount of money saved up, they never make a big deal of it.

In 1955, Brooklyn wins the World Series over the New York Yankees: 4-3. Rudolph Flesch publishes 'Why Johnny Can't Read.' Dr. Martin Luther King, Jr. leads the first major civil rights movement event. Albert Einstein dies, and Jo becomes pregnant for the third time. In an era when women are still considered somewhat less than a man, Kit continually berates her and believes she exists to take care of him.

Jo decides this must be how life works and does her best to comply. She keeps the house and yard in order, cooks and serves Kit. She always wanted to be married and have a family, so if this is the best it is, then it is what it is. But they do hang out with their friends which gives Jo some solace. It's especially fun to take the model A on an outing. With a rumble seat installed in the trunk area, four of their friends ride along; two in the back seat and two squeezed in the rumble seat.

One day Kit decides to sell their Model A Ford with the rumble seat and comes home with an MG model TC sports car, a two-seater. He can't understand why Jo is so upset. It never occurs to him that he should ask her opinion about anything.

In May of 1956, Jo safely passes her sixth month mark, and the baby is healthy. Then, in mid-August, she goes into labor and delivers a baby boy christened Howard Mitch Conner, keeping with the family name of Howard. Due to Doctor Benjamin Spock's writings, some women believe babies should not be breast fed, but instead should be fed entirely on formula. This idea leads to unfortunate consequences in the Conner household.

At first Kit is happy that his wife is finally able to have a baby. But he isn't happy about helping to care for the baby. That's supposed to be Jo's job. But at three o'clock in the morning, Kit feeds the little tyke. The baby is colicky and cries incessantly. Then, every time Jo feeds the baby a thickened formula, Kit has to ream out the rubber nipple with a needle, because the grainy fluid stops up every few minutes. Kit follows Jo as she walks around the house feeding, singing, bouncing, and trying to calm the wailing child. During the day, Kit works like a zombie, wondering if he will ever get a full night's sleep again.

Somehow things finally calm down. They moved through the terrible twos, and then, when toddler Mitch is a little over three years old, Jo becomes pregnant again. Kit doesn't say much, but he is clearly not thrilled at the prospect of another baby in the house. The pregnancy continues uneventfully, and Jo gives birth to her second boy, christened Curtis Lee Conner. This time, she breastfeeds her baby, and Kit is overjoyed that he can sleep through the night. Not even a crying baby will interrupt Kit's loud snoring.

One Friday, Kit walks up the crumbling concrete sidewalk to another dilapidated house. He is glad for this final interview of the day. The house is in worse condition than he thought. Paint peels on the heavy wooden door, and as Kit pounds on it, a few pieces fall to the faded green porch. Several piles of trash are heaped up on the porch and a couple of windows are broken out. After a few minutes with no response, Kit turns to leave. The heavy iron security bars over the windows makes it seem like more of a prison than a home.

Just another bad area of town. Kit's mind is on dinner and a nice nap on the couch as he pulls open the driver's side door and climbs behind the wheel. Reaching across the seat, he pulls his briefcase over as a writing surface and begins to take notes. Before he finishes the first line, he hears the click of the passenger door and looks up to see two big men simultaneously open the front and back doors and quickly jump in. With the briefcase across his lap and up against the steering wheel, Kit is pinned in and unable to react quickly enough to lock the doors or jump out. Turning toward the back seat, his vision explodes as the man in the back seat pistol-whips him across the side of his head.

"Don't turn around," the man in the front passenger seat commands. "Let's have the cash now and make it fast!"

Kit reels from the blow to his head and feels blood flow down his neck and onto his formerly white collar. As he starts to pull out his wallet, the man grabs his arm.

"I told you… the cash now. Right now."

Releasing Kit's arm, he jerks open the glove compartment and throws everything onto the floor. "Where is it?"

Next he grabs the briefcase off Kit's lap and dumps it out, growing more angry and louder by the second. "I said where is it?"

"The only cash I have is in my wallet."

Passenger man squints at him with a mean look.

"Alright then, pull it out nice and slow."

Reaching into his back pocket, Kit knows he's in a bad position. The guy in the back seat has the control and the brute in the front is the commander who doesn't even need a gun. Kit complies and hopes for the best. He pulls out his wallet which is immediately snatched away.

"What are you trying to pull? There's only thirty dollars here. Where's the rest of it?"

"The rest of what?"

For a moment there is silence.

"You're an insurance salesman collecting payments. I'm not going to ask you again for the cash, so you better hand it over."

"I'm an investigator, not a salesman. I don't have any more cash."

More silence, then cursing.

"Of all the stupid, idiot ideas…"

Turning to address the man in the back seat, the front man unleashes another string of profanity.

"You idiot! I told you he didn't look like no salesman."

Then he turns back to Kit. "Give me that wedding ring. What's that in your front pocket? Give me everything you got."

Relieved of his wedding ring, cigarettes and lighter, the man finishes going through Kit's wallet and flips it back at him.

Kit speaks up, "Do you think I could get a cigarette from you? I'm kind of nervous."

The man pulls out a cigarette and hands it to Kit.

"Sorry, but you have my lighter, can I get a light?" After lighting Kit's cigarette, the front man tosses the lighter back. "Go ahead and keep the lighter. Here's your cigarettes, too. Only a couple left anyway and the lighter's worth nothin'."

As long as he's asking, Kit decides to try for more.

"You know, my driver's license isn't much good to you, could I get that back?"

As the man flips the license into Kit's lap, he says sarcastically, "What do you want next, the cash from your wallet?"

"No, but that wedding ring isn't worth much. Plus my wife will kill me if I come home without it."

"Is that right? Well what makes you think I won't kill you right here and now?"

"You don't seem like the killin' type to me."

The man in the back suddenly pipes up. "Somebody's coming up the street!"

Both passenger side doors open as the two men exit. The rear door slams, but the front man leans back in and tosses something onto the seat beside Kit. "Here's your ring — count yourself lucky that you're a good judge of character. Get out of here while you still can."

Kit doesn't have to be told twice. Later, at the police station he files a report of the robbery and the same detective sees him.

"Hey, Conner, not you again. What happened this time?"

After a lengthy conversation, the detective shakes his head. "You're about the luckiest guy I've ever seen. Not only did you come out with just a bump to the head, but they get a measly thirty bucks and give you back your wallet, driver's license, cigarettes, lighter and wedding ring. If I hadn't heard it from the horse's mouth, I wouldn't have believed it."

That night, Kit describes what happened while Jo holds a damp cloth to his head and cries. Pushing her hand away, he walks over and flips on the TV. "I'm fine, go read a magazine or something."

"First, I'd better tell you what happened today with the kids."

"What do you mean, 'tell me what happened today'? Better not be anything serious, 'cause I've had enough for one day."

"They've been arguing all day long. Then Mitch ran down the street and wasn't looking where he was going. He ran face first into the back of the Smith's pickup that was parked in front of their house. He knocked out his two front teeth."

Suddenly she has his full attention. "What? Oh for cryin' out loud! How much is that going to cost? I'm telling you, Jo, these kids are going to run us out of house and home with all this expense for one thing or another. Last week it was Curtis running down a sidewalk full force into a parking meter and now Mitch knocks his front teeth out. We'll never get ahead like this."

Jo migrates to the kitchen during Kit's tirade and yells back, "Do you want a whiskey sour?"

Kit holds his head in his hands and shakes it slowly back and forth. "Yeah, better make it a double."

Kit stares blankly at the TV as music from another episode of "Rawhide" plays through the tinny speakers of the Magnavox. His thoughts rattle above the noise and he pushes them away in irritation. *Is this the good life that we are supposed to be living? Working all day and all night for this? Is this it?*

* * *

As I get out of bed to go to the bathroom, a nightlight illuminates the short path from the bedroom door, where I sleep with my brother. The tip of my tongue runs over the empty place where my two front teeth used to be. They were there just this morning, and now they're gone. It makes me sad. I miss them. Everyone is upset, and it makes my heart beat hard. I feel sick. I just want things to go back to the way they were this morning. Why can't I go back?

As I pad back into the hallway, the sound of shooting and yelling waft in from the living room. I creep over to the edge of the living room door and peer around the corner, careful not to be noticed. The changing black and white images on the television cast shadowy monsters on the walls. Dad sits on the couch, staring into space. A cigarette glows in the darkness as he takes a puff now and then. Mom is in bed sleeping. She has to get up early to go to work.

It never occurs to me to run in and climb on his lap. He isn't really a 'lap' kind of dad. So I just watch him, unseen from the shadows, until I finally get tired enough to go back to sleep.

The Sergeant

Chapter Seven
The Gift

Peering through the window of the kitchen, I see my mom swinging her hoe as she tears through weeds in the garden. Dad's hunting dog jumps around nearby, a Springer Spaniel that provides monotonous, constant yelping as he jumps and strains at the end of his chain. The dog never hunted a day in his life. He is more of a pet than anything else. Maybe not really a pet either because he is relegated to spending his life imprisoned in the yard on the end of a chain. He lives in a home-built dog house, complete with leftover shingles for a roof. He isn't trained, so he isn't allowed in the house.

Dad would say, "That's a hunting dog, he shouldn't be kept in the house."

But Dad never took him to hunt either. Just spent his life trying to get rid of the constraints of the chain, living in a small muddy circle in our back yard.

My mind wanders to mighty hunting fields. Does our dog dream of running through fields, free? Retrieving that downed bird, bringing it to his master with pride and hearing the satisfying exclamation, "Good Boy!"

Maybe even a special scratch behind the ears? The sound of his barking brings me back to reality. I can't get close enough to pet him because he's so wild. He jumps on me and makes a mess with his muddy paws.

He barks and jumps around as my mom throws a bunch of weeds to the side. Aggravation mixed with compassion force a tear to my eye. I get rid of it with a jerk of my hand. Turning my thoughts back to the great hunting field, I'm suddenly startled by the voice of my mom, "Ah, There's nothing like a good smoke after working up a sweat in the garden."

She doesn't seem to notice I am trapped in my daydream.

Dad doesn't work up a sweat in the yard, garden or the house. Those are Mom's jobs and she never seems to mind working full time outside the house and working at home as well. Of course, it doesn't prevent Dad from also comforting himself with a nice cigarette or pipe and blowing the smoke into great plumes that waft around the rooms. Mom sticks to cigarettes, and when friends come over, they all fumble through a pack and pass them around.

Actually, no one is supposed to smoke in the house because I have a bad case of asthma. But some things in life you don't mess with and smoking is one of them.

"Ah, a little smoke now and then never hurt anyone. You get more smoke from a fire than you do from a cigarette."

I don't know who said that, but I guess it makes some kind of sense. After all, it isn't just the cigarette smoke that bothers me. I am allergic to, just about everything: bananas, tomatoes, rye, dust, pollen, mold, cats, dogs, animal dander in general, cigarette smoke, milk and anything with milk in it (like ice cream). You name it and I am probably allergic to it.

I sit in the allergy doctor's exam room on the cold steel table. Doc Allergy turns to my mom and intones in his most somber, low-pitched voice, "Don't smoke in the house. No pets in the house. Especially no birds or cats. Keep him in his room with the windows closed and an air filter machine running all the time. No milk, no ice cream, nothing with milk products like cheese or mashed potatoes, no bananas, no tomatoes, no cheese, nothing with mold on it..."

As he drones on, my mind imagines, *No bread, no water, make sure he wears his collar and keep the chain short so he can't escape from his muddy circle...*

My hands and feet are chained to the wall of some dungeon and my only food is green beans, which I hate. In fact, at the dinner table when no one is looking, I stuff them into my pants pocket then make an excuse to go to the bathroom and flush them. A dim light filters into my cell from some overhead grate, and the air filter machine drones in the background. I sneeze myself to death. A click of the door brings me back to reality. Doc Allergy is gone, and Mom stares at me curiously.

Of course the doctor's orders never stopped us from having a dog in the house or other pets like birds, and it never stopped mom or dad from smoking in the house. In those days everybody smoked. No one seemed to know or care that it was bad for you. Bowling alleys, grocery stores, buses, or wherever people congregated — they handed out cigarettes and shared a lighter.

Allergies never prevent me from enjoying some of the events I like to participate in, such as the rifle range where I shoot targets. If the weekend weather is fair, our family goes to the shooting club. We barbecue hamburgers and hot dogs over an open fire. Dad tries out some new hunting rifle and he always gives my brother and I a chance to shoot targets, too.

My brother and I have grown up with guns. As youngsters, we learned gun safety and how to shoot. But I look forward to the day I am old enough to join the 'men' on one of their big hunts. I have fished with Dad for as long as I can remember, but the great event of the year is the deer hunt.

Today is my twelfth birthday and I'm thinking this is the year I'll get a rifle of my own. I'll get to hunt with the men. After wearing myself out watching Mom work around the house, I sit on the couch, lost in a memory of last year's hunting season. It was a week after Thanksgiving when...

...Stretched out on the couch I read 'The Swiss Family Robinson'. The door bursts open and Judd, my dad's hunting buddy, rushes in. Obviously not a man to lack food, he nicely fills out a down-filled camouflaged jacket, matching pants, boots with a spot of mud, and a red hunting cap which he throws onto the wooden table in front of me. He swears and complains about some newfangled piece of hunting equipment he bought. My dad is not far behind him, laughing about some new situation Judd managed to get himself into. Mom comes in and shooshes them into the dining room, making Judd pick up his hat as he goes.

Everyone congregates in the dining room. I guess they would sit in the living room, except I am there and everyone is smoking, dad with his constant cigarette, and Judd with whatever new cigar he happens to like. Since I have asthma, they do try to smoke in other rooms as if the smoke will confine itself against an invisible glass wall between the two areas. As the dining room fills with smoke, Judd fills one of the chairs with his girth and gestures towards me with his cigar.

"I don't know what it is about your old man, but he is the luckiest son of a gun I have ever seen, and he always comes out smelling like a rose."

I act like I'm reading my book because kids are supposed to be seen and not heard. They really shouldn't be seen either. But I'm all ears as Dad and Judd sit around the table entertaining Mom with talk about their latest hunting trip. Getting no attention from me, Judd shifts his verbiage to my mom.

"Jo, your husband has once again managed to get the biggest

buck in the Northeastern part of Lewis county. To hear him tell, the thing walked right out in front of him, not even 50 yards away, then just stood there while he took a shot. Now me, on the other hand, I'm slaving away in my tree stand all week long and don't even see one lousy buck, only a couple of doe's!"

Dad pipes up, laughter in his voice, "Go ahead, Judd, tell her what else you managed to do."

Judd looks disgusted and shakes his head like a sad bulldog. Then he points and wags his finger up and down.

"Well, I just want you to know that it's not my fault, Jo. I bought this new tree chair a couple of weeks ago and thought I'd like to try it out. Now the way it works is that the chair has a couple of bands that wrap around the tree to hold it in place. I screwed my tree steps in place and put this chair about fifteen feet up the tree on the edge of a field. You have to keep in mind that I'm right on the tree line in this field and there's a barbed wire fence below me.

So I go out in the morning, just before it's getting light, carefully climb up the tree and situate myself on this tree chair, waiting for a deer to pop into the field. I've been sitting there about two hours when suddenly I see these two doe's cross the field, and I'm thinking there's going to be a nice-sized buck coming behind them any minute. Just as I raise my rifle to get a look through the scope, this Mickey Mouse chair takes that opportunity to completely collapse and dumps me on top of that fence."

By this time mom is laughing and shaking her head, trying to conjure up sympathy.

Dad pipes in again. "That's not the worst of it."

Dad is now laughing so hard, tears run down his face.

"Judd limps back to the house and tells us what happened. When he turns around to show us, he has a big Z on the back of his pants where the barbed wire sliced it. Everybody said it was like the mark of Zorro."

At that point I lose all pretense of reading as the house enjoys the echoes of our laughter.

The voice of my mom interupts my thoughts and brings me back to the present. "Mitch! Hey, Mitch! Snap out of it and come on. It's time to eat."

Everyone sits around the table and stares at me. My face turns red as I try to divert their attention.

"Oh, is it time to eat?"

"You didn't hear us calling you? Come on. We can't start without you on your birthday."

I rush through dinner. It can't end soon enough as I anticipate opening my birthday presents. Forget the food and cake, let's get to the gifts! Birthdays were always fun but, like I said, I have the sneaking suspicion that I am now old enough to accompany the hunters on their forays and that means some hunting-related gifts.

Twelve years old is a difficult time for a kid. I am not really a child any more but not a teenager either. Just kind of caught in this never, never land where I'm too old to play with little-kid toys and too young to play with the really neat toys, like dad's car.

Dinner is finally done and we do my birthday cake and candles. My brother who is three years younger, Mom and Dad sing to me, and I'm so excited! I tear open some gifts, but there's nothing associated with hunting except a pair of nice hiking boots. I don't know what I expected, but somehow I can't help feeling disappointed and let down. I try to not let anything show, because I know how hard my mom and dad work so that we can have good food on the table and nice birthdays. I'm not ungrateful… well, maybe a little. Dad goes into the kitchen to get something, and he comes back in with a long package.

"Mitch, you're old enough now to have this. It means a lot of responsibility, but you've earned it."

As I tear into that package and open the box, I gasp. There it is! A premiere hunting rifle, scope and all; and not a cheap one either. I look up at my mom and she tilts her head towards Dad to indicate it was all his idea. Dad isn't really the huggy type of person. He just nods and looks pleased that he has surprised me.

This year I have the grand privilege of accompanying my dad and his hunting buddies up to Northeastern Missouri where this old lady has about a hundred acres of wooded land that she lets only my dad and his friends hunt on. She's an eccentric old gal, about five foot three, a bit stocky and tough as leather nailed to oak. She runs a farm of about forty head of cattle, twenty or thirty hogs, some horses, and probably two hundred acres of tillable land in soybean, wheat and corn. A tiny one-room shack stands behind her house with a wood stove in it where this old man named Otto lives. He looks older than she and works the entire farm for her.

The story is that she lived in Chicago during the roaring twenties where she worked as a singer in one of Al Capone's nightclubs. I've heard the story that every year, in the spring, a limousine shows up at her farm. During that time some pretty rough characters can be seen around town. About a week later, they all cram into the car and it disappears down the road. I guess it's just their way of checking up on her and making sure she's okay.

How my dad met her, I don't know. But he and my mom seem to be the only people she trusts. In the end, she would sell her land and the farm only to them. Dad and his friends have been hunting up there long before I was born, and I always remember knowing the great Nona Shaw. Even though she is one tough old gal, she is always kind to me.

On this particular hunting trip, I'm with my dad and Judd as they go through their pre deer hunting ritual. They walk through the woods and look for deer tracks to see how the deer are moving. They do this so that we can sit in the right place where deer pass by. When we hunt deer, we sit and let the deer come to us. Some guys run the deer with dogs to force them into certain areas, but that is kind of illegal and bad practice. My dad and his hunting buddies won't do it.

Over the years I learn a lot of wisdom from Dad and his hunting buddies. They welcome me into their group, but at the same time, they make sure I know we are not on equal footing.

One particular time, I have to learn that painful lesson.

The leaves crunch under foot, and the nearby artesian well lends a smell of rotten eggs as a small stream bubbles past our feet. I'm holding that beautiful rifle Dad gave me. As I look up, I see my dad and his hunting buddy just ahead, climbing over a barbed wire fence. My dad holds the top wire down so I can get over it. After I scramble over, I watch him as he walks easily with his rifle in the crook of his arm. Our orange vests flash in the late afternoon sun as it filters through the trees. The orange vest is pulled over a nice camouflage jacket with matching pants. Good tough boots from the Cabelas sporting catalog completes the ensemble.

As Dad and Judd look for deer track, I observe — not really sure I belong here. Dad and Judd trade insults at each other. I think that I can do the same; hey, you know... I'm a part of their team. So I throw in some weak insults of my own.

"I guess Judd's going to have to lose some weight to make it over that next fence."

No one laughs. After a few more lame attempts at humor, my dad kind of lags behind a bit, then stops and calls me over.

"You know, I've known Judd a long time and we are good friends. We've earned the right to kid around with each other. You're just a young man here and what you're doing isn't respectful. Now I want you to go and apologize to him."

I hang my head in shame and turn away quickly so he won't see my red face and the tears that betray me. It isn't so much that I don't want to go and apologize to Judd; and I *really* don't want to do that because now I'm embarrassed. But the worst part is that I feel I've somehow disappointed my dad. He made it clear that I'm here by his grace alone. Not that I'm not a member of their team — I am. But, at the same time, he lets me know I'm not on an equal footing with them. I look at him again and am proud that he wouldn't let me get away with that disrespect.

Years later, I fail to do the same with my daughter. I never teach her about the gap between myself and her that can never be bridged; a respect she owes me as her parent and elder. I try too hard to be her friend and too little to be her parent. As she grows into a teen, and then a young adult, there is a disrespect. There are no boundaries to make her bow her head in honor.

I walk with my head down when suddenly a small tree branch slaps me in the face. I look up again at my dad, but the sun filters through the trees, becomes brighter and blocks my view. I struggle to say something to him. I want to tell him that I appreciate him. I want to let him know he did a good job and I love him. But the words are stuck in my throat and cannot be spoken. I look down to clear my vision and when I look up again, Judd leans against a barbed wire fence post, scans the tree line for any sign of a deer breaking into the field. My dad is nowhere in sight.

Chapter Eight
Second Chances

Dad is a great hunter and fisherman. Besides my mom, hunting and fishing are the two loves of his life. Mom never tries to compete with them. Whatever Dad hunts or fishes for seems to walk right in front of him or jump onto his fishing line.

He and a few other like-minded men create the core elite hunting and fishing team of Northeastern Missouri. Although not as lucky as my dad, they are men of honesty, honor, integrity and sincerity. They grind, shape, and mold each other's lives, thoughts, and actions — and they all come out the better for it. They stand by each other in every circumstance, bound together by their friendship and loyalty.

After Dad upbraids me, I shift my weight uncomfortably from foot to foot. Judd puts his boot against the barbed wire fence. It screeches in protest as he shifts his weight and leans on his upraised knee. A puff of smoke slowly drifts as he exhales from some new brand of cigar he found. "You know Mitch, you can learn a lot from the simple things in life," he says as he continues to scan the field.

When I'm lost in thought, I might as well leave the room because I'm not aware of anything going on around me. Once in second grade, I stared out the window at the clouds and thought about flying to the moon — anywhere but in that classroom. Suddenly the voice of the teacher snatched me back from the outer reaches of the universe.

"Earth to Mitch! Earth to Mitch!"

She apparently asked me some stupid question which I totally did not hear. As my vision cleared, I found myself the center of attention. All my classmates laughed at me. After that I learned to keep to myself.

Lost in a daydream after my dad's scolding, I'm surprised by Judd's voice. The barbed wire strands jerk me back to the present as they screech like a badly-tuned violin. Judd takes his foot off the fence and looks at me. I pretend to examine the weather-beaten fence posts which seem dangerously close to falling over.

Judd starts in with some crazy story of the fence. "Now let me tell you something here. You would think, given the age of it, that this whole fence row should just fall down, much less keep the cows inside the field. But each post creates just enough tension on the other posts to keep the entire thing standing and functional, and the cows seem to pretty much accept it for what it is; the boundaries of their home."

Judd finishes another long draw and exhalation of fog from his cigar, then starts up again. "All of these fence posts and wire cooperate together to make a complete fence. Many a time, we hafta' do the same thing. We hafta' work together for a bigger purpose in life. Very little is gonna' come from the effort of one person alone."

I feel my eyelids get heavy as he drones on.

"The problem is that relationships become filled with tension; differing personalities, disagreements, misunderstandings and just plain busyness. You see this barbed wire on each post?"

Judd doesn't pause for an answer.

"There is positive and negative tension here. That very tension on each post makes the whole thing work. Sometimes we forget that one post isn't gonna' reach its destiny."

Suddenly, I really have to pee and shift from foot to foot again. Judd can go on and on, so I hope he finishes up real quick.

"Mitch, a lot of people think they're the center of the world. Think they're the biggest and brightest of all the fence posts, and the fence wouldn't exist if not for them. They think they must be the greatest fence post of all, better than the rest; the center of the world. If only these other fence posts would get outta' the way. They're for sure keeping me from greatness."

Judd looks down at me. "Don'tcha' think if we could get free of it all, we could soar and be successful?"

By this point, the only success I want is the success of finding a toilet. Turning to look behind us, Judd motions with his cigar at an old fence row that has fallen over. Ashes and sparks fly from the end of his glowing cigar as he continues, oblivious to my plight.

"You see that fence post over there? It strained so hard that it disconnected from the rest of the fence. It's fallen over and leans at an odd angle. It's unstable, plus, it isn't useful anymore. It's just a stick in the mud that doesn't have any purpose. More importantly, its absence put more strain on the rest of the fence and you can see that the whole thing fell over. When life gets difficult, it sometimes feels like we should just pull away from whatever creates tension. But, when we do that, we may end up disconnecting from an important purpose and making it harder on those around us. One fence post by itself can't keep the cows in the field."

Looking down at me again he asks, "Mitch, do you know what I'm telling you?"

As I continue to prance from foot to foot, my head dutifully nods up and down even though I don't have a clue.

Judd stares at me. "What's wrong with you?"

"Is there a bathroom around here somewhere?"

Judd shakes his head and points to a nearby tree. As I

immediately scurry to the far side of it, he calls out, "Don't let a rattlesnake getcha."

Judd exhales another cloud of cigar smoke like a train engine pulling into its last station. A slight breeze scatters the last wisps as I return, snakebite free. I think once again about my dad and remember Judd's words that day at our house. They seem branded into my memory.

"I don't know what it is about your dad, but he is the luckiest guy I've ever seen. He always manages to come out smelling like a rose."

I knew it was true, but Dad never tried to be that way. He just had a penchant. Just as I begin to fear that Judd will launch into another interminable speech, I hear my dad yell, "Mitch!"

Grateful, I look up to see Dad walking towards us.

"Mitch, follow me," he commands.

As we follow him along a creek bed, the sound of a bleating noise becomes louder. Dad stops and raises his hand, then stoops down in the leaves. Suddenly, something thrashes around and I see a small fawn, a baby deer maybe less than a year old. Dad makes a shushing noise and puts his gloved hand on its neck. It calms down a bit, but it's breathing hard, eyes wild with fright. Judd comes around the other side and crouches down.

"Well, I'll be doggone," says Judd. "Looks like someone has been hunting out of season. Look at that."

He points to a small bloody hole on the back leg quarter and Dad nods. "Yep."

Although a man of few words, I hear the anger in Dad's voice. One thing he doesn't cotton to is breaking the law or something unfair. I remembered what he taught me about hunting.

When I was younger, schoolteachers taught us a song about a rabbit who tried to hide from a hunter. The last line of the song went something like, 'Little rabbit come inside, safely here abide.' After that, I was upset when my own dad hunted and killed an animal. So he took me aside one day and we had this talk.

"Mitch, hunting is definitely a sport, but there's another side of it, too. If deer or any animal populations are left unchecked, they will soon overrun the ability of the land to sustain them. They'll damage the farmer's crops much more than they do now. It's never good to shoot something just for the sake of shooting it. There are rifle ranges and targets for that kind of thing.

When we go hunting, we're careful to only fire that weapon when we have a shot that will minimize the suffering of the animal. Also, we never waste anything. If we aren't going to eat the meat, we don't shoot it. Many times I just sit quietly and watch as animals go about their business. You can learn a lot from sitting quietly and watching, whether it's an animal or a person." Later I found out Dad's team of hunters often gave deer meat to poor people that lived in the area.

Now as I watch my dad with this wounded animal, I understand the values he lives by. He could easily take out his pistol and put the animal out of its misery. But he has something else in mind. As Judd and my dad crouch there, Judd looks across at him.

"You can't be serious! What are you going to do? Carry it out and put it in the car?"

Dad slowly shakes his head and purses his lips together, deep in thought. "Carry it out, yes. Put it in the car, no. Otto has that old pickup truck with the cover on it. We can put some blankets in the back and..."

So that's how the luckiest deer in all of the surrounding area ends up in a little game preserve area at a nearby old folks' home. Dad carries that deer out of the woods and Otto transports it to a little wildlife area where the deer is treated and cared for. It's a buck, a male deer, and later, he sports a nice rack of antlers.

Dad often visits the deer which he calls Bambi, naming him after a fawn in the Bambi movie. Bambi comes up to the fence and nuzzles my dad's hand, looking for an apple or some other handout my dad always produces. It took many years before I could reconcile this behavior with Dad's love of hunting and fishing.

On the one hand, he expends great effort to save this injured deer. On the other, he expends great effort to hunt… deer. Dad never let much of his true feelings leak out. But a couple of other times his true heart peeked through that tough exterior.

In the early 1960's President Kennedy was assassinated and NASA took a shot at landing on the moon. I was eight and didn't care about all that. But there was this frog. I caught this great frog, actually a toad, and I made this great shoebox for it with grass and water and even a few bugs. It was like the Ritz!

But this kid down the street talked me into selling that frog to him for three quarters. When I got home I felt like I had sold my best friend (the frog, that is). So I went and gave the kid his money back and got my favorite toad back. It was great… until I got up the next morning, opened up that box and discovered my toad was gone! Guess he didn't know what a great friend I was. I was heartbroken. Anyway, Dad took time to write a letter to me.

"Mitch," he wrote, "I know how much that frog meant to you. But the thing is, you can't hold on to an animal like that and close it up in a box. Animals, like people, have to be free."

Later in life, I thought of that concept when it came to people and a certain girl.

The only other time I see Dad's heart leak out happens after I'm married and we take our two and a half year-old daughter, Allia, on her first fishing expedition. We drive up to the country where the fishing is good, hook the old flatboat and rusty trailer onto the truck, and pull it to a nearby lake. Probably more of a cow pond than a lake, about thirty yards across and maybe fifty yards long. This particular time of year, a lot of moss grows up against the shoreline, so it isn't possible to do much fishing from the shore.

Our crew consists of me, my lovely wife, our young daughter and Dad. There isn't room in the boat for all four of us. By all rights, as the expert fisherman of fifty years, Dad should take my daughter out on her first fishing expedition. But he insists that we do the honors. We climb into the small aluminum craft, Dad hands over our gear then teaches a small lesson on what lures to use. Lifting up the shore-bound end of the boat, he pushes us into the water.

During the course of the afternoon, we get a few bites but nothing of note. Every so often I catch sight of my dad throwing in a line but the only thing he catches is the moss that drags in with his lure. After a while I don't see him any longer. A couple of hours later, as it starts to get dark, Allia hooks a three and a half pound bass and is thrilled with her catch! She looks up and claps, bouncing up and down on her seat. "Can we keep it as a pet?"

After some discussion, she decides to let it go rather than eat it or keep it. I help her hold it as we lean over and place it back in the water. With a lazy wave of the fin, the water swirls as it disappears from sight. By the time we reach the shore, darkness has fallen. I pull the boat out of the water and notice the faint glow of Dad's cigarette as he leans against the truck. He comes over and we heft the boat over to the trailer.

"I didn't know you were waiting for us. Why didn't you call out that you were ready to go?"

"I wanted Allia to have a chance at her first fish," he replies.

He waited several hours. I am touched that he would stand there and silently wait for us to run out of fun.

I am jolted awake as the car bounces into our driveway. We are home from my first hunting outing with the guys. Once inside, I sit at the table with Mom, Dad and Judd as they tell stories about the weekend and tell about rescuing the deer. My lack of respect and comment to Judd is never mentioned again. As we talk and laugh, my brother, who is three years younger, comes into the room. After listening for a moment, he shouts, "Mitch didn't flush!" then he runs.

I chase him through a couple of rooms, both of us yelling and screaming like banshees. Finally, I catch him by the arm and thump him a couple of times on the head. Turns out he was kind of jealous because I got to go off with the guys while he had to stay home with Mom. But we never needed an excuse to aggravate each other.

With all of Mom's side of the family living in the Southern city of Memphis, we take a yearly vacation to visit them. In the 1960's only two-lane roads run in this part of the country. No interstate highways, so this is a seven hour trek. No air conditioning, and my brother and I don't make life any easier with our love of conflict.

Our family car is an old 1950's Hudson with a rusting floorboard. Sitting in the front passenger seat, we can watch the road go by through the holes in the floor. Mom puts a scrap piece of carpet over the hole with a couple of bricks to hold it in place, thinking that will make it safer. No seat belts or car seats for infants are in vogue yet, but somehow we manage to survive, in spite of the lack of safety.

Everyone is excited about taking this trip, but the real thrill is the annual battle between my brother and me. Today is no exception, and we get an early start. As Mom packs our luggage into the trunk, my brother and I race for the same car door.

"I'm sitting on this side!"

"No, I am!"

"No, you're not! Mom, Mom, he won't let me sit on this side."

We fight back and forth, holding the door shut and blocking each other until Mom gets tired of hearing it. "We aren't leaving for two hours. Get back in the house."

Later, the problem of who sits where is resolved at Mom's command, and Dad backs out of the driveway. We are officially under way. Sternly lectured to leave each other alone, my brother and I last a record-breaking thirty minutes until the war begins. We never resort to fisticuffs as we're too sophisticated for that. As the older brother, I make it my prime goal to aggravate my younger brother as much as possible without getting caught. My first tactic is known as 'perimeter breach,' and it goes like this:

Dad drives, Mom is in the passenger seat, and my brother and I are in the back. In those days, children are to be seen and not heard, and we really shouldn't be seen much. On a trip, we know nothing about this rule and if we did, we ignore it. My brother is on his side of the seat but inches closer to the middle demilitarized zone. I quickly place my hand on the seat with my pinky barely in the zone. "He's on my side! He's on my side!" screams my brother in an attempt to gain advantage.

Within a microsecond I have both hands on the book I'm reading. Mom turns around, but is too late to catch my lightning fast move. We repeat this tactic over and over as the heat boils our blood. After my Mom has had enough, Dad adds his refrain. "You two knock it off right now, or I'm pulling this car over!"

We are never sure what will happen if Dad does pull the car over. He never did. It was just his part of the entertainment. After we tire of playing 'perimeter breach,' the next tactic involves 'the breathing game'. In this scenario, I breathe in and out just loudly enough for my brother to hear, but not loud enough for Dad or Mom to hear over the sound of the wind that roars through the open windows.

"He's breathing! He's breathing!" screams my brother.

This time Mom chimes in, "What do you mean, 'He's breathing?' Of course he is!"

So it goes, for seven hours of misery on the way down, then seven hours on the way back. The only positive thing is that it teaches us great creative thinking skills as we try to outdo the other. I suppose it also taught my mom and my dad patience.

Mom and Dad show a lot of patience as they raise us. Dad spends most of his time working as a private investigator, researching and investigating insurance claims. I hear him typing on an IBM manual typewriter at an impossible speed; a talent left over from his time as a Radioman in the Navy. He works on the street, investigating all day, then types his reports late at night. Often I wake up to the sound of 'Gunsmoke' on our black and white Zenith television as Dad tries to de-stress from the events of the day. Mom works as well, but also takes care of the house, the yard, the cooking and the washing, yet tries to reserve some time to spend with us kids.

During the late 1950's, a particular family lives next door. The lady is about Mom's age with two kids about the age of me and my brother. In the morning, in order to get all her housework done quickly, she locks her kids in their room. Then she brings her kids over to our house to visit with my mom for the rest of the day. At night when my dad comes home, he can never understand why mom hasn't finished her housework. She's too kind to say anything to the lady and finally takes a part time job outside the home, so she can break the cycle and get something accomplished around the house.

My dad goes ballistic when he finds out she applied for and got a secretarial job at the local dentist's office. In spite of Mom's quiet subservience, when she gets something in her mind she does it no matter what the consequences. I hear my dad complaining until the wee hours of the morning — over, and over and over again.

As we grow into teenagers, my brother and I fight less as we find other, more interesting pursuits. I join a falconry club whose purpose is to teach about these birds of prey, and also to capture and train hawks for hunting. This sounds like great fun to me and Mom does her best to support the whole idea. We even keep a small hawk in our nicely finished basement. This is before I am able to drive. Catching a hawk requires the use of a car, so I'm happy for Mom's assistance at a time when teens usually don't want to hang out with their moms. There is a certain art to trapping a hawk and nowadays it requires the proper licensing.

We start out with a trip to the hardware store for chicken wire mesh, fishing line, a couple of weights, then on to the pet store for a mouse or two. At home, we fashion a cage out of chicken wire. A quarter inch square mesh wire sheet, once formed into a cage, stands about two inches high and sixteen inches square. I cut myself several times on the unwieldy wire mesh. Next we take the nearly invisible fishing line, create a loop at one end and attach the other end securely to the top of the cage. We repeat this about fifty to one hundred times until the top is covered in these loops.

After finishing the last loop, my fingers cramp. This isn't as much fun as it first appeared to be. Two heavy weights, secured to the bottom of the cage, ensure the hawk doesn't fly away with it. Finally, a small door is cut into the side of the cage and the mouse is inserted. It runs around a bit, poops on the wire, then cowers in the corner of its temporary quarters.

Mom drives along a deserted road as I watch the sky. This is where the months of study and training come in handy. I have to be able to tell the difference between different species of hawks, because some are protected. There's a difference between a falcon and a hawk. We look for hawks, not falcons. I spot one ahead as it lazily drifts on the wind, looking for its meal.

The trick is to not completely stop the vehicle and thus scare off the hawk. Mom slows down to about twenty miles per hour while I open the door and throw out the trap. Looking back, I see it bounce once and land upright on the side of the road. We continue up the road for about a mile, then turn around and go back. The hawk is gone and the trap is empty. As the car rolls to a stop, I jump out, retrieve the trap and get back in.

We do this about fifteen times that afternoon with nada a catch. This is more work than I realized, and I'm beginning to feel a bit guilty about taking up so much of Mom's time. She encourages me to try one last time. Slow down, open the door, toss the trap, close the door, look back and watch it bounce, then drive up a mile. I'm starting to feel badly for the mouse who is punished every time I throw the cage and it hits the pavement.

We turn around and drive back… and bingo! There's my hawk, unhappy and entangled in the monofilament fishing line. Now I have to get the hawk out of that trap, into a hood and into the car. I was instructed as to how to do that, but seeing it done and doing it are two very different things. As I approach the hawk, it flaps its wings in desperation and fights, but it can't fly away.

The weighted cage is too heavy.

After a short struggle, with its hood on, the bird calms down. Returning to the car with my prize, we drive home where the real work begins. The hawk must be carefully cared for and the training is time intensive over a period of months. As a teenager and a dreamer, I found that I like the 'thought' of doing something much better than actually doing it.

After a couple of months with the hawk, I'm moving on to other things. My parents remind me of my responsibility. As we sit around the living room and watch television, Dad's mouth is moves and his voice drones on as if speaking a foreign language. "Ou cat tha aw do the e ingca fit. Mo as enough to do out ha ean up hat mess. Yo no ve at fa o jueav at bird ooped up ho."

I try to concentrate on what he's saying, but the television commercial seems more important. Suddenly I realize the room is silent. The television is on mute and both of my parents stare at me like aliens.

"Did you hear what I just said to you?"

It doesn't seem like a question, yet my head nods up and down in response to their alien power.

"This is your responsibility and you need to make a decision to do the right thing."

A couple of weeks later I do the right thing. In a country field of freshly harvested wheat, I carefully cut the leather thongs from my hawk's legs and release it into the air. It arcs around the field and passes over me once as if in tribute, then soars into the heights, finally disappearing far above the earth.

As I watch its form disappear among the clouds, I feel strangely empty. On the one hand, a weight has been lifted from my shoulders. The responsibility is gone, and I won't get yelled at any more. On the other hand, I feel betrayed. I poured so much of myself into caring for my hawk but it left me on the ground, forgotten in the choice of ultimate freedom.

Chapter Nine
Boot Camp

High School seems to fly by as unremarkably as my grade point average. College starts out with all the excitement of a new beginning and quickly becomes the old drudgery of work and study.

Before the semester is out, so am I. As a 19 year-old college dropout working a go nowhere job in a cafeteria, I don't have a clue where my life will end up. A couple of my friends enlist in the Army to pursue law enforcement in the ranks of the Military Police.

I drive through our little shopping district and contemplate my life when I see a blonde girl on the side of the road with her thumb out. I pull my orange 1967 Plymouth Barracuda toward her, and she hops in without asking me where I'm going.

"Uh, where are you going?" I ask her.

"Just keep going straight," she answers.

Keep going straight? Things are never simple. Here I am, a lonely teenager, and suddenly this girl jumps in my car and starts giving me directions. So I drive down the road.

After a few minutes of silence, I finally ask, "So-o-o, is there a particular place you're going or did you just want to take a drive down this road?"

"I need to go to my apartment. Turn left here."

"You mean back there?"

"You didn't turn left!"

"You didn't tell me until we were in the middle of the intersection!"

Less than five minutes and we already argue as if we've been married ten years. I turn the car around and manage to navigate toward her apartment.

"Wait here," she states without waiting for an answer, then jumps out and heads into an apartment.

"What is this, taxi service?"

I'm talking to myself because she moves fast. A minute later, before I decide to put the car in gear and leave, she walks back to the car with a box and sets it on the hood of my car.

Gesturing, she looks at me like I'm an idiot. "The trunk… open the trunk and load up."

Then she's back in and out of the apartment with another box.

Jumping out of the car, I try to stop her. Instead, she dumps the box into my arms and heads back to the apartment. This time, she comes out with a small suitcase which she flings into the back seat. Then she gets into the passenger seat and sits there, staring straight ahead.

Suddenly, I hear this guttural yell. This drunk guy stumbles out of the apartment, looking unhappy. I shove the boxes into the back seat, jump in the front seat and away we go, as fast as that Barracuda can accelerate. Drunk guy is left in a trail of exhaust. My only hope is that he's too inebriated to make out my license plate. Once we're in the clear, I pull into a parking lot and turn off the engine.

"Can you explain what you're doing in my car with two boxes and a suitcase with a madman chasing after us?"

She doesn't speak. Minutes tick by. This is the strangest situation I've managed to get myself into.

"Hello there, where do you think I'm going to take you?"

Still no response.

"Look, Mister Drunk Madman isn't around. I'll give you ten dollars if you get out and call a taxi."

I finally get out, go around and open her door. "Hey, I've got stuff to do. I can't sit here with you for the rest of the day, okay?"

Tears slide down her cheek and I think, Oh no, not the tears, anything but the tears. Sighing, I close the door and go back to the driver's seat, hand her a tissue and wait.

After a few more minutes, she finally speaks. "Okay, that's my ex-boyfriend, see? He beats me up and I can't go back there, okay? I don't have any place to go."

"You don't have any place to go," I echo, feeling like I've found someone's pet in the street, and they don't want it back. The problem is, that guy probably does want her back.

"Well, what am I supposed to do with you?"

This is a bad question. I should take her to a women's shelter or something. But no, I'm too naïve to realize what I'm getting myself into.

She wipes a tear and looks at me imploringly. "Can I stay at your house for a while?"

"Look, I live with my parents so that's probably not a good idea."

"Can't you just ask them if I can stay a while?"

As I slowly drive home, I wonder how in the world this is going to go over. I have the uncanny feeling that it can't end well. The driveway appears too soon and I take her inside. Unfortunately, both my mom and my dad happen to be home, watching television, so I have to face both of them with this girl in tow. Of course, by this point I still don't realize that I'm the one in tow.

"Mom... Dad...

Mom seems intrigued while Dad does a double take. I'm not the type to show up with a girl.

Dad speaks first, "So, who is this?"

I can tell by his tone that his mind is processing a thousand scenarios. As an investigator, he doesn't easily trust anyone and he's already picking up that something isn't quite right.

"Ah, well, this is ah, someone I just kind of met today, ah…."

Dad never messes around.. "Mitch, spit it out. What's going on?"

I explain the situation as best I can, leaving out the part about the Mad Drunk Guy. Dad isn't falling for a line of it and starts giving the blonde the third degree.

"Exactly how old are you?"

I'm surprised to find out she is twenty five, but then, at nineteen, I'm not a good judge of age or character.

Mom rescues the girl, or me, with a simple, "You can stay for the time being."

And that's the end of it.

Dad, frustrated, blows out a lungful of cigarette smoke. "Alright then," he says, "but don't say I didn't warn you."

A few weeks later, Dad is proven right as rain. I'm in the middle of a conversation with this girl when suddenly, Mom marches into the room, madder than I've seen her in a while and says, "You, get out of this house now!"

I try to protest, but that's it. When Mom speaks, Mom speaks. What I don't realize is that this girl is not only freeloading, she's stealing as well. It's never a good thing to bite the hand that feeds you. Mom and Dad wouldn't put up with the blonde, but at the same time, they allowed me to learn my lesson the hard way.

Ah, the pains of youth.

By mid 1976, I'm approaching my twentieth birthday with no more direction in life than the man in the moon. The only career that interests me is law enforcement, but I'm too young to join the local police department. After thinking about my two friends in the Army, I drive downtown and talk to a recruiter.

That turns out to be a mistake. I drive home and realize the Army recruiter just talked me into signing up for three years. I never broached the subject with either my mom or my dad. I only meant to get some information on the Army, but now — I'm signed up.

In the driveway, I bang my head on the steering wheel a couple of times. How do I manage to get myself into these situations? I crumple then smooth out the enlistment papers and wonder how to announce my latest madness. Although my family doesn't communicate well, this is probably a little over the top. I should have talked to my parents before I took such a life-changing step.

Mom is in the kitchen and I hear pans rattling around as she soaps them up, gives a rinse and arranges them in the dishwasher. I slide past her and head to the living room thinking my dad will take this better than she will; a correct deduction.

Dad sits in his chair and watches the television show 'Mash'. He puffs on an ever-present cigarette. Every so often he grabs a tall glass off the round oak coaster and takes a few sips of a whiskey sour on ice. I sit on the couch and watch until a commercial break appears.

"Uh, can I talk to you for a minute, Dad?"

"Sure." He mutes the television, then turns to me. I'm sure he already knows something is going on. I rarely sit and watch television with him.

He gestures to the papers in my hand. "Whatcha' got there?"

I've almost forgotten that I'm still clutching them. I'm amazed. My dad never misses a tiny detail. Never.

"Ah, uh, well…"

Colors from the muted TV bounce around the room and I struggle to say anything coherent.

"Mitch, spit it out. What's going on?"

Finally I take a deep breath, square my shoulders and dredge up courage from somewhere.

"Well… Dad, I joined the army today."

A dish drops and shatters on the kitchen floor and I hear my mom gasp. I'll never forget the hurt look on his face as he slowly nods. This announcement seems to have temporarily stunned him. Mom is crying in the kitchen. To their credit, they both quickly recover. Dad congratulates me, and Mom hugs her boy.

Sleep doesn't come easily that night, so I open the curtains in my bedroom and look at the stars. I wonder, is there an answer to the madness and foolishness of this life we live? Of all the people on the whole earth, no one loves me more than my mom and dad. Yet, in order to appease a stranger, I sign my life away without even a word to them, and, in the end, hurt them more than I can fathom.

Only years later, when I became a parent, did I realize how much my parents loved me. After my daughter was grown, I understood my dad lost his hunting buddy that day. He was always so quiet. He never said it, never showed it, and I never, ever saw him cry. He just took it in stride and never mentioned it again.

A month or two later, Mom, Dad, and my brother bid me farewell as I ship out to Basic Training and submit to the subjugation of military life. We play all kinds of games like 'Drill Sergeant, may I do fifty more pushups?' We hang out in an airtight house full of tear gas. The Drill Sergeants take special pleasure in running us through exercise paces designed to wear us down and wear us out. One particular trainee decides he's too good for the rules, and he's caught smoking a cigarette in the barracks. The drill sergeant makes him stand at attention where everyone can observe him. He's issued a pack of cigarettes and a lighter. The Drill Sergeant, wearing his Smokey the Bear drill instructor alien hat, gets right up in the guilty trainee's face.

"Ok trainee, you want to smoke in the barracks? Let's have a good smoke then. Light up a cigarette."

The trainee fumbles with a cigarette, then lights up.

"You will now smoke as I give you commands. In, inhale…

The trainee inhales.

"Out, exhale."

As the trainee moves his hand towards the cigarette to take it out of his mouth and exhale, the Drill Sergeant stops him in mid motion.

"I didn't say touch that cigarette. I said exhale out. Here we go… in…out…in…out…in…out."

The Drill Sergeant picks up a regular marching cadence. The trainee looks a bit green, but the fun has only begun.

"Ok, now, let's knock out fifty, eight count pushups. Come on! One, two, three, four, five, six, seven, eight — that's one. Two, two, three, four, five, six, seven eight — that's two..."

After finishing fifty of these killer pushups, it's time for… another cigarette. Drill Sergeant picks up the cadence.

"In…out…in…"

Then fifty more pushups. Then another cigarette, until the entire pack has been smoked. By this time, the trainee is sick as a dog. His final task is to clean up the ashes and his dinner off the floor. I believe that was the last cigarette that boy ever smoked.

Another entertainment for the Drill Sergeants seems to be our field marches. Wearing a full pack of about 60 pounds and carrying our rifles, we set out for a five or ten mile march at a constant jog. No matter what we do, the Drill Sergeants do it right along with us and some of them don't look young. But they outrun and out-exercise all of us.

We head to the tear gas range. None of us know what to expect. As we jog the five miles to the range, the Drill Sergeant chants his cadence song, "Left, ha ha, left, ha ha, left, right, left, ha ha. I don't know but I've been told."

The trainees repeat the cadence loud and clear, "I don't know but I've been told."

"Charlie Company's made of gold."

"Charlie Company's made of gold."

"I don't know but it's been said."

"I don't know but it's been said."

"Delta Company's still in bed."

"Delta Company's still in bed."

"Sound Off."

"One, Two."

"Sound Off."

"Three, Four."

"Bring it on down."

"One, two, three, four, one, two…Three, Four!"

One of the Drill Sergeants notices that country-boy Trainee Martin bounces up and down as he jogs.

"Martin, stop bouncing. This is a military march, not a dance."

Martin manages to stop bouncing for about five steps then gradually begins bouncing at full speed again. The Drill Sergeant circles around him, yelling at him to stop bouncing. Marching to the beat of a different drum — that was Martin.

On it goes for mile after mile until we arrive at the tear gas range. We file into a gray building and take our seats at a series of long wooden tables. A large muscular drill sergeant with a slight hanging lip and a face like Swiss cheese begins his oration.

"Alright, Trainees. I'm not here to be your friend or to make you feel comfortable. I'm here to scare the shit out of you and then make you wipe it up. What you're about to see is a film demonstrating the adverse effects of nerve gas."

As the film starts to roll, they place a slender green injector in front of each trainee. Nerve gas affects the human body by shutting down the various nervous system functions. It starts with a runny nose and tightness of the chest, and then moves to nausea and drooling, accompanied by the total loss of other bodily functions. This quickly progresses to death by asphyxiation. We are informed the gas smells somewhat like juicy fruit gum. Once the film concludes, our attention is directed to the injectors on the table before us.

"Judging by your dumbfounded expressions, you now have a clear understanding of the dangers of this toxin. Your gas mask and these injectors are your best friends. I will now demonstrate how to use the Atropine autoinjector. Atropine is a chemical used as an antidote to nerve gas. Within this pen is a two inch razor sharp needle which, when applied, will pierce your tender baby trainee skin and inject the antidote into your thigh. Watch carefully as you will have to practice this with your injectors."

The drill sergeant clutches the pen and visibly tenses his muscles. I watch a vein pop out on his neck. Inhaling sharply, he slams the pen against his thigh with a loud grunt.

"Now it's your turn to practice. Trainees, pick up your needles! On the count of three, hit the pen against your leg as hard as you can to ensure the needles obtain full penetration."

A number of the trainees look fearfully at each other. I feel my heart pound against my chest as the sergeant counts down. When he reaches 'one' I close my eyes and slam the pen against my thigh along with the rest of the platoon. I hear a few shrieks and trainee Martin falls off the end of the bench. The drill sergeants laugh. There is no needle and only a spot of water on my green army pants. The autoinjector pens are fakes. When depressed, they squirt out only a bit of water.

Next stop is the tear gas house where we receive instructions for putting on our gas masks. One of the drill sergeants addresses us as we stand at attention in perfect formation.

"This house is full of tear gas. You will enter the house, remove your protective mask, take several deep breaths, and then walk, not run, to the exit door where a drill sergeant will be standing. You will take another deep breath and loudly state your name and serial number before you are allowed to exit. Be sure to keep your eyes open at all times."

Martin is the first one into the house and stumbles half way through. The others behind trip over him and sprawl to the ground. The Drill Sergeants drag them out of the gas-filled environment. By this time I am too tired to care if we are breathing tear gas or nerve gas. I come out of the building with eyes and nose running half way down my shirt, all too glad to start the five mile forced march back to the barracks.

Only once do the drill sergeants transform their behavior. At the grenade range, we receive instructions on how to throw a grenade, and then we pull the pin and actually throw it. I guess drill sergeants figure it isn't a good idea to upset someone holding a live grenade.

"Okay you Trainees, listen up. Today you are going to practice throwing a live grenade. This is a 'Live Grenade' and I repeat; This is a live grenade. You will follow our instructions exactly. You will not make any movement or do anything until you are told to do so. Have I made myself completely clear?"

It is not a question. Thirty wet behind the ears trainees, still in their late teens yell out, "Yes, Drill Sergeant!"

"Now, this is how we are going to proceed. First, we will demonstrate the proper method to throw a grenade. Watch Drill Sergeant Magoo carefully as he demonstrates. He will walk up to Drill Sergeant Dakes. When you walk up to Drill Sergeant Dakes, you will state your name and serial number. Drill Sergeant Dakes will repeat the instructions to you. Then Sergeant Dakes will hand you a live grenade. At this point you will hold the grenade in your right hand. I don't care if you are left handed or right handed. For this practice you will hold the grenade with your right hand. Everyone hold up your right hand."

One guy never quite gets it.

"Trainee Martin, I said hold up your 'other' right hand."

There is muted laughter as Martin's face turns red. He lowers his left hand and raises his right hand.

"Did I tell you to laugh, trainees? Well, did I?"

"No, Drill Sergeant!"

"The only time you move, speak or think is when I tell you to do it. Do you understand me, trainees?"

"Yes, Drill Sergeant!"

Normally this would result in the entire platoon doing endless eight count pushups or some other punishment. But not at the grenade range. Drill Sergeant pushes on with the instructions.

"You will hold the grenade firmly in your right hand with the lever facing away from you with your four fingers on the lever. Do not let go of the grenade or the lever. With your left hand you will grasp the ring of the pin. Everyone raise your left hand."

Once again, Martin is confused.

"Martin… Your 'other' left hand."

This time there is no laughter.

"Grasp the pin with your left hand and hold the grenade

'firmly' in your right hand. Move your hands apart and pull the pin from the grenade. Then throw the grenade over the concrete wall as far as you can. Drill Sergeant Magoo will demonstrate."

Drill Sergeant Magoo is handed a grenade, pulls the pin, and throws it in a beautiful arc into the valley below. Three seconds later, we hear a muffled explosion.

"Notice that Drill Sergeant Magoo threw the grenade 'like a baseball.' He did not lob it like John Wayne in a pansy girly throw. You will not lob this grenade like John Wayne. You will throw this grenade like you are throwing a baseball."

Drill Sergeant pauses and looks around to ensure he has our full attention, then he continues.

"One more thing. You will notice that on our side of the wall, there is a concrete gutter, and in that gutter are several holes. This is not for water drainage. If you happen to 'drop' the grenade, turn and throw yourself on the ground. Drill Sergeant Dakes will recover the grenade and direct it down one of those holes, where it will roll beyond the wall and detonate. Sergeant Dakes will grab you and throw both himself and you to the ground if you are not already on the ground. We have only lost one trainee so far, and we don't intend to lose any today. Is that clear?"

"Yes, Drill Sergeant."

It is a weak response but Drill Sergeant lets it pass.

The first few trainees do a fine job of throwing the grenade far out beyond the wall. Then it's Martin's turn. Drill Sergeant Dakes' voice is a murmur above the wind as he repeats instructions to Martin, then hands him a grenade. Martin pulls the pin and starts to put his arm back for the throw. Suddenly he fumbles, and the grenade falls to the ground in front of him. In one swift move, Drill Sergeant Dakes scoops it up and pops it down a hole. Martin, stunned, stands there until Sergeant Dakes grabs him and they both hit the ground with a thud. The grenade detonates a second later.

As they stand and dust themselves off, there is no yelling, no reprimands. Martin simply walks sheepishly back to the platoon and takes his place in the formation. That was the last day we saw Martin in our platoon.

The three months of basic training pass quickly and we are discharged to our secondary training. For me, this means three to four additional months of Military Police school. Once finished, I am sent to a stateside duty station for a year where I find military police work isn't all that great. We are required to pull both road duty: write tickets, direct traffic, keep the peace, as well as field duty: go out and practice soldiering. Our work schedule is nine days of twelve hour shifts, then three days off. The days off aren't bad, but the endless weeks on field duty sleeping in a tent is no fun.

Domestic disturbances are always a dangerous dispatch. Two on-duty military police are always dispatched together. This is for good reason. The disturbance usually starts as the wife or girlfriend makes a frantic call to the station and screams that she is being attacked by her boyfriend or husband. We respond and arrive to the angry shouts inside the house or trailer. The first thing we automatically assume is that both parties are probably drunk.

Entering the premises, the first task is to separate the two parties. Easier said than done. Invariably, when we restrain the husband, the wife attacks us, thus the reason behind two military police personnel sent together. Or if we restrain the wife, then the husband attacks us. It's just the protective nature of couples. Even if they are beating each other to death, when you intervene and restrain one of them, the other comes after you. I've had more than a few beer bottles cracked over my head.

It is important to stay uninvolved with their problems. As law enforcement personnel, we see some of the worst behavior, and we are generally only involved in someone's life for a brief moment. It isn't possible to fix the human condition in those brief moments. It's difficult to see the worst of human depravity day after day, because these situations very seldom turn out well. Maybe one in a thousand ends okay.

But the rest can wear you down. As a child, I grew up watching cartoons and television programs that were resolved in thirty minutes and always worked out for the best. The reality of raw life is a shock, but then another event makes me wonder if I'm cut out for this type of work.

On the military base, the main gate is manned by the military police. Every vehicle is stopped and only military or civilian personnel with a military ID can pass through. One night, I work with my partner who has been stationed at this particular base for almost two years. I'm a 'turtle' or newbie, because I arrived a couple of weeks ago. Four hours into our shift, at 2200 hours (ten p.m. civilian time), a car races up and screeches to a halt just outside of the gate building. A woman jumps out and runs into the gatehouse.

"Help me! My husband is trying to kill me. You have to help me!"

I'm stunned and don't know what to say or do. The gatehouse sits on a concrete island between incoming and outgoing traffic. Another car screeches to a stop. An army officer gets out, then strides angrily in our direction. Within a moment he charges through the door, nearly ripping it from the hinges, grabs his wife's arm and starts dragging her out of the tiny office. I'm just about ready to intervene when I feel a hand on my arm.

My partner warns me with a shake of his head. "You don't want to get involved with that."

Confused, I shake off his hand. "What are you talking about? You can't let him drag her off like that!"

He spends the next hour, between incoming traffic, lecturing me, in a kind way, about the world and our role in it. He ends with some advice. "That situation has been going on as long as I've been here. People have tried to intervene and they're not here anymore. I'm telling you to choose your fights carefully and never let anyone choose them for you… like with that situation."

Frustrated, I shake my head. "If we can't make a difference, then what are we here for?"

My partner isn't much older than me, but he is a lot more

street savvy. With a wry smile he shakes his head.

"We aren't here to make a difference. You have to know when to speak and when to stay silent. You know, like: 'there is a time for war, a time for peace; a time to tear, and a time to mend'?"

I shake my head.

"That's in the Bible, man. You've never heard of that? That's like famous stuff."

Jerking my head at the window, I cut him off, "Cars." I feel relieved he doesn't bring up the subject again.

Life drones on as I endure the sometimes conflicting life of the Military Police Corps. These issues don't seem to bother anyone else and I'm left to contemplate the word 'Justice'.

Our barracks are old wooden buildings in a remote part of the military base. Used during the Korean war, they are slated to be razed. But the base commander thinks it is a great place for the military police to live so we can be separated from the rest of the troops. Law enforcement personnel shouldn't have to live with the people they are enforcing.

The barracks consists of a large open area with bunks in a row down each side. The only privacy is a set of metal lockers set up between each area. A tiled common shower area is complete with a bunch of showerheads, and the toilets all stand in formation in a straight row. Having no privacy is part of being in the Army. After a difficult twelve-hour shift, any kind of bunk is nice.

On any one day, everyone in the barracks works a different shift. While some get ready for their shifts, others are off, or some, like me, come off the night shift. With all the commotion, it's difficult to sleep. During the day, any number of people play their boom boxes, talk, and laugh or just make noise. Then some guys see someone sleeping and sneak over to slam their hand or nightstick against the bed, then run before anyone jumps up and beats them. I learn to quickly fall asleep under many circumstances. Either I learn or I don't sleep.

I sit on the side of the bunk and pull on my combat boots for our next work shift. Just as I wonder if I'll be stuck in this place forever, Private Jenkins walks over to my bunk and throws an official looking letter on the bed beside me.

"Conner," Jenkins says, "check this out. We have orders for Korea as dog handlers."

My heart leaps with excitement. Any place seems better than this dump, and an overseas assignment is even better.

"Really? Wow, that's fantastic! When do we ship out?"

Jenkins has befriended me and helped me to evade trouble while teaching me the ropes. When a new troop arrives, the rest of the guys play any number of tricks including short-sheeting his bed or stuffing road kill under the sheets. They may even give him a shower beating and shove his head in one of the toilets. Even so, when out in the field on maneuvers, those same troops will give up their life for another guy.

As Jenkins and I transfer for our new assignment, we first report to the K-9 training school in San Antonio. We receive a canine partner and learn how to work with a dog. The dog also learns how to work with us. For a short period of time, the military tried breeding their own dogs. For some reason they closed that operation and returned to donated dogs. We see a variety of breeds, large German Shepherds to small dogs weighing under ten pounds. It's quite a sight to see a big MP walk with a miniature poodle. However, the small dogs are useful in bomb detection because we can put them in the luggage compartment of an aircraft where they can easily navigate.

In my training, the German Shepherd is the standard dog of choice. My dog is particularly stubborn. If I turn right, he turns left. If I turn left, he sits down. If I encourage him to attack, he rolls over so I can scratch his belly. It's embarrassing. But after a couple of weeks, he starts to get the hang of things and shapes into a better canine soldier. For the most part, the dog and I have great fun.

We have to take care of the dogs twenty four by seven, so there isn't time for other forms of entertainment. However, before we leave San Antonio, a few of us want to see the sights, especially the River Walk area where all the girls hang out. So one Friday after class, we rent a car and head out the gate.

When we first arrived on base, Sergeant Coy gave us the standard briefing with a little bit of a twist to it. "Most of you have heard this type of briefing before, so I'll be 'brief' if you'll pardon the pun. But first, I'll give you some important information you'll need to know when visiting the surrounding community. This is Texas and just about everyone around here carries a weapon. They may also have a few rifles in their pickup trucks. So when you are at a bar getting sloshed to the gills, you'd better maintain a real low profile and stay out of trouble. If you get in some bar fight, you might get shot and end up either in jail or in the morgue."

At dusk, three of us motor out of the base gate and turn onto the crowded road. A car pulls up fast on our tail. The driver slams on his brakes and hits the horn. Then he pulls around us real fast, cuts in front and hits the brakes. We slow down. As he speeds up and then slows down again, I flash my hi-beams at him a couple of times. Then seeing an opening, I pull around and get in front of him. Traffic is stop and go, and soon he's right on my tail again.

Jack sits in the back seat and watches through the rear window. Suddenly, he pipes up, "Uh oh, he's leaning over to the passenger side. Looks like he's trying to grab something out of the glove compartment! We'd better get out of here. He's probably got a gun! Let's get out of here!"

Concentrating on the traffic in front of me, I glance in the rearview mirror. The guy is definitely leaning way over and grabbing something, but in this traffic I have nowhere to go. We're all nervous. First of all, I don't want this rental car shot up and secondly, I don't want to get shot.

"Turn around and see what he's doing Jack! Keep an eye on him, will ya'?" I try to find an opening on either side, but we're packed in tighter than sardines in a can. Suddenly Jack yells, "He's got something. He's got something! He's pointing it our way!"

With a racing heart, I'm ready to duck when I look at the rearview mirror and start laughing. The other guys crouch down and look at me like I'm crazy. "Guys, take a look at this jerk. He's got a flashlight. He's shining it in our window."

Sure enough, the guy waves a small flashlight around He points it through the windshield then wiggles it up and down, apparently trying to blind us with it. At that moment, the traffic opens up and I take off down the road, leaving him in the dust. We all have a good laugh at our close call.

Before shipping out for Korea, I take some leave time to travel home and visit my family. Once home, I find Grandfather Conner in the hospital, and not doing well. At seventy six, he's slipping downhill fairly quickly, and I'm not sure I'll have an opportunity to see him again. Over the years, I spent a lot of time at Grandma and Grandpa Conner's house. In spite of Grandma Conner's rough edges, both she and Grandpa have been good to me, treating me better than their own son, my father.

On the day I'm scheduled to leave for a foreign land, I slip away from our house early and make my way to the hospital. My ailing grandfather's mind slips away with his life. I stand next to his bed, unable to speak. He barely whispers, "Kit," as if he thinks I am my dad. In my uniform, I bear a striking resemblance to my father, so this must be confusing him. For ten minutes, I try to explain who I am, but it is evident I am not making headway. Frustrated, I bend down near his ear. "Grandpa, I'm going to leave for Korea today. I just wanted to say goodbye."

Something in me wants to give him a kiss, but I can't bring myself to do it. Like I've said, our family isn't really the touchy, feely type. We are more of the uncomfortable hugging kind of family. Turning from the bed, I walk to the door but I can't leave. It feels as if all of heaven stands in that doorway and blocks my exit. I can't shove past. Behind me, I hear my grandfather whisper as loudly as he can, "Goodbye, Babe."

Closing my eyes momentarily, I grit my teeth. It takes everything in me to turn and walk back over to his bedside. Leaning down, I give him an awkward kiss on the forehead. "I love you, Grandpa."

On the long flight to Korea, night falls quickly. In the darkened cabin, I stare out the window into the blackness. My heart is heavy with sadness. How does time pass so fast? It seems like only yesterday that Grandpa Conner sat in his chair and watched the baseball game, yelling instructions to the players on the television while downing a beer. Is this what life is all about? Getting through whatever days we have only to grow feeble and bedridden with half a mind? A tear forms and drips onto my starched green military shirt. Everyone around me is asleep so I just let the flood continue as we wing our way toward morning.

Chapter Ten
Mitch Meets Korea

Climbing down the steep stairs of the plane, my feet step on land a world away from the United States in terms of distance, time, and culture. The wind hits my face and the air smells fresh after being cooped up in the Boeing 747 for 19 hours.

Making my way into the terminal for customs, the stark differences begin to emerge. Pairs of soldiers toting machine rifles march the terminal building while others walk with German Shepherd dogs, patrolling for explosives and drugs. Once through customs with my duffle bag and footlocker, five or six different cab drivers vie for my business and try to grab the luggage. I wave them away but they are very persistent and buzz around me like flies on a carcass. The luggage I have with me is not what I started with.

When I received my orders and instructions for travel, the paper looked like it had been printed with ink long overdue for replacement and was quite faded and barely readable. There was a specification for luggage allowable weight and it looked like it stated

"150lbs". After my dad and mom dropped me off at the airport, I was standing at the counter with my duffle bag and a large rectangular footlocker. Having never really travelled much, I knew nothing about weight restrictions or what to take or not take. So I just threw a bunch of my stuff into the foot locker, which was heavy in itself, and my Army uniforms into my duffle bag. The agent at the counter announces I am over by twenty five pounds.

Being confused by this I pull out my orders and show her the instructions with the weight allocation.

"This says the maximum is a hundred and fifty pounds."

She sighs loudly and points to what I though was a '1'.

"That's not a one, its a smudge. You only have fifty pounds unless you want to pay for the extra twenty five pounds you are over."

My face flushes quite red. Although my parents wanted to wait with me at the airport, I had adjured them to leave. This is 1978. There are no cell phones so I can't call my mom and dad to turn around and come back to the airport. The best I could possibly do is wait until they get home and then try to reach them using a nearby pay phone. By the time they get back up here, I will have missed my flight. I've never had a credit card, and I'm not really willing to spend what little cash I do have on this. The counter agent sees my hesitation and dilemma and tries to move me along.

"If you don't want to pay for the overage, you can step out of line and get rid of the extra weight."

The line behind me is now longer. It took forty five minutes to get this far to the counter and I don't relish standing in it again. I turn again to the young woman behind the counter. She is wearing the typical airlines uniform but her peace symbol earrings and disdain for me is fairly obvious. This isn't too far removed from the Vietnam War and military personnel are not well favored in American society. Pulling my luggage off to the side, I spend a few minutes pitching half of the contents of the footlocker into a nearby garbage can, until I am sure to be well within the weight limits. It takes another hour to again reach the counter. There is no security to go through, so after I get my ticket, it's just a straight walk to the gate to board my flight. Now that I'm in Korea having to lug this footlocker around, I'm wishing I had left it at home.

Walking out from the terminal, I locate the green army bus for transport to the nearby military base, stow my gear, and climb aboard. The thirty minute trip to base winds through the narrow city streets of Seoul. Everything is very different, from the ladies on the streets throwing water on the brick sidewalks and whisking it away with a broom, to the flowing, fluted architecture. When we arrive at the large military base, I go through the normal processing of coming in to the country and receive my secondary orders of where I will be stationed; a small compound where I will provide security. At the processing station, the Staff Sergeant looks curiously at my footlocker.

"What's that?"

He is a man of few words.

"That's my stuff I brought with me."

"Get rid of it."

He gestures off to a corner of the room where there is a large trash container piled with suitcases.

"Get rid of it?"

The activity in the room stops and a hush falls. Looking at the Sergeant, I see his neck flush red and not from embarrassment. I figure it's best to not create a big scene on my first day in country.

"Yes, Sergeant. Absolutely... get rid of it." I can't really remember what was in that footlocker, but I guess I didn't miss it too much. I felt worse about all the work it took to lug it here rather than because of what was in it.

Climbing into the back of a deuce and a half army truck, I feel curiously light with only my duffle bag. The trip to the small compound is dusty and the infrastructure of the city gives way to rolling fields of rice and barley. No wheat, corn or such. After a while we pull into a small army base with a medium sized village built around it. Eighteen of the twenty soldiers disembark here. Then the two of us who are left continue on with the driver for another trek to a tiny village with an even smaller Army compound located at the fringe.

The truck pulls through the gate and grinds to a stop. Jumping out with my duffle bag, I see there is a two-story apartment-like building, and four smaller buildings housing the medical office, the captain's office, the mess hall, and the motor pool. Off to one corner there is a very small storage building known as a quonset hut. The first sergeant's orderly comes out of the office and heads over to the two of us as the truck pulls off for the drive back to Seoul.

"You must be the new guys."

After traveling for almost two days, I'm not in the best mood and feel like saying, "Duh, what gave you that idea." Instead I smile and respond politely to the private.

"Yes, where should we take our gear?"

"Which of you is Private Jenner?"

The guy next to me responds.

"That's me."

The orderly points to the low apartment building.

"You're in room twenty three."

I pick up my gear to follow him, expecting the orderly to provide my room number.

"You must be Sergeant Conner."

"That's right."

He turns and gestures to the tiny storage building in the corner. It's the quonset hut which looks very similar to a coffee can cut in half and turned on its side.

"The MP's stay in that building over there. We keep you guys separated from the general troops. I think there's a spare bunk."

I'm about to ask why the MP's stay in a storage hut but he turns and goes back into the office as I realize the only thing this storage hut stores are MP's. Hefting my duffle bag for its final trek to my home for the next year, I trudge over and enter the tin building.

The door is a crude wooden screen door with some plastic over it to keep the wind out. Inside I blink to adjust my vision after coming in out of the bright sunlight.

The interior is divided in half by a small thin partial wall open at both sides. There are two bare bulbs for illumination and one is burned out. In the first half there are a set of double bunks on each wall with an oil drum type heater in the middle of the room, its stack reaching up to the low ceiling. A five-gallon can of diesel fuel with a metal feed tube in it hangs off the side for fuel.

In the back section, there are four double bunks along each wall. Each bunk in both sections is accompanied by an old rusty metal locker with double doors. At least the floor is concrete and not dirt. It's more of an enclosure than a building and it was definitely meant to be a supply hut before they threw some bunks and a heater in it. It's worse than I came from but, for the experience of being in Korea, I don't mind it too much and feel lucky to be here.

The showers and toilets are twenty five yards down the fence line in another quonset hut building about three times this size. The apartment building where Jenkins went turns out to be a paradise compared to our quarters, complete with individual bathrooms with modern showers for each room.

As I'm standing in my new quarters trying to take this in, a Korean MP looks up from sitting on his bunk and points to the back.

"There a bunk in back of it."

He is part of the KATUSA program where the Republic of Korea (ROK) army provides Korean personnel to the US army for assistance with translation and other tasks. KATUSA is an acronym meaning Korean Augmentation Troops to the United States Army.

Nodding, I walk into the back section where an empty and somewhat crooked metal locker leans against a set of stacked bunks. It doesn't take long to unload my meager gear into it. The doors don't really stay closed too well so I take a metal folding chair from the corner and prop against them.

Lying across the empty mattress I quickly fall into a deep

sleep, exhausted after not sleeping for almost two days. The next morning I wake up around five a.m. Even though I slept for about twelve hours I still feel groggy from jet lag. A couple of MP's are just coming in from the night shift, and several others are sacked out in the other bunks. The back room where I am is chilly in the September pre-winter air and I can smell the aroma something cooking in the front room. After introducing myself, I change into a clean uniform and head into the front room.

A couple of KATUSAs are sitting on one of the bunks, using chopsticks to slurp up noodles from bowls perched on their knees. A small pot of noodles and spices is cooking on top of the diesel-fired heater. Although the back room is chilly, this room is uncomfortably hot and I'm glad there were no spare bunks in it. A sergeant is sitting on the other bunk. He stands and extends his hand as I come into the room.

"Hi. I'm Steve Slice. You must be Conner. Welcome to Korea."

He shakes my hand then introduces me to the two Korean soldiers seated on the other bunk.

"And this is Sergeant Na and PFC Kim Chon, but everybody just calls him Kansas City for short."

The acronym 'PFC' is for 'Private First Class'. They look up from eating and smile and nod at me.

"After you get ready, I'll give you the grand tour of our little compound here."

"Let me grab my jacket and I'm ready. When does the mess hall open for breakfast? I haven't eaten for a while."

Sergeant Slice laughs then follows me back to my bunk. "Mess is open at zero six hundred hours, but you don't want to eat there. The food's pretty bad."

Zero six hundred hours means six a.m. civilian lingo. Moving the chair holding the doors of my metal locker shut I reach in and grab my jacket.

"Well, I'll eat just about anything right now. On the drive in, the village looks to be pretty much just a crossroads with some shops around it and that's it. Didn't appear to be a lot of choice in restaurants or eateries."

"No, not a lot. A couple of little chophouses and a bar is about it. Come on, I'll show you around."

The compound is no larger than it appeared yesterday. There is a nice concrete block library building and some much larger quonset hut buildings that I hadn't noticed. We stop in front of one of them and Sergeant Slice points out a faded sign over the entrance: 4077th MASH.

"This used to be the Mash unit that they modeled the TV show after. These quonset huts were a hospital back in the 1950's."

There is a small chapel near the gate entrance and we end up at another tiny concrete block building wedged in the corner of the compound which turns out to be the NCO club, 'NCO' standing for 'Non Commissioned Officers'. Even though it has the title of 'NCO Club' over the door, it is the only other place to eat close around and everyone from privates to officers frequent it. There are a few tables and a pinball machine in the corner leaving room for about twenty five people. It is a good place to have a party and celebrate birthdays.

We take a table and a middle aged Korean woman comes over and bows slightly in greeting. "Whachu eat jis moning."

I look at Slice questioningly.

"She wants to know what you want to eat."

"Oh. Well, how about a couple eggs over medium and some bacon with toast."

Slice smiles and looks up at the waitress who is also the cook.

"Give him some Ohm Rice."

"Ahhh, very goot."

She backs away from our table bowing, then turns and heads into the kitchen area. In a moment she returns with two cups and a ceramic pot of tea which she carefully pours into our cups.

"You drink. Very goot."

Raising his cup, we clink in a toast and I sip the hot liquid.

"Umm, very unique taste. What exactly did you order?"

"That's barley tea. I ordered you vegetable rice with an egg over it. You're not in Kansas anymore, Dorothy. There's no bacon and she doesn't know what you mean by, 'eggs over medium and toast.'"

In a few moments she brings out a large plate of Ohm Rice. It is indeed a mound of rice with some carrots, peas, and onions in it, all covered by what can only be described as a thin egg omelet with ketchup on it in the shape of a happy face. Taking a tentative bite, it is better than I feared it would be and I quickly devour it.

"Hey, slow down there. No one is going to take that away from you and there's no hurry here. We're in the middle of nowhere."

"I'm used to a standard fifteen minute meal break with ten minutes spent standing in line and five minutes left to eat. What's our agenda for today?"

"There is no agenda." Seeing my confused look, Sergeant Slice continues. "This isn't like the States. For the first week, take some time off and do whatever you want. Visit the surrounding villages, see the sights, acclimate yourself. Then we will put you on Tac site rotation."

"Tac site rotation?"

"Tactical. As a dog handler, your schedule is pretty easy. There are five dog handler's including yourself. You work one twenty four hour shift on the Tac security site team, and then you get four days off. The truck leaves this compound at zero eight hundred hours with everybody going up and it takes about twenty minutes to get there. Then, whoever is finished with their shift comes back with the truck. Pretty simple. But for now, acclimate yourself and get familiar with the area. And rest up."

As we get up to leave, I find out my breakfast is a whopping seventy five cents. I pay with a dollar and tell her to keep the change. Then I reach into my pocket and throw a couple of dollars extra on the table, thinking to give her a nice tip. As I turn to leave I catch a glimpse of Sergeant Slice picking up the bills and sliding them into his pocket.

"What are you doing?"

"Oh, you have to understand you're in a different country here. These people make less than twenty dollars a month. That would be like getting a hundred bucks."

We walk out as he continues to talk about the culture and customs but somehow keeps the bills in his pocket, and I let it go.

For the next week I sleep off my jet lag and get to know my fellow MP's. As the Sergeant said, four were dog handlers like myself, five others were line MP's pulling gate duty and patrolling the nearby villages to keep the ruckus down to a minimum, and there are the two MP KATUSA's attached to our small squadron helping out where needed. Travel is either walking or by bus. There are a few taxis if you can find one. We are pretty far out from any city of size and almost no cars or taxis are here at all. I think the size of our village is barely a thousand including all the troops stationed here.

Traveling by bus from village to village is a good way to see the lay of the land. There are little villages every so often, mainly around an Army base, then mile after mile of rice and barley fields. Farmers tend the fields using cows to pull carts and plow. There is no mechanization. They plant and harvest all by hand. It's like stepping back in time a hundred years.

After a week I'm feeling better and am ready to get to work having pretty much seen what there is to see. The covered army truck turns off the narrow asphalt road onto an even narrower gravel and dirt road and begins winding its way up a small mountain. At one point the road changes to concrete on a particularly steep and dangerous section right before the gate to the Tac. There are no safety walls and the narrow road drops off several hundred feet on either side. Looking out the back of the truck there is only rock, vegetation, and a lot of dust.

Pausing at the gate, the guard comes around and checks the back to ensure only properly cleared personnel are aboard, then we start up again. The truck pulls through the gate and drops us off before rumbling back down the way it came.

Once out of the truck I walk down a small hill past the generator shed to the kennel to meet my new working partner, a one hundred and ten pound German Shepherd named Charlie. The dogs really have it a lot better than we do in terms of working hours. They have someone to care for them twenty four hours a day, and there are very strict regulations concerning how long the dogs can work before taking required rest breaks, and how long to rest before returning to work. They can only work several hours before taking a required hour's rest time. Then they can work a few more hours. After that though, they have to be given a twenty four hour rest period. No one ever told me that I had to rest after working a few hours. Quite the opposite, someone would probably yell at me and say, "What are you doing resting? Get back to work." So the dogs have it good.

Getting ready to patrol with the dogs in the evening, we announce to everyone to head indoors and stay there. This is a necessary precaution when we patrol with these German Shepherds. Most people think of police dogs and how highly trained they are. The dogs walk patiently next to their handlers, they are well behaved, and when they are released to attack, with just one command they will freeze in their tracks. These Shepherds are not like that. They are trained to do one thing, and that is to attack. Once we release the dog, there is no stopping it; the dog is going to hit the target and there is no easy way to call them off. The dogs don't know the difference between a friendly Korean guard, an American GI, or an enemy North Korean. To minimize the risk someone getting bitten, we advise everyone to stay indoors.

There is this one incident when a Korean guard doesn't get the message. One of our team is walking up the hill from the kennel area with his dog when suddenly a Korean guard crests the hill on his way down. The dog catches wind of his scent. Within a second the dog lunges, rips the leash out of the handler's hand, crosses the fifty feet to the guard, and is in the process of tearing his arm off. There are two saving fortunalities.

The first is the handler responds quickly and is able to choke the dog off of the frightened guard within seconds after the attack. The other is that it is rather cold out on this particular night and the guard is wearing a heavy coat. Although the coat sleeve is pretty well tattered, there are minimal puncture wounds and no broken bones. He has some pretty good bruises which he later proudly displays as evidence of surviving an attack by one of our dogs. There are a few other incidents, but, as is usually the case, it is more a result of stupidity than anything else.

The kennel area consists of a concrete block office building with an oil fired drum heater, a desk, a bunk, a supply cabinet containing medical supplies for the dogs, and a large fifty-gallon metal trash can with a wooden lid containing the military issue dog food. The fifty pound bags of dog food are Army green with the words, 'DOG FOOD' in large, plain, black print.

Outside, there are five dog kennels or pens where the dogs spend their off time during the day. Each kennel consists of a caged area with a heavy gate and latch on the front of it. In the back part of the kennel caged area is a wooden doghouse that can be separated from the rest of the pen by a sliding metal door. This makes it possible to clean the pen of 'you know what' while the dog is kept in his house.

There is a very specific procedure that must be followed when cleaning the kennel pen. First, it is important to only work with one pen at a time. Second, you put the dog into its house by saying the appropriate command, and then slide the metal door across the house opening. This leaves the dog contained in the house and allows the front pen gate to be opened to clean and disinfect.

All the dog handlers are trained to use this exact process: one: put the dog in the house, two: slide the door closed, three: clean the cage, four: close and lock the gate, and then five: release the dog from the house. That way there can be no error of a dog escaping its pen. The one thing we want to avoid at all cost is for multiple dogs to escape their kennels at one time. The dogs are trained to attack and they don't like each other at all. So if multiple dogs are out at one time, they could attack and injure each other and these are expensive animals.

It is much faster, however, to lock all the dogs in their houses at once, open all the pen gates at the same time, clean all the pens at one effort, close and lock all the gates, then let all the dogs back out into their pen area one after another.

The only problem with this faster method is that it is easy to get distracted and forget to lock all of the kennel gates before letting the dogs out of their house. Thus it is possible for several dogs to get loose. With only one handler on site, this could be a disaster. However, when there is a safe, slower method and a fast, riskier method, you know what everybody does. They do it the fast way, not the safe way.

One particular incident occurred after I had been in country only a couple of months. Being a certified veterinary technician, it is my responsibility to do the monthly medical exams on the dogs and to handle any medical emergencies… for the dogs, not humans.

Normally, there is only one dog handler manning the Tac Site kennels on any certain day. It is an unusual situation on this particular day because the on-duty dog handler is on site pulling his shift, and I am also there doing medical exams on the dogs and updating their military records… Yes, even the dogs have full military records. It turns out to be a very lucky thing I am there.

Remember, the rule is that we never ever take more than one dog out at one time and we only clean one pen at a time. The dog handler on duty that day is barely twenty years old and this is his first assignment out of dog training school. Having arrived a few months before me, he should certainly know the procedures by now. After assisting me with the medical exams, he goes out to wash down the kennels.

As I sit at the office desk finishing up some paperwork, I hear this commotion outside. Dogs are barking like crazy and someone is yelling for help. I know right away what has happened and grab a spare leather leash as I leap over the desk and slam out the door in a flash. Time is going to be very critical to minimize the damage.

I can hear dogs fighting in the back behind the pens. Rounding the corner I assess the situation without slowing. King, a very large one hundred and twenty pound Shepherd is embroiled in a battle to the death with Budzo, a smaller eighty pound Shepherd. To his credit, Budzo has the upper hand and has King's throat solidly between his teeth and isn't letting go. King is slinging the smaller dog back and forth, trying to escape and attack. The dog handler is standing in shock, leash hanging from his hand and his mouth gaping open.

There is a saying, 'he who hesitates is lost' and this is not the time to hesitate. We must get both dogs under control as fast as possible and it's going to take both of us to do it. As I charge past the young troop and right up on the dogs I yell at him. "When I get a leash on Budzo and choke him out, you get that leash on King. Then when I say 'Now', you pull King off."

At the same time I'm yelling commands at the two fighting dogs, trying to get them to stop. I take a quick glance at him and he gulps and nods. My plan is to straddle Budzo, get the leash around his neck, and then choke him out so he will release King. At the same time, Private Goofball is going to have to have to get his leash around King's neck and pull him back at the exact moment Budzo releases his clamped jaws. Otherwise, when I pull Budzo off, King will lunge forward and attack Budzo or me.

The dogs are dancing around and trying to pin each other to the ground making it difficult to get the leashes in place. Taking a chance, I leap forward and thrust my hand between the fighting dogs in an attempt to restrain them. I get lucky and manage to clip the leash onto Budzo's collar. Like a cowboy wet behind the ears, the PFC is trying to sling the leash around King but he is too far away. Grabbing the end of his leash with my other hand, I clip it onto King's collar.

Now I'm holding both leashes and restraining both dogs which

I can't do for long. PFC finally moves in and grabs King's leash allowing me to let go. Both dogs are now somewhat leashed but next comes the tricky part: getting them separated with the least amount of damage.

Still holding Budzo's leash with my left hand, I use my right hand to choke him out of his death grip on King. Budzo's breathing gets raspy and he finally releases his mouth and I yell, "Now!" at the Private who hauls back on King's neck with the leash.

Suddenly, as he is pulling back, King lunges forward and nails my right hand and thumb between his sharp teeth. Private Goofball has recovered and starts pulling back again on King but now my hand is coming with him, being clamped in King's mouth.

"Stop, stop!"

Now we really have a dilemma. With my left hand and arm, I'm restraining eighty pounds of Budzo, and now my right hand is trapped by King. I can't let go of Budzo or he will attack King again. But he's wearing me out fast and I won't be able to hang on to him much longer. The PFC is going to have to choke out King so he that he will let go of my hand. That means he has to grip the leash in one hand and use his other hand to choke him out.

King is a lot of dog to handle with a choke collar on when he is calm, and now he only wearing a leather collar and is anything but calm. Right now he is whipping my hand back and forth like a piece of meat and straining against the collar. I know I am going to tire out in seconds.

"Grab the leash in your left hand and choke him out with your right! Then yank him as hard as you can away from me!"

"I can't!" PFC doesn't want to get any closer to King's sharp canines than he already is.

"Do it now Soldier!! We only have seconds!"

To his credit, he snaps out of it and chokes out King. As soon as King releases my hand, Private manages to wrestle him back to his kennel and slam the gate into place, locking it this time.

Wrangling Budzo back down to his kennel I manage to secure

the gate. There are multiple puncture wounds on my hand and blood is all over my hand and arm. I can't tell if it's my blood or the dogs, but I have to get the bleeding stopped quickly. As I jog by King's kennel, I see he is lying on the concrete and a bit bloodied. Bursting into the office I grab the first aid kit and begin to pressure-wrap my hand. PFC is leaning against the desk shaking.

As I wrap my hand with some gauze I address the young recruit.

"Private, we've got two problems here and every minute is critical. One is King has been injured and the other is I've been bitten. I need you to run up the hill and tell the duty lieutenant that we need an ambulance in route for one of the dogs. See if there is a jeep or something up there. Somehow we are going to have to get king up the hill for pickup and he's too heavy to carry."

The PFC takes off up the hill. Grabbing the med kit, I head out of the office to King's kennel. As I open the kennel gate and latch it behind me, King remains lying on the concrete. He moves his head slightly to look over at me and wags his tail a bit as I inspect the damage. Although some blood is oozing out, it doesn't look too terribly bad. However, King barely moves as I clean up the wounds, which isn't a good sign. Finishing up, I scratch him behind the ear and his tail sweeps across the floor a couple of times.

"Well buddy, it looks like you and me took a beating on that one didn't we."

Private G arrives with the lieutenant's jeep and parks it outside the kennel office gate. For safety, there are two sets of gates. Each pen is enclosed and gated, then the entire kennel area is surrounded with a 10 ft. high fence and entry gate with concertina wire across the top of it all. Hearing the jeep pull up, I exit and lock King's kennel, then unlock the main gate. PFC has brought a couple of guys down to help, but I have to ask them to move off and stand at a distance. If King sees them it would only rile him up again and we need to keep him calm for now. The Private and I map out our plan.

"What did the LT say?"

"He called for a medevac."

"A medevac? Are they sending a truck up?"

Private G shakes his head.

"Negative, a chopper."

"A chopper!!?"

Closing my eyes I slowly shake my head. It's going to be hard enough to explain this situation in the first place. But to scramble a medevac helicopter for an injured dog to boot makes it worse. Especially if the dog isn't outright dying which I don't think it is. Goofball hangs his head.

"Sorry Sergeant Conner, I know I've made a mess of things."

"Well that's an understatement! It's too late now. Okay, let's talk through this first. I've got the choke chain on King so we only have to clip the leash to it and we're ready. I'll go in his kennel and close the gate. When I pick him up, you open the gate, and then run ahead and open the main gate, and close and lock it behind us. After you lock it, get in the back of the jeep and I'll hand King over to you. Hold him still while I drive up to the helipad. Then you can hand King over to me."

Although he isn't happy about handling King, it goes off without a hitch. King is in no mood to fight and stays fairly calm, only bucking a couple of times. We pass the LT and a retinue of people headed up to the helipad to watch us. This is the best entertainment they've had in a while.

At the helipad I park the jeep a safe distance away and Private G hands King over to me. Hefting him up I stumble backwards and almost fall but luckily catch myself. Then I lug him closer to the pad and collapse. This is a heavy dog. The helipad is the highest point of the Tac site and offers a stunning view of the countryside. I can see the helicopter headed our way; army green with a red cross on it. In a few minutes it maneuvers in and lightly touches down. The flight medic hops out of the back, trots over with his head down to avoid the rotating blades, and crouches down. We have to yell over the sound of the jet engines.

"How bad?"

"Not as bad as it looks, just some secondary bleeding."

"Alright, bring him over and let's get him strapped in. Keep your head down under the blades."

By now it's getting more difficult to pick King up and he's starting to get feisty with the noise from the chopper. Plus my hand is beginning to throb badly and I realize I should have popped a couple of aspirin while I was at the kennel. I manage to get King up to chest level but I'm having trouble standing up with the added weight. Private G runs over and helps support some of the weight so I can get to my feet.

Looking back I see the LT and about twenty guys watching the circus of us stumbling around with this large German Shepherd. The LT mouths something about 'better have a good explanation' but I can't hear it over the blades and engine noise.

The flight medic and I get King strapped in, then I turn and motion for Private G and he jogs over, keeping his head low. I have to yell to make myself heard, even though he's no more than a few inches away. "Phone down to the compound and tell Sergeant Slice what happened. Have him send a truck down to the clinic in Seoul to pick me up later. I'm sure I won't be coming back the way I'm leaving."

Nodding, he jogs clear of the chopper. There's one more thing before we can lift off. I have to be strapped in. The problem is, I've never flown in a chopper before, and can't quite figure out how the four safety straps clasp together. King is strapped in. The flight medic is strapped in. The pilots are waiting and everyone on the Tac site has gathered a bit down the road to watch this rare event. The flight medic leans over but, being strapped in himself, can't reach far enough to help me.

"The pilots can't take off until you're strapped in. You have to strap in or get out. We're burning fuel."

I was never good at puzzles and the pieces just don't seem to make any sense, plus I keep dropping them out of my bandaged hand which has gone numb and won't grasp. Finally, the flight medic has pity on me, unstraps his harness and helps buckle me in. It's very embarrassing. Then back in his seat he pulls on his headset and gives the clearance. The jet engines whine up and the blades pitch and cut through the air as we leap off of the small mountain, make a tight turn, and head for the veterinary clinic in Seoul.

Within minutes we are landing at the helipad closest to the veterinary clinic. As we are coming in, I see they have an ambulance and several medical and veterinary techs standing by with a stretcher; not for me, for the dog. Again I groan inwardly as this seems to be getting more out of hand as the minutes tick by. How am I going to explain this mess?

Once on the ground, they inject King to knock him out so they can handle him, then trundle him off in the ambulance leaving me standing by myself. Hiking across base about a quarter of a mile, I get my hand stitched up and then head back over to the Vet clinic. Turns out King had only minor gashes and it looked worse than it actually was.

After spending a night at the Yongsan Base in Seoul, I meet up with a truck sent from our compound and King and I are on our way back to the Tac site; King to his kennel and me to face the music. The commander is none too happy about the entire incident from the point of view that we airlifted a dog to a vet hospital, and now it becomes a huge problem to explain. Many reports are to be written and someone's head is going to roll.

In the end, Sergeant Slice helps explain the situation to the captain. The PFC and I manage to avoid official punishment, but PFC is confined to the Tac Site for three days and I agree to implement a complete refresher-training program for all the dog handlers.

The one other incident that I will mention involves a disgruntled soldier that has just arrived at our lovely compound from the States. By the mid seventies the Vietnam War is mostly over and the military service has gone from a draft to a volunteer system. This means that incoming personnel no longer represented a large slice of society, but a much smaller section of just those willing to volunteer. Additionally, as mentioned, society is not kind to military personnel during these years and many soldiers who fought valiantly are treated worse than a junkyard dog. This doesn't lend any attractiveness to join the service and sometimes the quality of personnel reflects that attitude if you get my drift.

In this particular case the disgruntled soldier is mad because he got shipped to Korea and had to leave his girlfriend back in the states. So he thinks he will pull a little stunt in an attempt to get himself shipped back to the states.

The motor pool of our compound contains a retinue of vehicles from small jeeps to large two and a half ton trucks known as a deuce and a half. The look hasn't changed much and you've probably seen them on TV or driving down the road; painted camouflaged green or sand color with the arched tarpaulin across the back. Standard procedures state that in order to use one of the vehicles it is necessary to have the commander's office fill out the necessary form, then take it to the motor pool sergeant to check out the keys for a vehicle.

Disgruntled GI sneaks into the motor pool area and waits for the sergeant to head up to the latrine for his midmorning constitutional. The latrine door slams shut. Waiting another minute, he then breaks the lock on the key repository, grabs one for a deuce and a half, then jumps in the truck and starts it up. Clouds of diesel smoke pour out as he slams it in gear and takes off. Normally the engine would have to be warmed up pretty good first or it would stall out. But this one had just been returned to the motor pool and it is piping hot and ready to go.

The motor pool metal chain link gate is shut, but there's no time to waste getting out and opening it. The front of the truck hits the gate in second gear and it flies partially open as the wheels roll over it and flatten it to the ground. Motor Pool sergeant hears the truck start up and comes running out of the latrine while trying to buckle his belt, toilet paper caught in his pants and streaming behind him.

Just outside the door he sees the truck bearing down on him and jumps back inside just as the truck bursts past taking the latrine door off with it.

Just past the latrine to the left is the mess hall. A sidewalk is between it and the former MASH quonset hut. There are two entrances to the mess hall from the sidewalk, and each has a canopy cover extending from the door over the sidewalk perpendicular to the building. The truck has gained some speed as Private Disgruntled swings the wheel hard to the left, pumps the gas, and shifts into a higher gear.

Inside the mess hall, the tables are currently filled with all the commissioned and non-commissioned officers from the compound for their monthly status meeting. The CO, or Commanding Officer, a captain, stands at a portable chalkboard as he gives his briefing. Suddenly there are two quick explosions directly outside and the exit door and frame disintegrate in a shower of dust and splintering wood.

Everyone dives under the tables and several senior NCO's yell, "Incoming! Incoming!" The captain ducks down and turns into the base of the chalkboard causing it to fall on top of him.

Outside, the truck has taken out both mess hall door canopies, hit and damaged the corner of the library building, knocked down both baskets on the basketball court, and is headed toward the main gate at full steam. The gate guard, an elderly Korean man hears the truck coming and waves his hands for the driver to stop so he can check the paperwork. He barely has time to jump back and falls through the office door into the small guard shack as the large truck hits and snaps the chain across the paved drive. It's a good thing he trips and falls into the shack because the force of the chain snapping whips it against the wall, shattering the glass windows, and would have cut him in half.

As it is, Private Disgruntled gets to the end of the drive and manages to flip the truck on its side as he attempts to turn too fast. He has left in his wake a stream of destruction but fortunately no one has been injured except in their pride.

Several hours later Captain Quigley's nerves have calmed down and Private Disgruntled is called into his office, escorted by two MPs. The MP's are dismissed and stand outside of the closed door listening to the muffled yelling as the captain vents his feelings about the event. Later, in Top's office (the first sergeant is known as Top) the 'conversation' continues.

"Do you think I'm sending you back to the states after that little Sunday afternoon drive? Well, do you? I've got better things to do than to sit around and babysit your sorry self. Is that what your mommy and daddy taught you to do when you don't get your sorry way? Throw a little fit and destroy some property? Well it may have worked at home but I can guarantee you it ain't gonna work here. I'm confining you to the TAC site for three days. During that time you will spend your days washing dishes and picking up every cigarette butt on the entire TAC site with a pair of tweezers. Then, when you get back down here, you can clean every single vehicle in the motor pool with a cotton swab. Then, after that, you can drive the captain around in his jeep so we can keep a close eye on you at all times. Is that understood, Private Stupid?"

Private Disgruntled makes the mistake of responding.

"I don't think you're supposed to call me 'stupid.'"

"Oh Yeah? Well, how about if I hear one more comment out of your stupid mouth, I'll take you out back of this office and beat you to a stupid pulp? Does that work for you?"

Seeing the private start to open his mouth, Top cuts him off for his own good. "Not one more word, private. Not One… MPs! Get this idiot out of here."

True to his word, about three days later the private is back down from TAC site duty and, to everyone's amazement, becomes the captain's driver. This led to the saying, "Screw up, Move up," but it was termed a slightly different way. Most of the GI's didn't know the whole story and thought they would like being the designated driver for the captain.

Chapter Eleven
The Missing

Within a few months, Sergeant Slice is due to leave and I'm 'selected' to take over management of the MP squadron which includes the dog handlers. Basically, I'm the stuck-ee for team lead duty. I don't realize how much of a 'stuck-ee' I am until a month after the Sergeant leaves.

But before he leaves, we inventory all the equipment that will now be my responsibility. Most of it is kept in a large metal storage unit known as a conex, located near the basketball court. Sergeant Slice accompanies me to the container and pulls a set of keys out of his pocket. He unlocks the heavy padlock on the door.

He looks me in the eye and holds out the clipboard with the inventory sheet and a pen. "Really no need to go through this — it's all here. You can just sign and save us both some time. You trust me, don't you?"

My face tinges red as I'm not real good at standing up for myself, but I know better than to pass on the inventory. "If it's all the same to you, let's just do it anyway."

Shrugging his shoulders, he pulls open the door. The hinges screech. We use a flashlight to go through everything inside and mark it on the inventory sheet. I'm thinking that he is trying to pull something over on me, but everything is in order.

After completing the inventory, he closes the door with another screech, secures it with the heavy lock and hands me the two keys. We each keep a signed copy of the inventory and another copy goes to the captain. A couple of weeks later Sergeant Slice returns to the states. Everything seems just fine until the next month's inventory with the supply sergeant and the captain present.

We stand in front of the storage unit as I unlock it and swing open the rusty door. As we step in and sweep the flashlight around, my jaw hits the floor! I look at the supply sergeant and the captain.

They look back at me. "Sergeant Conner, I hope this isn't some kind of practical joke."

My heart pounds as I stare at the completely empty container. "Uh... I... Uh..."

Captain Quigley asks, "Where is your inventory, Sergeant?"

"Uh... I don't know. It was here last month when I did the inventory with Sergeant Slice." I'm dumbfounded. How can the container be empty? Where did everything go? Did one of the guys move it or are they pulling a joke on me? Several scenarios run through my mind, but the truth never occurs to me.

Suddenly I snap back to reality as I realize the captain is addressing me again. "Hey, Sergeant Conner, did you hear me?"

"Yes sir, I mean no, sir. Sorry, sir."

"I want a full report on the location of your inventory on my desk by seventeen hundred hours today."

They both turn and walk out. As I exit and lock the door, I'm praying this is simply someone pulling a prank on me. I can't imagine any other scenario, until a couple of hours later when I call a meeting of our team. No one confesses about a prank, although I notice a couple of them try not to smile.

After I dismiss everyone, Corporal Bay, who I count as a friend, approaches me. "You really don't know what happened to that inventory?"

Defeated, I shake my head and sigh. "If it isn't a prank by one of the guys, I don't see how someone could steal it and get it through gate security. If I can't come up with that inventory, the Captain and Supply Sergeant are going to hang me, and I'll end up having to pay about two thousand dollars out of what little pay I get."

Bay puts his hands on his hips and looks down at me as though lecturing a child. "Mitch, who else do you think had the keys to that conex?"

"No one else has the keys except me. Sergeant Slice gave me the keys right after we did the inventory."

Bay laughs. "Don't you get it? What makes you think those are the 'only' two keys to the conex lock?"

The light begins to dawn on me and I look up at Bay. My mouth hangs open. "Huh? What are you saying?"

Bay looks around to make sure no one else is listening. "Look, you didn't hear this from me, but your supposed friend, Sergeant Slice, cleaned out the conex, took it off base and sold it right before he left."

I stare at him, more dumbfounded than when I saw the empty container. "What? He did what?" I can't believe that someone would pretend to be my friend and yet do something like this to me.

Bay shakes his head. "You can't trust people, Mitch. Most of these guys will stab you in the back given half a chance. Slice didn't care anything about you. He saw an opportunity to make a quick buck and he did it. That's all there is to it. You better wise up to life, my friend." Then he turns and walks out of my office.

Now I'm in a fix. I have no inventory and some silly story that I can't prove to anyone, and no one who will back me up. Later as I stand in front of the captain's desk, he pokes out his lips and stares at me with a sideways look.

"So, you're telling me that Sergeant Slice went into the conex after you did the inventory, took it through the security gate and sold it in the village. Is that it?"

"Yes, sir."

"And why should I even begin to believe that?"

"Sir, I can only give you my best estimation of what happened. The inventory was there, and I didn't open the lock again until today. It never occurred to me to change the lock or that there might be more than the two keys Sergeant Slice gave me."

"Are you aware, Sergeant, that I can give you an Article Fifteen punishment for this? And you will have to pay back the one thousand eight hundred dollars in inventory that needs to be replaced?"

I hear no hint of mercy in his voice. An Article fifteen is a step down from a court martial. I will lose my rank as sergeant, my pay for several months, my position as the team leader, and probably be confined to the Tac site, picking up cigarette butts with tweezers. What can I say? As far as the captain knows, I could be the one who sold off the inventory. I reply the only way I can. "Yes, sir."

The sound of defeat is clear to both of us. Captain Quigley stares silently at me. Finally he nods. "Okay. You may be naïve, but I don't think you're stupid enough to take that stuff and sell it, knowing that you have to produce it for inventory. I'll suspend any punishment for this incident, but you're still going to have to pay for the inventory that was lost. It was in your care, and it is still your responsibility. Work with the supply sergeant to order replacements and get with Finance to arrange a payment schedule. Dismissed."

"Yes, sir. Thank you, sir."

Saluting, I do an about face and exit the office. Once outside the small building I take a deep breath of the cold December air and blow it out in a fog. Fortunately, no one is around and it is fully dark, hiding the tears that sting my eyes. I don't know how I'm going to pay for this. I only make six hundred dollars a month. I'm going to be flat broke for a long time. But, more than the money, I realize I've been betrayed and feel like a fool. Leaning against the side of the building, I wipe my eyes with the back of my coat sleeve. I've always known I tend to take people at face value, and usually it's a mistake.

Still, I'm somehow surprised every time I end up betrayed. I don't know why I can't learn my lesson. I clearly remember my dad's advice, 'Mitch, you've got to learn not to wear your heart on your sleeve.' But I just don't know how.

"Sergeant Conner."

My reverie is broken by the voice of the night duty orderly. "Top wants to see you in his office right away."

"Sit down, Sergeant Conner."

The first sergeant sounds unnaturally nice, and I wonder what's going on.

"Sergeant, there's no easy way to say this, so I'll tell you straight out. We received word that your grandfather passed away sometime last evening. I'm sorry to have to break the news to you."

I guess I was expecting it. I'm so far away — it doesn't seem real.

Top continues. "Why don't you catch a ride down to Yongsan tomorrow and call your family. I'm confident that unless you actually lived with your grandparents, the Army can't let you take personal leave to attend the funeral.

So my grandpa died and I can't go back for the funeral. I can't even talk to my mom or dad until tomorrow. I'll catch a ride to the main base in Seoul. There are no phones in these parts where I could place an international call.

In my last moments with Grandpa, I'm so glad I kissed him and told him I loved him. After I left, he told all the nurses and doctors that his son kissed him and told him he loved him. That was his story even up to the time of his passing. Although he mistook me for my dad, that goodbye moment had a tremendous impact on him.

Looking up at the starlit sky, I wonder if there isn't something greater than myself involved in this life. What made me turn back and do something so out of character? What kind of relationship did Dad really have with his dad that my action would have such a dramatic effect on Grandpa?

Later that evening, I head down to a nearby village to drown my sorrows at a local bar. One pretty Korean woman comes over and sits down next to me. "Hey Conner, how 'bout buy me drink?"

It isn't really a question and I'm surprised she knows my name. But then, it's no big mystery since I haven't changed out of my uniform complete with my nametag. After a few minutes, I discover I am in no mood to sit around and drink. After downing the cheap beer, I realize that with all the excitement of the day, I forgot to eat lunch or dinner.

As I head across the street to the only open chophouse, a light snow begins to fall. It's Christmas Eve, and I'm about to get the best gift of my life.

Chapter Twelve
Chophouse of Destiny

Still reeling from the betrayal by Sergeant Slice, I walk across the narrow dirt street and into the chophouse café. Brushing the snow from my coat, I take a seat in one of the booths against the wall. Given the late hour, only a couple of people slurp soup from ceramic bowls.

A girl comes over from the small bar area and, in grammatically perfect English, asks, "What would you like to eat?"

This is kind of unusual up in this remote area. I study her while she jots down my order of chicken fried rice and a beer, then turns and walks back to the tiny kitchen area where I occasionally catch a glimpse of her long black hair and beautiful figure.

A few minutes later she brings my beer and sets it on the table. No perfunctory greeting or slight bow. Just, "Would you like anything else?"

As I drink my beer, my heart begins to pound, and I gasp for breath. I start to sweat even though my hands feel clammy. I hope I'm not coming down with the flu.

The girl comes out again with my plate of fried rice and several bowls of vegetable items. In an attempt to help her, I reach up to take the plate and manage to knock my bottle of beer over. It spins lazily on the table, dumping beer all over me. Jumping up, I accidentally knock her arm. The plate of fried rice and some of the vegetables join it on the table before they fall and shatter on the floor.

I set the bottle upright and mop up the mess with a couple of cheap paper napkins, then stoop down to join her as she cleans up the floor.

"Oh, I'm so sorry, miss." My face is beet red, but I can't stop staring at her as I pick up several pieces of the broken plate.

She looks me straight in the eye with a wry smile. "You're kind of a klutz, aren't you?"

For several moments, we stare at each other and I begin to realize my condition may not be the flu. Suddenly our reverie is broken as the older cook comes over with a broom and dustpan which he throws down on the floor next to her.

"Aaigooo! You make big mess. You pay for food. You pay." He clicks his tongue and shakes his head. "You pay."

"Oh, sure. No problem. I'll pay for everything."

As I grab for the dustpan he kicks it away. "You no clean. Woman clean it."

He walks back to the kitchen, still clicking and shaking his head. I grab for the dustpan again but feel a jolt of electricity. Her hand is on my arm. She's staring at me again.

"Sit down," she says, "and let me clean this up. Don't bring shame on me."

Living in another country can be challenging. It is easy to insult people without realizing it, to create problems just by doing or saying what seems normal to me.

It isn't polite to look someone directly in the eye. When in conversation look at the chin area. Don't call people by their proper name. Don't stoop below your station in life. Don't help a girl.

As I sit back in the booth and watch her clean and ferry my mess back to the kitchen, my mind wanders out the door. I think about Korea and the people that call this peninsula home. Some might call it "The Land of the Morning Calm." But as a sergeant in the United States Army, I know Korea is not calm.

First and foremost, the country is bitterly split between the North and the South, and technically still at war; thus the reason I'm there as United States Army support personnel. The people... well, they are just people the same as me. They go through the same struggles of daily life with each other and with their kids.

"What are you doing still in bed!" a mother screeches loudly. It isn't a question. "The bus is coming in 10 minutes. Now get up before I beat you with a broom!"

She grabs the twelve year-old boy by his ear and wrestles him from the bed onto the warm floor. He rolls around and complains about the need for more sleep, while she thrusts a book bag at him. This scene happens around the world every day, and the Orient is no exception.

In the village surrounding our military compound, the homes are typically small, a couple of rooms at most. At night, some blankets on the floor create a bed while during the day this area converts to the eating and living space. Heating and cooking are accomplished as they burn a large cylindrical charcoal with holes drilled down the center in a heating system called ondol. Because the hot gases are forced into a space under the floor, it is particularly dangerous due to the carbon monoxide. If there is the slightest crack in the flooring, the deadly gas can seep into the room. The military advises us to keep a window open when sleeping in the village and, unfortunately, not everyone listens to good advice. Several have died. But this system heats the rooms well, and it is nice in the winter.

There is nothing like sitting on a hot floor with a thick and cozy mink blanket wrapped around you. Thus part of the reason for sleeping directly on the warm floor. The kid who is pulled out of bed and onto the floor doesn't have far to fall.

Life is difficult in many ways. During my tour of duty, I live in a rural area. Families work the fields from four or five a.m. till sometimes after midnight. In the spring, they borrow money to plant crops that will make it through till harvest. The main staple is rice and if the harvest is good, they pay off their debt with enough left to make it through the coming winter. In the spring they have to borrow again to plant, and so it goes.

In the late 1970's, the median monthly income for a family is about twenty five or thirty dollars or less. It is hard work. Few of them own machinery, so everything consists of manual labor. The kitchen is outdoors as is the bathroom, which may consist of a couple of boards across a hole in the ground. Water from a well is the norm, so clothes are washed at the local stream by beating them with a piece of wood.

In the United States, I spent my youth playing and watching TV. The locals don't own even half the things we own in America, but they do possess an unconquerable spirit and families that stick together. I can learn from them.

Americans are generally tolerated by the locals but somewhat shunned in other ways. Look but don't touch. You don't want that white or black to rub off on you. It is the same with some of the troops. The GI's are always willing to carouse in the towns and villages, but in private (and sometimes in public depending on the percentage of inebriation) they believe these Orientals are of a lower caste.

As I grew up prior to and during the civil rights demonstrations of the 1960's, I remember asking about things that didn't make sense to me. Certain times of the year, Grandma Conner took me to the city to shop or to see the Christmas decorations. As a child, I was primarily interested in the toy section where I could buy some new treasure.

Grandma Conner was old as far back as I can remember. Of German descent, she was a woman of few words with even less tolerance for monkey business from kids or adults.

On one of our city excursions when I was eight, we sat about three quarters of the way back in the bus. I wore my dress slacks while Grandma wore her netted hat and carried a big leather purse. We planned to shop at the Famous & Barr and the Sears store where I hoped to get a new toy.

The bus swayed and stopped. A few people in front stood up and exited at the stop. That left empty seats up front. Then an elderly black woman got on, dropped a few coins in the coin meter, and carefully made her way to the back of the bus as it swayed into traffic, belching thick black smoke. She walked to the back of the bus and stood there because no seats were open in the back.

Grandma stood up, grabbed me by the arm, and moved us to one of the empty seats up front. I looked back as the elderly lady sat down in the seat we vacated. A kind of gasp went through the bus. My heart started beating real fast as if we had somehow wandered onto a stage into the spotlight.

I looked up at my grandma, but she didn't say a word. For the first time, I realized there was a kind of dividing line in the bus. At the front of the bus, no black people. At the back of the bus, no white people.

In the big department store downtown, there were two sets of bathrooms; black and white. Two sets of drinking fountains. Grandma wouldn't let me drink out of either one of them. No black patrons lunched with us at the sandwich shop either.

I wondered about this. At church, all of us white people sang, "Red and yellow black and white, they are precious in His sight, Jesus loves the little children of the world." But something was wrong! Why couldn't we even touch black people?

When we treat each other differently, this is what happens. We don't think, "What is wrong with me?" Instead, we think, "What is wrong with them?"

When I asked Grandma, she said, "That's the way things are and they ain't likely to change." Fortunately, in some aspects, she was wrong. The Jim Crow laws did eventually change, but no one can legislate people's hearts. It takes a lot longer for our attitudes to change toward each other, and we are still working on it. But Grandma did teach me that even though 'things are the way they are,' you still have to do what is right by people. In the end, we are all just people, no matter how we look or act.

During my tour of duty in South Korea, I found that as I treated others with respect and kindness, ninety nine percent of the time they tended to return the same. Many of the people in our local village became like family and invited me into their homes and lives where we shared joys and sorrows. The joy of a new baby or marriage, the sorrow of a death or a fire that destroyed a home. In Korea it was rude to call someone by their proper name, so they called me MokSaNim which means Pastor. I felt honored.

As I sit in that tiny restaurant chophouse thousands of miles from home, I feel lonely. I realize my loneliness is not just because I'm in Korea, but I'm also lonely in life. Not just at this moment, but always. The girl comes out with another set of food. I sit quietly while she sets it on the table in front of me. Then she sits down across from me and stares again.

"You don't mind if I sit with you, huh?"

Back to the present, I swallow hard to cover the sudden onslaught of dizziness. I can only squeak, "No, not at all."

After eating a bit of food and polishing off another beer, I begin to calm down and think a bit more clearly. I can also hold an intelligent conversation without my squeaky voice.

Before I know it, the cook comes out again and announces he wants to close up. Looking at my watch I realize it's after twenty three hours or eleven p.m. I've got to catch a bus back to my compound before the midnight curfew or I'm in trouble! The gate is secured at midnight and I'll catch hell for not being in before they close it. That would be the topping on the cake after my trouble with the inventory today. Korea has a midnight curfew for all citizens from midnight to four a.m. No one can be out except on-duty military personnel.

But I'm not on duty. Through the window I see a bus pull up. I run for the door. Then I turn back. The girl is watching me. "Hey, what's your name?"

"I'm Young."

Misunderstanding, I try again. "No, no. Not your age. I mean your 'name'. What is your name?"

She smiles and points to herself. "I told you. My name is Young."

The bus begins to pull off and I have to run over and pound on the side to get the driver to slow and open the door. I leap aboard. As I take a seat and look back, she stands outside and watches the bus roll down the road.

Later, after everything is cleaned up, she sits on the floor of her tiny room and smoothes out a piece of notepaper with flowers on it, then contemplates her actions. Should I really do this, she wonders? Many people comment on her beauty and men have tried to woo her. Some even want to marry her. Sighing, she talks to herself, "They come and go but they're all the same."

No one seems to really care about her. So why even think about it? Still, something about this guy keeps intruding into her mind. Finally, her curiosity wins. As the candle flickers across the floor, she takes her only pen, a quill. Dipping it into a small ink jar, she touches it to the paper and begins to write, "Dear Conner..."

Chapter Thirteen
Taking Chance

I make it safely through the gates with eight minutes to spare, but barely drift off to sleep when someone talks to me in a terse voice. "Sergeant Conner... Sergeant Conner."

Forcing my eyes open, I respond groggily. "Huh?"

"Sergeant Conner, Private Turley no show up for gate duty shift. Need gate duty."

"Ughh. Yah, okay."

My eyes begin to close again. My head is too heavy to lift from the wonderful pillow.

"Sergeant Conner! Wake up! Nobody on the gate duty."

Finally sitting on the side of my bunk, I look around. No one is here except Kansas City Kim, the Korean KATUSA MP.

"Where is everyone?"

"Skoshi Joe and Sergeant Na on Tac site. Everybody else in village. No here." 'Skoshi' is kind of Korean slang for 'little'. We have two guys named Joe and differentiate by calling one Little Joe and the other Big Joe.

Groaning, I shake my head to try to clear out the overwhelming desire for sleep. At least twice a week, someone doesn't show up for a shift and no one else is available... except me. It's like a carefully coordinated show where everyone knows the script... except me. Only one or two people have overnight passes with permission to be off the compound.

But tonight, five people are gone which means at least three of them are out illegally and will get an audience with the commander tomorrow. One of those three will have to answer for not showing up for his shift, which I now have to work. Kansas City just came off a twelve-hour shift on the gate, so I can't put him back on it. No one else is available.

In the small gatehouse, I flip off the little heater unit and open a sliding window. The cold December air blusters in and helps keep my eyes open. A hard swallow of hot coffee provides a contrast to the cold air but only keeps away the next 30 minutes of boredom.

The base commander, Captain Quigley, won't do much except lecture the soldiers staying out all night. This is one reason they continue to do it. There's no real consequence. But of course, it is that same Quigley attitude that saved me from a more severe punishment earlier when I lost my entire inventory. Unfortunately, that kind of attitude doesn't help create order in the ranks.

I imagine Quigley as a pirate captain, standing on the main mast. He swings his sword and yells at the crew below. "Ahoy there, mateys. Swab the deck and turnabout. Thar be an island and rocks coming up starboard. Turn hard to the port bow."

As he yells and screams from his perch high above the deck, no one pays a bit of attention to him. They're too busy drinking the rum and fighting with each other as the ship bears down on the deadly rocks and shoreline. Actually, the captain probably isn't even on the mast where he can see the danger. More likely, he's in the supposed safety of his cabin, sitting at his wooden desk writing interminable reports that never end. Suddenly a crewmember bursts through the door, his pirate voice grave. "Aye, Captain.

Turlock's not back on base yet and it's shift change for the Tac. The deuce be leavin' in thirty minutes."

"Huh?" Rubbing my eyes to clear my vision, I see one of the contract Korean guards standing in front of me. The coffee is long cold and the sky is just turning from black to gray with a covering of clouds that hint of more snow on the way.

"Sergeant Conner. Private Turlock..."

Waving a hand I cut him off. "I know, I know. Turlock is late for the truck going up to Tac and someone has to take his place."

Signing off the change of shift to the elderly man hired as the day shift gate guard, I jump up on the back of the deuce and a half truck as it slows for the gate to swing open. During the day we use contract guards at the gate, but at night we have only military personnel on duty. Minutes later the truck is signed through the gate and rumbles down the road for the trip to Tac site duty. Eight other soldiers sit on fold-down benches on either side of the green canvas-covered truck. Pulling myself up against the cab, I remain seated on the floor, lean my head back, and catch a few more minutes of sleep before pulling a twenty four hour shift on the Tac.

And so it goes, week after week as I try to determine what in the world I can do to change these people around me who seem to not care about anything, except getting out of work. At least twice a week, I'm in the same position. Call them into my office for counseling. Do it again. Then, after the third counseling session, send them to the commander. They work well for a couple of weeks or a month and then they don't show up. What's the answer?

"Hey Conner, hello... Did you hear me?"

I'm still pondering the shift situation as I sit in the little cafe where I met that girl. I look up to see her waving her hand in my face.

"Oh, I'm sorry, what did you say?"

It's getting late and I have to leave to make it back to the compound in time. Seems like I end up at this place every chance I get. February is just around the corner. A month has gone by since

I first met her and I do my best to see her whenever I can. Usually, I manage it three times a week.

"I said it's snowing really hard, and the bus probably won't run."

I look out the window. The previously light snow has turned into a storm and is now piled up at least a foot against the door. "Oh, no!"

No taxis will run in this weather. It's after eleven p.m. and there's no way I can slog it the five miles from this village to my compound. I always scored well on the Army PT (physical training) test, and I can average a seven minute mile. On a good day I could make it back on foot, but not in this snow.

As I stare at the snow that piles up against the door, she sits across from me and whispers. I don't hear a word as I imagine the first sergeant rolling me up in a giant snowball and then giving it a push down the side of the Tac site mountain. Then he strings me up on the flagpole. The flag flutters in the wind as I await my fate.

A slight touch of her hand jolts me back.

"Huh?"

"Conner! Snap out of it. Listen. Go around to the back gate and wait. I'll open it and you can sleep in my room. But be quiet so no one hears us. Okay?"

After thirty minutes of waiting, I shiver and wonder if I've been abandoned, a seemingly normal event when it comes to girls and me. Fortunately, there is an overhang next to the gate which keeps the snow off of me. I would give up and just walk back to the compound, but not in this snow.

Suddenly the metal gate creaks, which sounds tremendously loud in the snowy night. Her face appears in the dark and she waves me in. As I slide through, we creep to a rice paper-covered door, slide it aside, and jump inside. She quickly closes it behind us. A single candle flickers on a saucer on the floor. This room is barely the size of a small walk-in closet with cheap linoleum on the concrete floor. Are we hiding here until we can get to her actual room?

A towel hits me in the face. "Just whisper. No talking or someone will hear. Take your boots off on this towel, so everything doesn't get wet. Hang your coat up there." She gestures to four wooden pegs on the concrete wall. I'm used to taking orders, so I quickly comply. We continue to whisper. "Is this your room?"

"Yes. Sorry, so small."

Opening a black, mother-of-pearl closet door, she throws a pillow down on the floor then sends a beautiful mink blanket after it.

"Uh, like... where do you sleep?"

It's a silly question, but we don't know each other that well and I'm wondering how this is going to work with limited space.

She stares at me with gorgeous brown eyes. Her long, lovely black hair cascades across her shoulders, shimmering in the candlelight.

"It's either in here or out there in the snow. Come on, if you're lucky I won't bite you. You have to get up and be gone before Aujoshi and Aujima wake up or I'll be in real trouble."

Aujoshi and Aujima are names for Sir and Maam. She uses this to refer to the husband and wife owners of the cafe. It's rude to refer to someone by their proper name. We lie down together, sharing a pillow, blanket, and the floor as the stars seemed to explode in the sky and our lives become sealed together for better or for worse.

I'm awakened from my blissful dream when someone shakes me. "Okay, okay. I'm awake."

What am I doing on the floor? Did I fall off my bunk? Shaking the sleep out of my head, I sit up and see... her! "Where am I?"

Instantly I know it wasn't a dream. I'm really in her room and... "Oh no. What time is it?"

"It's almost five. I think the buses are running again."

As I slip out through the metal gate and hear it close behind me, neither Young nor I see Aujoshi watching us from the cafe doorway.

The bus pulls over at the compound gate. There's no hiding from the situation. I simply get out and stride up to the gate to take my chances. It is just after six a.m. Many times the first sergeant waits at the gate to see who stays out without an overnight pass. It's a throw of the dice as to whether this is one of those times.

Unfortunately, I am never good at poker, dice, or any other luck-based game. As I walk through the gate, I can see the first sergeant shake his large head. Might as well face the music. Pushing through the door, I begin to make an excuse but he cuts me off with a flick of his hand.

"Well, if it isn't Sergeant Conner! No, no... don't say a word. My office at zero eight hundred hours!"

All I can do is say, "Yes, First Sergeant," and go to my bunk to contemplate my fate. Promptly at zero eight hundred hours, I stand in front of Top's desk.

"Well, Sergeant Conner..."

Top draws out the word 'Sergeant' to make sure I get his drift. "How many times do I have one of your MP's in here for breaking regulations? Aren't you and your crew supposed to be enforcing the regulations instead of doing your best to break them?"

It isn't a question and I provide no answer as I stand at attention in front of Top's desk.

"And now you! Do you have any clue as to the fact that you happen to be in a leadership position here and just maybe it might be appropriate for you to set some kind of small example for the rest of the troops?"

"Yes, First Sergeant."

Again, it isn't really a question but it seems the right time to add something to the conversation.

"Now I'm sure if I let you blather on, you'll give me some sob hearted story about how the snow storm kept you from getting back to the gate last night. And, if I know anything, I'd be willing to bet that some girl was involved as well."

On the advice of others who had been in this position, I don't give the expected answer. "No, First Sergeant."

Surprised, Top is momentarily derailed from his well-practiced monologue. "No? No it wasn't the storm... or no it wasn't a girl or...?"

"No, there is no excuse for this and I take full responsibility for the penalty."

Top grins and shakes his head.

"That won't get you anywhere either, Sergeant. Even if I wanted to, I can't let you off easy. The good news is that I won't pass this on to the commander and it won't be on your record. No one knows that anyway except my orderly and if he breathes a word of anything that goes on in this office I'll personally make him wish he was dead before he gets half a word out of his mouth. Isn't that right, Corporal Snidely?"

The office door is closed, so I'm surprised to hear the shifting of feet just outside the door and Snidely's muffled reply on the other side. "Yes, First Sergeant."

All I can do at this point is reply, "Thank you, First Sergeant."

Top continues.

"The bad news is that I'm confining you to Tac site for two weeks. That means you'll stay there for a duration of fourteen days and pull duty without coming back down for any reason. So you'd better take enough uniforms and supplies. You leave immediately on the next deuce and a half."

He stands and plants both meaty hands on his desk, then leans way across and launches several missiles with his eyes. "Do I make myself completely clear, Sergeant Conner?"

My heart sinks as I give the best, "Yes, First Sergeant," that I can muster. The only thing I can think about is the girl in the cafe. I won't see her for two weeks and she won't know what's happened to me.

Back at my bunk, everyone gathers around to hear the results. As I'm stuffing my duffle bag, I wonder how they can all manage to be here now but not when it's time to pull duty.

They badger me but I ignore it. Finally I turn and face them all. Unable to resist the moment, I fall into my typical comedy routine. "Men, I've gathered you together as we go out to face the enemy. Don't let them drink you into a stupor but instead, hold your beer until you see the whites of their bloodshot eyes."

They groan and complain, so I get a bit more serious. "Well, do you want the good news or the bad news? The good news is that everyone working Tac site gets a two week vacation. The bad news is that I'm taking your place for those two weeks."

I expect cheering but everyone is at a loss for words. They stare or look down at the floor before dispersing. No one has ever heard of being confined to Tac site for a week, much less two. There are some bathrooms on Tac and bunks to sleep in but it's pretty primitive and there are no showers or other niceties. Plus, a row of large generators power the site and the constant droning day and night can drive you crazy. But I soon learn that Top has other intentions in mind.

After I'm on Tac site for three days, I get a message, "Report to Top's office right away."

What's going on now? I hope it's not another bad report about my family. If nothing else, Top is a man of his word and if he says 14 days on Tac, then that's exactly what it is. Why would he call me back down after just three days?

"Sergeant Conner, have I got a deal for you."

Standing at attention in front of his desk again, I'm sure this isn't going to be something I'm going to like.

"How would you like to have your two week sentence suspended?"

Although I would like that a lot, I'm not sure what it's going to cost me. I'm also sure there won't really be a choice one way or the other. I remain silent.

Top continues. "Captain Quigley has to provide four candidates for a three week leadership class in Osan. If you accept, then you can be relieved of the penalty immediately and will be expected to report to Osan on Monday."

As he drones on, my mind calculates this news. Top isn't stupid. He knows I want to go see a girl in the next village. There are no secrets on this tiny compound nor in the small surrounding village. News travels fast and people know what you are doing before you do it. Everyone seems to know everyone else's business and it's often better than a soap opera. That is, unless you're one of the main characters.

Since this is only Thursday, that gives me three days to see Young and then travel to Osan. Career wise, I would be stupid not to take this opportunity. Plus, Osan Air Base is like a five-star resort compared to my current living conditions. Unfortunately, I won't see Young for those three weeks, but at least I'll have the chance to let her know what's going on.

Suddenly I realize the office is silent as Top waits for me with his hands folded on the desk. My face feels red.

Top says in a mild voice, "Ah, Sergeant Conner. How nice of you to return to us."

Suddenly his hand slams on the desk making me jump.

"How about staying with me for a few minutes here, Sergeant Conner! I'm trying to help you out, for God's sake."

"Yes, Sir... I mean yes, First Sergeant," I recover quickly even as Top does a double take at my calling him 'Sir'. Non-commissioned officers hate being addressed as 'sir' and the standard reply is, "Don't call me 'Sir' because I work for a living." Top lets it slide without giving me the standard reply.

"I asked for your response to this generous offer, Sergeant, and I don't like repeating myself."

"First Sergeant, I would be honored to attend."

A few days later, I repack my duffle bag, but this time for the Osan trip. Removing a recent picture of Young and myself from my locker, I place it in the bag before clipping it closed.

Skoshi Joe sits on his bunk and watches me. Finally, he pipes up. "What do you think you're going to do with that girl, Conner? You can't really be serious about her are you?"

When I don't respond, he continues. "You know these Korean girls just want to get to the States, and they'll do anything to get there. Then after they get to the U.S., they dump you like a hot potato. Don't get trapped into something you'll regret. If you're smart, just lead her along until you're gone and then you won't end up sorry, my friend."

Joe doesn't always have something to say, but when he does, there's usually some kind of angle to it. As I ponder his words, I wonder why he's saying this. He doesn't care a flip about me.

On my way to the showers, I give the sad news to the Tac site crew that they are back on the duty roster. After the expected moaning, whining, and complaints, I clean up and head down to the village to see Young.

Although she never openly displays affection, it is evident she is happy to see me again. She pours me a cup of tea from a colorful pot and sits down across the table as I speak. "Did you miss me?"

"Miss you? I didn't know you were missing."

Seeing she is serious, I have to laugh at her unintentional humor. Although she has a better grasp of the English language and slang than anyone I have met, there are occasions when the gap between us is evident. Over the last month or two, the owners of the cafe have become more tolerant of my visits and of my taking Young's time away from the café. It's okay as long as I spend money and there aren't any other paying customers or messes for Young to clean up. Sometimes the owners will even clean tables themselves while we sit and talk. I am about to find out the reasoning behind their unusual kindness.

I leave the cafe early since I have to get ready to depart for Osan. The owner follows me out and walks toward the bus stop with me. This is highly unusual, and I wonder where he is going at this time of the evening. Suddenly, he grabs me by the arm. I'm thinking to myself, this guy doesn't even speak English, What's he going to say to me? Then I'm shocked when he does speak some English.

"What you wanna' do with girl?"

"You mean Young?"

"Yas, Young. Who you think I speaky, uh?

I'm momentarily at a loss. I've never really thought about it. Well, actually I have thought about it — every single day. She's in my mind all day long and I dream about her at night. But I'm not about to confide that to the cafe owner.

So I tell him, "I don't know. I haven't really thought about it." Probably the wrong thing to say. I should have said, "Not interested," and walked away. But that doesn't occur to me. I always think of great responses an hour too late.

"Aigoo. Young like only you. She care a lot of you. You take her."

I am momentarily stunned and feel my face start to turn red. I wish that bus would hurry up.

"Aujoshi, look, I haven't even talked to Young about this. How can I just 'take her'? Now I've completely forgotten about the bus which pulls up and then away again.

"You take her. She like you. She care much of you."

Riding the bus to Osan is more comfortable than riding in the back of a truck. As I lean back and close my eyes I think about what Joe told me. He couldn't have known of my future conversation with the cafe owner. What odd timing!

I didn't bother to explain to the cafe owner about my cash flow. It's barely one hundred dollars a month. There's no way I can afford to rent a place and move her. It would cost about seven or eight hundred dollars. Paying back the inventory month after month has stripped me of most of my cash. I don't earn much as a sergeant.

I once calculated all the hours I put in compared to my monthly salary and it averaged a little under fifty cents an hour. Where could I possibly come up with eight hundred? I can't believe I'm even considering it. What am I going to do, call Mom and Dad and say, "Hey, guess what? I'm moving in with this girl and I need about eight hundred dollars. Can you send it over?"

I laugh at the absurdity of it, then realize people are staring at me. Although I try to push the whole thing to the back of my mind, it's with me every moment of every day during my three weeks of training. I'm mad at myself for thinking about it all the time. It's wearing me down, so I decide to talk to the owners and Young when I get back. That gives me a little solace.

The weeks of training pass quickly and soon I'm standing across the street from the cafe, contemplating my next action. Even after three weeks, I haven't made up my mind as to how to approach her. Does Young know about this? Young and I only met three months ago. I watch them through the window. Suddenly Young looks up and catches a glimpse of me. She does a double take and says something to Aujoshi. Then she takes off her apron and hurries out the door and across the street.

"Conner, did you miss me?"

Before I can tell her I didn't know she was missing, she grabs my hand and leads me to a bar down the street with some private tables. After we are seated and she orders a couple of beers, she turns to me and holds her hand up before I speak. "I'm going to say some things to you that I never say to anyone. If you believe me, then believe me. If not, then you and I go separate ways."

She sticks out her hand across the table. "Deal?"

Slowly, I take her hand. "Yes, deal."

She pauses as the waitress brings us our drinks. Young pays before I can speak or reach for my coins.

"After you left, I found out what Aujoshi said to you and I basically 'let him have it' as you say. Korean traditions are much different than America. People usually go through a matchmaker and Aujoshi was trying to help me. So I will tell you the truth. I know you wonder if it's true. But you have to decide yourself. I lived on a farm all my life and wanted something better than just working on a farm in a little village."

The afternoon sun shines through her glass of beer, making a little rainbow on the table.

"I'm here because I ran away from home. I want something more than that, so I ran away to Seoul and then I came here. Now I want to run away from here, too, but I can't right now."

When I start to open my mouth, she raises both hands to stop me. "Let me finish, because this is hard. Korean people don't share their feelings or talk like Americans do. Because there are a lot of American GI's here, many girls come so they can try to go to America. That's like their dream to go to America, because they think it's some fairyland where they can be rich and do anything. But when they get over there, it's not what they thought. Sometimes they end up as slaves. Many Korean people have warned me about this. These girls marry GI over here, have a baby and then the GI just leave them here. Or they go to America and get divorced and have a hard time. My intention is not to marry some GI or go to America or leave my family behind. Even if I think that way I get scared about it."

As she lifts her glass to drink, the rainbow disappears.

"I know some men think I am beautiful. I think they're crazy. Many want to date me and some want to marry me but I always say no. They want to take me out of cafe and live with me and I say no.

They bring me gifts sometimes and always talk and talk about how great they are. But they don't care about me."

As she looks down at the wooden bar, she gives a wry smile.

"But now you come and start all kind of problem for me. You make me think you really care about me and I start to really care about you. I try not do it, but I can't help it. Every moment you're away from me, I think about you, Conner."

A tear escapes her eye. She raises her hand again to stop me as I reach over to wipe it away.

"So I'm going to tell you truth about this because I trust you even though we only know each other three months. If we move in together, it would cost about eight hundred dollars to get started. I have three hundred saved up for long time. I was waiting to save more so I could go back to Seoul and find a job."

"But if you want, I will give my three hundred dollars, and you give four hundred dollars, and we get a hundred dollar discount, yeah?"

She smiles. Everything in Korea is a discount. No one buys anything without a discount.

"So I take a chance on you, Conner, and you take a chance on me. That's what I can tell you. I can't promise you anything more than that."

She finishes off her beer and stands up. This certainly isn't going anything like I planned.

"Conner, you take time and think about it. If you come back to see me, then you see me. If not, then okay. Okay?"

As she walks out of the bar I try to make sense of it all. I think back to that evening we met. That night my heart skipped a beat and it's never been the same. Then I remember what Joe said to me a couple of weeks ago, "Don't get led away by a girl." My heart is beating like a freight train as I polish off the rest of my beer and contemplate something a bit stronger. Instead, I leave the bar and see her a distance away as she walks back to the cafe.

"Young, wait."

When I catch up I see tears combined with eye liner in little streams down her face. I take her hands in mine and pull her towards me. "I've thought about it every day for the last three months."

Then echoing her broken English, I give her my answer.

"I take chance on you. Okay?"

Chapter Fourteen
Fire

Funny how sometimes things just seem to work out. A few days later, we make plans on how to proceed. My intention is to rent a small place in the village near the Army compound. Trouble is, I still owe for the 'lost inventory.' Beyond that, we need household stuff as well like furniture and cooking utensils. That's going to take months to save up enough. But sometimes we just don't know anything beyond ourselves.

It's mail call and Mom is always faithful to send me letters. She lets me know what is going on back home. Almost every month there is some kind of great Care Package with cookies and all sorts of things.

We stand around on the asphalt as the mail sergeant calls out names. "Dewey, Calandro, Felix, Smith, Bay..."

Suddenly my thoughts are interrupted with my name.

"Conner."

I look up just as a box flies towards my head. Perfect catch, thank you. A couple of my team follow me back to our living quarters in the quonset hut to read letters and see what Mom sent this month.

Stale cookies, homemade brownies that are a bit hardened, some books, little games, and other mail; a couple are government envelopes. Well, at least they can't draft me! I open a few letters from some of my friends who are finishing college and lay on my bunk eating brownies and enjoying the reads.

As I get up, I kick the box under my bunk but then think better of it since I don't want the mice to share my prize food. Then I see the two government envelopes. The first contains threats about being in arrears on my student loans which are supposed to be in forbearance since I'm in the service. That's trash. The second is from the Treasury Department which I figure is just an arm of the IRS.

Certainly they can't be auditing me. There ain't much to audit. I open it up and see a check. Shaking my head twice, I look again. No way! What's this for? An enclosed note states there was an error on a previous tax return from a couple of years ago and they are sending a check with the correction. I examine the check again to make sure it really has my name on it.

Yes! The check is for a little over three thousand dollars! In shock, I sink onto my bunk. This means I can easily pay off the rest of the 'inventory mess,' get a place in the village for Young and me, save some and have plenty left over for a party. Pumping my hands in the air, I yell, "Yes!" and then explain my good fortune to those around me. Who says there isn't any God?

It doesn't take more than a day or two to rent a truck and move Young's stuff the few miles to my village. To 'rent' a place, we pay something called 'Key Money.' Pay one thousand dollars up front to rent the room, then at the end of the lease, we get our money back: all of it. I'm confused by this concept. How can we live there and not pay anything? Young explains that they invest our key money at a high interest rate.

We pay in the local currency because Americans are not supposed to be spreading U.S. currency into the local economy. I still need an overnight pass to stay outside the compound, but it isn't hard to get one since I am close by where they can find me if needed. Our little room is not even two hundred yards from the gate. It's ten times bigger than Young's room at the cafe so we have a bed and some furniture. I didn't realize all the other stuff we needed as well: a fridge, a little stove thing that's more like a camping stove than anything, dishes, pans, pots, and on and on. When I complain about the cost, this hurts Young's feelings. But she doesn't say anything about it to me and we start the culture gap dance. Relationships are hard enough in the same culture, let alone within different cultures.

A classic story brings this out. In the city there is a shoe shop and the owner makes custom shoes by hand. You go in the shop with a favorite pair of shoes that are worn out and ask, "Can you make me a new pair of shoes just like this?"

The owner says, "Yes."

The next week you come back to pick up the shoes but they aren't ready. Next week same thing; not ready. Eventually you manage to find out that the shop owner can't make the shoes and actually never could. But he couldn't say that because he would lose face and cause shame. So it was better to say, "Yes," than to admit he couldn't do it.

That's an extreme example, but it underscores that we are dealing with communication gaps and misunderstandings and I don't know what I don't know. So I keep on plodding along. Young and I are having problems, and I'm completely clueless what we are having problems about. Plus, I have to admit, I really don't have any idea how to pay attention to her. I just want to do what I want to do. I figured she would just fit into my life, but now I'm beginning to discover that she thinks I'm supposed to fit into her life. This ain't working out real well.

Additionally, she is now bored since she has nothing to do all day and much of my time is taken up with my military service. I do take notice that she likes to draw. The next time I make a trip to the PX, a military store, I see a beginning artist kit complete with paint, brushes, and a sixteen by twenty inch canvas. When I give it to her, she is thrilled and I gain back some lost points with her. The next day I'm off to Tac site for twenty four hours. Before I leave, she asks for some of my pictures which I happen to have right there in our closet. That has a nice ring to it... 'Our' closet. I give her a box of photos and leave to pull my duty.

Next morning, I walk in to our room wanting nothing more than to get some sleep after pulling guard duty all night. Before I can collapse on the bed, she excitedly wants to show me something but I'm really in no mood. She's dancing around like a little kid and you would think she was a cat on a hot tin roof.

That is one thing she seems to have not lost, an excitement and innocence of life; like a child. She sees something new to her and bounces up and down saying, "Conner, look, look! Isn't that amazing?" Sometimes at night I sit on the bed to read a book and she runs in from outside, grabs my arm in excitement, pulls me off of the bed and out the door. "Look, look! It's a full moon, isn't it beautiful?" Then we stand in wonder and gaze at the moon as it sails across the starry sea.

I initially resist and grumble. I'm busy reading my book. I don't want to interrupt my life and focus on hers. But I don't have the heart to crush her excitement and I let myself be pulled out the door.

So now she makes me sit on the edge of the bed like we're in a theater getting ready for the main attraction. The lights dim. The spotlights blaze and she pulls out this canvas and waves it around in the air.

"Ta Da!"

I'm stunned! It's a painting of me, standing on the Tac site with my dog, Charlie. There are mountains and a sunrise in the background. It's an exact, and I mean exact, duplicate of the actual picture except a hundred times better. I can see every blade of grass, the individual hair on the dog, and the sun exploding in the background. Suddenly

I've forgotten all about me and my tiredness. As I gasp, she smiles.

"Where did this come from?" I ask. Many local artists in the villages around the military compounds can paint a canvas from a photo, and some are better than others. But I've never seen anything like this before. "Who did this?"

"I did. With the paint set you gave me. I worked on it all night."

"No way! You did? How?"

That was just a little beginner paint set, for crying out loud. It doesn't seem possible. But she did it and in less than one day! Unbelievable! Who would have thought? As talented as she is, she never paints for other people or wants to sell her paintings. Her excuse? "It's not good enough for that."

We have our ups and downs and often, it seems the downs outweigh the ups ten to one. I mean, I really like her a lot and think about her all the time. But living with another person seems to bring out the worst in me. I often end up hurting her by my actions or words. I'm confounded by my own behavior and my inability to change it for any length of time.

We've been together about two months when something happens which changes my life. It's been hot, in the high nineties on the F scale. No rain for a while, so we are in a drought. Across the little dirt road from us, there is a sewing business that makes clothes. I'm reading a book when I hear this commotion outside the window. Did I tell you there's no air conditioning? Just a fan. I roll off the bed and saunter outside to… a fire!

Smoke is pouring out of the little textile business as a couple of Korean guys run in and out carrying sewing machines and whatever they can save. Without thinking, I run in and help carry stuff out. We do this for about five minutes as a crowd grows. We come out with some furniture as the flames start to take over the one story, one big room building. As I turn to go back in, Young grabs my arm. Over the sound of the fire I shout, "I'm helping them get stuff out."

When I turn to go back in, she won't let go. She tugs at me. I'm almost irritated but I see she's crying. Now I'm confused. "What's wrong with you?" But she just keeps saying, "Please don't go back in. Please don't go in there again."

There is something in her eyes besides the tears. Sometimes a person speaks with a warning voice, greater than that person. It stops me in my tracks. "Okay. I won't. You can let go of me."

Suddenly, an explosion almost knocks us off our feet with an intense blast. I look at Young in astonishment. I might have gone back in, for just some machinery and furniture. Fortunately, no one is injured although the building is a loss.

With my arm around her, we go back to our place and I wash up. Later, we sit on the bed together. "What made you stop me?"

She doesn't like it when I try to draw information or feelings out of her, but I do it anyway. After a while she manages to stop crying. "I love you now. I don't want to lose you."

Then it's my turn to cry. Big Army Military Police man brought to tears by a few words of a woman. It takes me a few days to process it all. I know I have to do something, but I'm not sure it's the right thing to do. I feel I'm at a real crossroads, and this decision is going take me down one road or another. But the scenery is different, depending on my choice.

In six months, I'm leaving Korea to return to the United States and my home. I know Young doesn't want to go. She's already expressed that, and I'm not one to change her mind. But it's a conversation I don't want to have. I end up in an unlikely place, the chapel on the compound. I've never been religious and don't know if there is a God. But I need advice, and I don't trust anyone else.

"Well, God, if there is a God I mean. I'm not really used to addressing you. In fact, I'm not sure I ever did. But if you are there, I could really use some advice right about now. There's this girl and... and..." A tear runs down my cheek. "And... I love her."

This is not at all what I had in mind to say, especially to God... if there is a God. I didn't intend to get into all of this and I'm kind of shocked to discover what I'm saying. But I suddenly realize that I actually love this girl. I think back on her actions during the fire and realize she loves me. Yet, she doesn't want to leave her family or country and my time here is short.

When I finally leave the chapel, it is dark outside and the wind blows a cool breeze from the North. Better to get this conversation over with. Heading down the street to our little room, my heart is heavy. Halfway there, a pelting rain begins and by the time I arrive, I'm soaked. When I step in, she has a towel waiting as if she was watching for me. She helps me out of my boots and wet clothes. Once I'm dry and dressed, I discover she has dinner ready, so we eat. Then she excitedly shows me another painting she finished, this time of me and her two sisters who visited last week.

I don't know how to tell her what I want to say, so I don't say anything. This doesn't work real well, because she can tell there is something bothering me. It's her, me, and the room. No TV, no place to hide from each other, and not much to do after we have talked about our day.

"What's bothering you, Conner?"

To be or not to be, that is the question. To be honest or blunt, or just how to start. As I'm struggling to say something, she speaks. "Are you trying to talk about our faith?"

Sometimes she confuses words a bit.

"Did you mean fate?"

She laughs, nodding. "Yes, I meant fate." She smiles, then adds, "I guess we could talk about our faith, but it would probably be a short conversation."

Then she laughs, and I have to smile in spite of myself. Pretty soon, we are laughing together over nothing. Then I'm tickling her and she's trying to get away. Then she's using Tae Kwon Do Ninja moves on me and finally we fall off the side of the bed onto the floor and stare into each other's eyes.

As I run my hand through her long dark hair, I try to get more serious. "I have to tell you something."

Sitting up she asks, "Is it serious?"

"Very serious."

"Is it about us?"

"Yes, Young, it's about us."

I feel tears coming to my eyes, but I force them back. I just can't do anything without these cockamamie tears! I even cry when I read a book or watch a movie and sometimes a normal conversation takes me to the edge for no apparent reason. Taking a deep breath, I continue. "You know I'm supposed to ETS in October and go back to the States."

As she looks down, it's as if all her happiness falls to the floor and drains away. "Yes, I know that. But we still have almost six months together before you have to leave." Even though she keeps a level voice, I can tell she is struggling to maintain her composure.

"Young, what are you going to do when I leave?"

"Go back to Seoul and find a job. I was trained to do electronics work and I was a nanny for a while."

"You were? Really?"

She always surprises me with these tidbits about her life that leak out every so often. Then she explains a little bit about working in a factory making electronic boards and she describes what it was like to be a nanny.

After that we are silent for a bit. Finally I speak again. "Young, there's something I want to talk to you about, and I just don't know how to say it..."

"Just say it, Conner. Just say it."

She is still looking down as I take both of her hands in mine.

"Young, I don't want to force you into anything, and I probably couldn't anyway because you are your own person. I've been thinking about this for what short time we've been together, and especially after the fire. The more I know you, the more convinced I am that I really want to ask you this question."

As she looks up, I ask her before she can interrupt.

"Will you marry me?"

Chapter Fifteen
Lessons Learned

Time is a funny thing. When you want it to go slowly, it goes faster than crazy. All the fun and joy of the present swirls like a memory down the drain of time. Trying to remember feels like dipping up water with open hands, only to have it slip through your grasp. When you want time to go by fast, it stretches out like a bad dream, on and on forever.

I sit quietly and let her think as time becomes interminable. The tick of the clock in the background seems to grind away at a favorable answer. Her head hangs down and her long black hair covers her face. Puddles of tears form on the floor; the mixed-in eyeliner makes little designs. My heart beats. The pressure of the blood pumps through my body and into my hot face and head.

After a while, she finally wipes her eyes with the back of her hand, then uses a towel to finish the job. After cleaning up the streaks on her face and restoring her honor, she comes back over and sits down across from me on the floor. Looking at me, she slightly nods.

"I should have figured you would do this. I shouldn't be surprised.

I just didn't expect it today I guess. You don't even know me, so how can you possibly ask me to marry you?"

Now it's my turn to look down.

"Mitchau." She rarely uses my given name but when she does, she always puts a slight au sound on the end of it.

"My family lives in this land. I don't speak English good. Our cultures, communications and thoughts are very different. What will your family say about this?"

I can answer fairly certain about my family. "They will really love you. I don't know about the rest of your questions, but I know my family will love you."

"It's a scary thing, what you are asking. I'm only nineteen. I have to get my parents' permission to marry you, and I can guarantee my dad is going to go ballistic."

"Really?"

"Yes, I can tell you for sure. One time I was pen pal with a boy in the next village. My dad found one of his letters to me. He tore up the letter and threw the table across the room. He screamed and yelled. I ran real fast to my friend's house to hide and wouldn't come home for three days. Finally, my sister came and told me that Dad said he wasn't mad anymore and he wouldn't beat me or anything. So I went home. But if he found out we were together he would be furious, not to mention if I asked to marry you."

With a nod and a sigh, I look down again. "I understand," It's about all I can squeak out. I hate any kind of rejection.

Now it is Young who takes my face in her hands and lifts my chin to look at her.

"Conner, I didn't say, 'No.' I'm just saying it won't be easy. Plus, I want more time to learn English better and to visit my family."

She wipes away my tears with the back of her hand. "But if you want, I take chance on you, okay."

Nodding, smiling and crying all at the same time, I say, "Okay."

Then she tickles me and it's another all-out fight as we each secretly contemplate our fate and our lives.

The very next day, as I deal with paperwork in my office, Big Joe comes through the door and crams his six foot five inch, three hundred pound frame into a chair. He tosses an official looking document across at me.

"What's this?"

As I turn it around to examine it, Joe slaps the desktop. "That, my friend, is an official Army communication for any 'In Country' military K-9 handlers and that just happens to include you."

I scan down the lines and read it to myself. 'Blah blah blah, any in-country military police K9 handlers will be allowed to extend for a period of twelve months or longer.'

"Oh, wow! Is this real?"

"Would I try to pull something over on you?"

At the narrowing of my eyes, Joe continues. "Well, I guess I would but this isn't one of those times. I just figured since you were getting married to that girl, you may want to extend for another year since you don't have time to get married and get a visa for her before you are scheduled to leave the country and ETS."

"How in the hell did you know I'm going to marry her?"

When he laughs, I figure he didn't know but was probing to see if that possibility was even in my train of thought.

"Oh ho! So you are going to marry her. I figured as much anyway, the way you treat her and all."

"How do I treat her…'and all'?"

"Come on, Sarge. You see the way most of these guys treat these girls they live with. It's terrible. They date a host of other girls while they live with one and get her to do everything for them, then they take off and leave without so much as a glance back. A lot of them leave with a big debt and rent due on the hooch." A 'hooch' is our village living space, maybe a room or three at most.

I look at Big Joe. "So what about you and Kim? You seem pretty tight with her."

Joe stands up and grabs the paper out of my hands in a quick move. He may be big, but he's lightning fast which comes in handy when we pull patrol down in the village with a bunch of rowdy drunks. They always think he's lumbering slow but he can take three men down in a minute or less.

"We're already in the process of getting married. You have to go through these Army classes which take a month, then fill out all kinds of paperwork, then go down to the Embassy and tie the knot. I already put in my paperwork to request a twelve month extension."

The next day I head to our battalion level military base to the South. We are such a small compound, there is no reenlistment sergeant. We do have a medic but no real medical facilities, so if someone needs to go on sick call they have to take the truck down to this particular base.

I ride on the sick call truck with several guys headed down to the medical facility. I haven't told Young about my intent to extend another year, because I don't want to get her hopes up in case it falls through. Once on the base, I wander around until I find the reenlistment office. I didn't call in advance, so I hope someone will see me.

The reenlistment NCO is a young guy but, by the looks of him, he's been in the service a while longer than I. However, he isn't cooperative. After looking at the Army communication about allowing any MP K9 handler to extend, he tosses it back across the desk to me. "Yeah, I know about that, Sergeant Conner, but we haven't had any luck getting anyone extended."

"Well, what do you suggest then?" I'm grasping after straws here, looking for some kind of solution to stay in the country longer and he knows it.

"I recommend you reenlist for another three years."

Often, I'm naive and people take advantage of me, but this isn't one of those times. I figure he gets a bonus if he writes a reenlistment on someone and he probably has some kind of monthly goal. So I'm wary, but willing to listen. I know if I go back to the states to ETS, I can reenlist and write my own ticket because enlistments in the

Army are down at this point in time, especially since the draft is no longer in effect. I'm fairly confident I can go to language school, get a bonus, go to officer's school or even become an instructor down in San Antonio for dog handler's school.

"So what exactly can you do for me if I reenlist?"

"Well, I can freeze you at your current duty station."

"You've got to be kidding. There's no way I want to stay at that place. How about line duty down at Yongsan in Seoul or at Osan Air Base?" I'm thinking of the five star accommodations and not having to pull field duty for a week every spring and fall.

"Naw, can't really do that. All I can do is guarantee to keep you at your present duty station."

After a little more conversation, I've had it with this guy. I know he's conning me and just doesn't want to go the extra mile to fill out additional paperwork.

"Look, Sergeant whatever your name is, I know that if I go back to the states to ETS, I can pretty well write my own ticket to any school or type of job I want to do in the Army and get a bonus on top of it. If you think I'm going to reenlist for three years so I can stay at my present duty station for an extra twelve months, you're out of your mind."

I stand up, but he just sits there and looks at me. Then he says, "You're the one who wants to stay in the country."

"Yeah, but not at any cost!"

With that I turn and leave, pretty steamed. What a jerk! After calming down a bit, I find the sick call truck and, with a heavy heart, make the trip back to base.

About a month later, I've pretty well given up on staying in Korea an extra year, but I haven't forgotten about my experience with that reenlistment NCO. It still steams me whenever I think about it. It's too late to put in for an extension now, because I'm just four months away from leaving and the communication stated it takes a little over five or six months to process the extension.

I'm not feeling well as I make the trip on the sick call truck again but this time to the medical facility. I wouldn't go near the reenlistment office if someone paid me. Skoshi Joe is also headed to the medical facility. As we sit in the waiting room, Joe asks me when I'm scheduled to leave the country and somehow we get on the subject of my experience with the reenlistment guy and the Army communication about K-9 handlers being able to extend. I finish my griping with, "But this reenlistment NCO wouldn't do it."

A heavy-set guy sits across from us in civilian clothes, also waiting to see the doctor. He's been reading the newspaper, but now he puts it down and leans toward me.

"Hey, explain to me again what happened with that extension."

I tell him in minute detail about the whole thing, and he can see I'm upset about it. He smirks while his eyes pierce with a narrow stare. Looking at my nametag, he asks for my full name and then inquires where I'm stationed.

So I tell him, not really thinking much about it.

Then he leans forward and nods his head. "Sergeant Conner, after you finish here, go back to your compound and see your commander. He will arrange for your extension."

I'm stunned. "What did you say?"

Then thinking of a better question I ask, "Who are you?"

"I just happen to be the Command Sergeant Major of this here base, and I don't much care for the attitude of that reenlistment NCO who will be promptly relieved of duty."

My face jets bright red. "Ah, oh...uh...hold on just a sec there, Sergeant Major. I'm not trying to get anyone into trouble, and if you contact my commander, he's not going to like it much."

He cuts me off. "Sergeant, I may be wearing civilian clothes, but I'm still the Sergeant Major of this base. Are you questioning me?"

"Uh, no, Sergeant Major."

"Good. I didn't think you were." Then he stands up and walks out of the building.

I wonder, *wasn't he here to see the doctor?* I'm dreading going back to compound cause this is not going to go over well. It's going to cost me one way or another. Joe and I finish our medical visit and bump along in the back of the truck as we head back to the compound. He looks over at me and laughs.

"I'll tell you what, Conner. You're something else. I've never seen somebody who always seems to come out on top in every situation. You are one lucky..." He finishes it with a few choice soldierly words.

Once back on compound, I jump out of the back of the truck, and here comes the captain's orderly out to meet me. "Sergeant Conner, Captain wants to see you in his office right away."

I nod and slump inside. Entering his office, I salute and stand at attention in front of his desk. "Sergeant Conner reporting, sir."

"Sergeaaaant Conner." He kind of draws out the word and nods at me with a grim look, then pushes some papers across his desk with a sigh. "Sign these here and here."

As I sign, I try to explain. "Sir, this wasn't my intention but I was down at..."

"No, Sergeant Conner, no need to explain at all, I know the whole story, for better or for worse. I've been instructed to have you sign these extension papers and then have my orderly drive them to Brigade headquarters in my jeep as fast as possible to ensure that these papers are processed ASAP. Those are my orders, Sergeant Conner. But next time you have some type of problem, could you please talk to me about it first?"

"Yes, sir."

Then saluting again, I slink out of his presence. I didn't mean for all of this to come down this way, but it happened. I'm still not sure they'll get me extended this long after the cutoff, but we will see.

Preparation for marriage seems to be a real chore and I get a taste of some of the Korean customs as well as some formerly unknown military requirements. We attend mandatory classes sponsored by the military which demonstrate how little we actually communicate. One of the exercises requires the guy to verbally instruct the girl to draw a simple diagram which only the guy gets to see.

With a three minute time limit, I talk fast. "Put the pencil on the left top quadrant of the paper. Draw a line straight down for about two inches and don't lift the pencil from the paper. Then make a straight line to the right for two inches..."

It seems simple when you think about it, but in practice, it's difficult. Most of the girls are at a loss because they haven't run across words like 'quadrant' and have never put phrases together like 'section of the paper' and 'move your hand in a straight line down.'

Young fares a bit better than others, but this does underscore that even though we think we communicate well, there's a lot we don't understand about each other.

It's the critical question that must be asked in many situations. "How do you find out what you don't know?" It's critical for war, for business continuity and a host of other applications, including relationships. "Grow or die" is the catchphrase.

Reams of paperwork need to be completed on the Korean side and we hire an agency to help us get through it successfully. The more we 'tip' the agency, the faster the process goes. I'm not used to this 'tipping' and I call it a bribe or highway robbery, which doesn't go over well. It causes consternation in our relationship. Young's standard comment is, "You asked for this."

The biggest hurdle is getting Young's parents' permission. Unknown to me, she sends a letter with my picture in it to her dad and mom back on the farm. Her younger sister later informs us of the reaction. "You can't believe what happened."

Concerned, Young asks, "Was it bad? What happened?"

"It was worse than bad. They were thrilled to get a letter from you. Mom said, 'Open it, open it!' Then when Dad opened the letter, this picture of a white guy fell out on the floor. Dad took one look and went ballistic. Mom cried and Dad shouted, threw things around, stomped around outside and shook his fists in the air. I thought he was going to have a heart attack."

I could never quite judge which way things would go with Young. Sometimes she fell apart and needed comforting while other times she acted like a warrior. This was a warrior time.

Holding a bottle of beer, she gestures forcibly. "Oh, yeah?! Well, they'd better get used to it fast cause if they don't give me permission, I'm going down there and there's going to be a big fight. Maybe I'll bring the white guy with me, too, and see how that goes over!"

Her sister, I guess, is used to talking Young down, so I learn a few things about communication from listening to them. I took a couple of college level courses in basic and advanced Korean. Even though I can't pick up every word, I get the gist of it.

"No need for that, they're coming here."

Young drops her bottle of beer. It crashes to the floor, but fortunately doesn't break. The bottle rolls around and dumps beer on the yellow-flowered linoleum. The rule is: don't wear shoes in the hooch/house/room and broken glass is a problem so I'm glad it doesn't shatter. I grab a towel to clean up the sloshing mess.

"They're what!"

We are almost as far north as you get in South Korea. They live almost as far south. It's not only a long trip by taxi over rock roads, then train and then bus, but it's also expensive. As farmers, they don't make a lot of money. They've never seen a white person before, much less the sometimes degraded behavior displayed around the American military installations.

Then the question is, why are they coming here? Are they coming to bless us or to take Young home — forcibly?

Unfortunately, we also don't know 'when' they are coming. Are they on their way, or will it be in a week, a month? One of the things I've learned, especially in a small village is the lack of concern over time. We Americans literally live by the clock. The Koreans in these parts are in no hurry. For instance, if we plan to go to a Korean home for dinner, my first question is, "What time?"

So Young gives me a time. "Oh, I don't know, about five." But five o'clock comes and goes, and she hasn't even begun to get ready. I'm vibrating like a racehorse in the gate, getting more stressed out by the minute. "Isn't it time to go? Don't you think we should be leaving? It will take at least twenty minutes to walk over there. Aren't you going to get ready? The food's going to be cold. Won't they be offended if we arrive late?"

Young simply ignores me, which makes me angry but I try not to say anything because it only causes a fight. So I sit and vibrate. Practice meditative, calming thoughts. Breathe in deeply, let it out slowly. Look at my watch, thirty seconds go by. Finally, about seven p.m., she's ready, and we begin our journey. When we arrive, no one is angry or upset. As a matter of fact, they haven't even started cooking. I call it Hanguk Shigan, or Korean Time. I have to differentiate between precise American time and Korean time which falls into a several hours or longer window.

In this case we don't have a clue when her parents will show up or if at all. In spite of her bravado, Young is frightened of her dad and this meeting. Three days later, they show up at our door. No warning, no letter or phone call — they're just here. Young gets down on her knees and bows before them, something she unfortunately didn't apprise me of, so I stand there like an idiot. However, I do resist sticking my hand out American style and instead give the expected bow from the waist to honor them. Then we invite them in and we all sit down together.

I manage a little conversation with her dad as Young and her mom go off to fix some food. We top the meal off with some Korean wine, and then I have to go to work so I leave them at the mercy of each other. Before I leave, her father hands me a box and I look over at Young but she shrugs her shoulders. I open it and see a beautiful pair of leather dress shoes. Her father gestures that it's a gift for me. I'm so surprised that I fall into my American traditions.

"Oh no, I can't take this."

Fortunately, I catch a glimpse of Young, standing a bit behind her father. She shakes her head and mouths, "No, no." Then she says in English. "You have to take that or else he will feel insulted."

She's banking he won't have a clue what she is saying and he doesn't. Later I find out he had the shoes custom-made for me but I never figure out how he knew what size to make them. They fit perfectly. It was his way of saying, "Welcome to the family."

As the days fly by, all our time seems taken up with wedding classes, travel to various cities to gather the appropriate information and paying everyone to do it faster. Finally, the day arrives and none too soon because I'm worn to a frazzle. But at least, everything has been completed on both the Korean, military and American sides. All we have to do is go to the American Embassy and sign the papers, and we will be officially married.

The Embassy is located in Seoul, and we end up leaving late for the trip. So I'm nervous before we even start. Once in Seoul, we meet with our marriage guide and his secretary. They have helped us navigate this entire mess, at a cost, of course. They talk with Young and I can't understand except I think it has something to do with eating. So when we arrive at the Embassy, I take Young aside and ask her about it.

"After we finish all our paperwork here," she says, "we are all going out to eat and celebrate."

That means Young and I have to pay for this celebration. We're not broke, but I just can't tolerate it anymore. We have paid a load of money already. She tries to explain that this is the custom to show our appreciation but I have no more patience for it. I come unglued. We argue for no good reason as tears spill out of her eyes. It isn't often that she cries, so I know I need to quiet down.

"This is our wedding day and you're ruining it," she sobs.

It's horrible to ruin an important event, and I can't undo it. I'm still mad about the whole thing and I can't shake it. I feel miserable and I'm making Young miserable but I charge ahead with my mouth and continue to blast out at her.

"I'm sorry we even came down here in the first place. Maybe this was all a big mistake. I've had it with all these expensive Korean customs we have to go through."

I want to stop. I want to apologize, but I keep on and on like an idiot, saying things I don't want to and I'm sorry before they're even out of my mouth. At the end of it all, we go back home and sleep facing different directions without a word to each other — on our wedding day. A big part of me wants to say I'm so sorry, but this little demanding part of me won't let me say it. The next morning I leave early without a word as Young lies in bed wide awake.

As I walk to the compound, I wonder at this person I am discovering. I always thought I was a nice guy who cared about other people. Yet, in this close relationship with another person, that image shatters like a broken mirror. Deep inside I'm self centered and it leaks out. Fortunately, Young won't just give in and let me have my way. I want to be different with her. Yet, somehow I can't seem to break free of my own bad behavior.

No sooner than I walk through the gate, I hear the orderly calling out my name. I quickly turn and try to duck into the gatehouse before he spots me.

"Sergeant Conner!"

Too late. He sees me before I get inside, so my duck and hide is a complete failure.

"Sergeant Conner." He runs up panting then pauses to catch his breath. "Got your orders here."

"Huh? What orders?"

"The orders for your extension. You've been extended another twelve months."

Now that is a surprise. I didn't expect the extension to go through at all, much less to go through in just a month. I can't wait to let Young know. She'll be thrilled. I'm not sure how to break the news to my family who are expecting me back this year.

Later, in my office, I finish up some paperwork. It's getting late and I snap on the tiny desk lamp against the oncoming darkness. As

I lean back in my chair, all of a sudden something occurs to me. I'm married, and I didn't even tell my family I had a girlfriend, much less that we were getting married. I hold my face in my hands, then bang my head against the desktop. I was so busy with everything, it never even occurred to me. How is this going to go over?

"Hi Mom, hi Dad, I've been busy for a while here. Nothin' much new. Oh, well there is one thing you might be interested in. I got married this week; just thought I'd let you know. Oh, and before I forget, I'm staying in the Army in Korea an extra year. How have you been lately?"

It's past dark and I finally finish up my paperwork. The joy of my extension orders washes away with the problem of how to break this news of my latest madness to Mom and Dad. If I was a drinkin' man, I'd surely be drinkin' by now. But that never seemed to do much for me except give me a headache the next morning.

Heading out the gate, I have to turn around and go back to my office to grab the extension orders lying on my desk. I almost forgot them and I want to show them to Young. I didn't tell her about the extension in case it fell through. But now that it's completed and I have the orders in hand, this will be a nice present and surprise to make up for my poor attitude on our wedding day.

Thinking about cheering her up puts life back into my step and my heart. I hurry home and open the door and... nothing is here. What is this? Am I in the wrong place? I back out of the door and look around to get my bearings. Yes, this is the right room. At least it seems to be right, but it can't be because it's empty. There is no furniture, no bed, no nothing.

As I snap on the light, I see that it isn't completely empty. A stack of uniforms and boots are in a corner with a box. I look at the uniforms to make sure they're mine and this isn't someone else's room. The nametag reads 'Conner.' Yep. They're mine. What happened here? My heart seems to fall to the floor but I don't bother to pick it up as I go back out the door and look around in a confused state.

"She go." An old woman washes cabbage in a large red tub. She doesn't look up but continues her work. "Not know where she go. She just go. Truck come, then she shoo, shoo. Go."

I'm at a complete loss as to what to do, so I go back in and sit on the floor. That's when I notice a paper on the floor with 'Conner' written on it. Hands trembling, I unfold it and start to read.

Dear Conner,
>   I never want to make your life miserable.
>   I want to make your life better. So you be happy,
>   I will leave and then you can be happy again.
>   Maybe someday you will meet a nice girl and
>   she can make you happy.
> > Love,
> > Young

Two little hearts sit next to the word 'Young'. I feel ruined. Silent tears course down my face and fall on the floor. I want to scream, but everyone lives in such close proximity, I don't want to share my pain with them. Instead I fall asleep on the floor and dream of Young holding my head in her lap and stroking my hair. She smiles and I reach up to touch her face. Then I wake up.

The light dawns, and I am alone. It was just a dream and I have to face my own consequences. I report in sick at the compound and go searching, asking questions, and widening my search patterns to the next village and the little cafe. But no one has seen her or at least they aren't admitting to it. Days go by and I have to return to my work drudgery. I hear comments as if in a fog. "Sergeant Conner, you look terrible. What's up with you? Are you okay?"

The words seem to come from a different dimension, only shadows passing by. At night I wet the floor with my tears while during the day, I move through the motions of work. A week passes. We go out to field duty which consists of taking all the Tac site equipment, including dogs, and living in worse conditions than the little quonset hut on the compound. While we 'camp' out, the monsoon season starts early and we are all soaked to the gills.

After the field exercise is completed, we traipse back to the Tac site, drop the equipment, get the dogs situated back in their kennels and finally pull back into compound. As I jump down from the truck, memory hits me in the face and the fog comes roaring back. Even though it's been over two weeks since I've seen her, I still sleep in the little room because it's better than sleeping in the quonset hut bunk on the compound. I bought a little mat to sleep on and a light blanket for cover, but it's so hot, I don't need it.

In my bunk in the quonset hut, I strip out of my wet gear and head down for a hot shower. Afterwards, I walk back through the mud which covers my rubber flip flops, but at least to some extent, I'm clean. Changing into dry clothes doesn't help my immense fatigue, and I'm tempted to collapse on my bunk.

But I really want to go home. Funny how I call it home now. Before we left for field duty, I put up some pictures of Young and some of both of us on the walls. I want to go and sleep in that room. "See you guys later. I'm headed down to the village to get some sleep."

"Okay Sarge. Give your girl a kiss for us, too."

They don't know or at least don't let on that they know. Kansas City grins at me and, as I pass by, he thumps me on the back, which is unusual. Passing through the gate, I give a half-hearted wave to the guards on duty then head out for the short walk through the rain.

Jogging the last fifty yards as if I'm not going to be as wet, I stop suddenly. Oh no, I've left the light on in the room all week. I see it dimly through the window. Oh well, just some extra electricity. I don't care. I'm just glad to be close to home and rest. I slog the last few yards, jump some puddles, and pause at the door to kick off my wet shoes.

Then I slide back the door. Wha-a-a-t?

I quickly slide the door closed behind me and try to get my bearings. This isn't my room. It's full of furniture and I hope no one is inside. I can't believe I just jerked open the door of the wrong place. No wonder I thought I'd left the light on. My heart pounds from embarrassment and I feel my face heat to jet red. My worst fears are realized as the door jerks open behind me.

Turning to apologize, I freeze. Time stops as I feel my heart struggle to find a beat. My mouth falls open, yet no breath enters my lungs. Time returns as Young slams her arms around me, nearly knocking me off my feet, Her head buries in my chest. My heart races again, and my breath becomes ragged as I wrap my arms around her. We stand together a long time, just breathing.

She finally lets go, takes my hand and leads me back into our fully furnished room. We talk almost all night, and I dream this wonderful dream. I don't want to wake up to my empty room with the pictures on the wall. Then I do wake up as the noonday light pours through the window. I grimace in the heat. Putting my hand out to push the blanket off, I jerk awake. I'm not on the floor. I'm on a bed — our bed!

Is she really there, smiling at me? Was it only a bad dream? Yet, she's back and perhaps we've both learned something. Somehow, a grateful prayer escapes my lips.

Chapter Sixteen
A Time to Die

Watch out! He's got a knife!

Weapons and drunkenness do not mix well. There isn't much to do around a small military base. About five American military installations operate within ten square miles. What invariably crops up in the surrounding villages are bars, food vendors, jewelry stores and other forms of entertainment particularly geared to the American GI. Take away the American military, and the businesses and population will disappear within a month.

On this Friday night we pull Military Police patrol in one of those small villages crowded with bars, nightclubs and hundreds of GI's looking for entertainment. Big Joe, KATUSA Kansas City, and I take a break from our patrol. The village is just a little crossroads near a military installation.

A strip of clubs and food vendors stretch down both sides of the street for six hundred feet. Add to these businesses a bus stop and some dingy buildings with rooms to rent. That's about the whole village, which probably sprang up around the base. There are at least ten different bars of all different themes: country & western, disco this and disco that, along with little walk-up booths housing food vendors, like a fairground, complete with enough colorful lights to mimic a miniature Las Vegas.

We stand at the Fried Onion Ring booth which is next to the Fried Chicken booth with the Aces Club directly across the street. For some reason, the Aces Club always brings trouble, so the onion ring vendor is a good place to stop for a break. As we munch on crunchy, somewhat greasy onion rings, Big Joe turns his paper onion ring holder around and peers at it.

Korea in the 1970's is mostly poor. The local community provides trash collection as a service to the military base. The trash doesn't go to a dump, but is carefully collected and used. Soda and beer cans make smoke stacks for the Ondol systems. Cut the top and bottom out, fit them together and voila! — a nice smoke stack. Some smoke stacks combine Budweiser or Coors-colored stacks, with Pepsi, Coke, and Seven-Up thrown in here and there.

Big Joe is curious about another innovative use of trash which is discarded paper. The military service runs on paper. All kinds of communications and paperwork require an unending supply from the paper mills. One type of communication is termed an 'order' which tells us what to do and where to go. For instance, when a soldier rotates to a new duty station in a different location or country, he cannot do so without a copy of his official 'orders.'

After popping the last onion ring into his mouth, Joe pulls out his flashlight and unfolds the paper cup that the onion rings were stuffed into. Even though the paper is greased-soaked, it is still readable. Suddenly he shouts, "Hey! These are my orders!"

I snatch them out of his hand and hold them under the beam of his flashlight, a long heavy metal cylinder that doubles as a nightstick. Sure enough, the paper is dated a week ago and states that Joe is officially extended for another twelve months in Korea at his present duty station. The light disappears as Joe does some kind of weird disco move dance in the street, most unbecoming of an MP.

"Yeah, Baby! I got my orders. Yeah, Baby!"

Kansas City and I move into the shadows so no one will mistake us as friends of 'Disco Joe.' That's one dance I don't ever want to see again. I shake my head and laugh at the craziness of it all. Joe's all happy that he got his orders to stay in the country another year. Actually, he didn't get his orders yet because no one officially gave them to him.

Instead, someone accidentally threw the paper into the trashcan and it ended up here in the village as an onion ring wrapper. The crazy part is that Joe isn't even mad about it. He's just thrilled about the orders. Tomorrow, back on compound, we'll have to sort it out and find something for the official records.

Shouts from down the street interrupt us, and a glance in that direction tells me break time is over. We hoof it down to where a small crowd gathers. The sound of breaking glass can be heard over the shouts of the crowd. Pushing our way through, we dodge a wine bottle that hurtles out the open door of a small room.

From inside, some guy yells and curses while a girl screams Stepping inside, we quickly size up the situation. A girl is on the floor screaming, a very large GI with no shirt is standing over her yelling in a drunken, guttural voice.

Two other MP's try to restrain him but he throws them off like paper towels. One lands against the wall causing the whole room to shake and the other crashes into us. We fall back through the small doorway as it splinters around us. The crowd breaks into cheers and shouts of approval as if this is the entertainment of the week. It probably is.

Joe jumps up and starts to go back in, but I grab his arm and we both back up. The drunk man lurches out the door, dragging the girl by her hair like some kind of caveman.

Kansas City shouts, "Watch out, he's got a knife!"

Drunk Man slashes a long switchblade through the air while still holding the girl by her hair. She continues to scream and wail.

Joe looks over at me and shouts at the top of his lungs, "Football! Seventy-two, twenty-one, thirty-five!"

At the word "Football," Joe and I crouch down in a line position. Drunk Man drops the girl and prepares for an attack. He waves his knife at us. On "thirty-five," I stand up, move in front of Joe and extend my hand to the guy. "I'm sorry," I say, "I didn't catch your name."

He's momentarily confused and lowers his knife hand. "Wha...?"

But as soon as that knife hand moves, I crouch down real fast. Joe hurtles over me and crashes into him, knocking the knife out of his hand and pinning him to the ground. Unfortunately, in all the times we practiced this move, Joe didn't wear a long, heavy metal flashlight on his belt. Now, as he jumps over me, the flashlight/nightstick combination slams into the back of my head. I'm on the ground with a good concussion; dazed and bleeding. It all happens in less than ten seconds. Then everything is over and the crowd begins to disperse. Kansas City, stunned by our moves, helps me to my feet and over to a large concrete block where I sit down.

He looks at me, shaking his head, "You guys really crazy."

"But it worked," I protest.

I suppose we were taking a bit of a chance because when I stood up and extended my hand. Mister Drunk Man could have cut me and charged and in his right mind, he probably would have done just that. We were counting on a certain amount of inebriation and it worked like a charm — this time. Except for the heavy flashlight.

By the time we haul Mister Drunk to the closest military installation with a lock-up (a jail), write up all the reports and paperwork, it is well after midnight. However, since we are on military duty, we have no problem with curfew. One of the night duty MP's drives us back to our village and compound in his jeep, then I head down to our room in the village. Young isn't feeling well today, and I'm anxious to check on her. If I could have called her, I would have done so several times, but there is only one phone in the village and it's not close to where we live.

Quietly, I slide open the rice paper door in case she is sleeping and find her lying on the floor. She has a fever, so I guess it makes sense because the heating is in the floor. Gingerly sliding the door closed, I whisper, "Hey, Yobo."

Yobo is a Korean word meaning sweetheart. Although she calls me 'Conner' most of the time, she begins calling me 'Yobo' after we married so I do the same.

"Why are you lying on the floor, Baby?"

I kneel down to pick her up and she's hot like she's burning up. I get no response from her and begin to get alarmed. "Young? Young! Hey, wake up."

No response. This is serious! Turning her onto her back, I see that she is whiter than me. This isn't good. She's barely breathing and burning up with a fever. I don't know what to do. We don't even have a thermometer to take her temperature. It's after curfew. The nearest hospital is over an hour away, and I have no transportation.

Then I remember a little Korean first aid station right down from the crossroads in our village. But it's at least a mile away. I don't have a way to get her there and I've got to do something fast. She's starting to breathe much slower and real hard and I'm not getting much of a pulse on her. Picking her up, I head out the door and begin an army jog down the street. About halfway there, I fall into a rhythm of putting one foot in front of the other and breathing.

The door to the med station is closed, but quickly opens after I bang on it with my foot. A sleepy-eyed nurse peers out, then motions me in. As I try to explain what the problem is, I quickly realize my lack of Korean vocabulary. I need medical terms.

Fortunately, the doctor comes into the room, pulling on his shirt. I'm sure I've wakened him. I lay Young on a metal table. The doctor examines her and listens to me explain the symptoms. Afterwards, he peers at me through thick glasses. "What eat today?"

"Uh, she was fixing chicken tonight before I left, but I didn't have time to eat with her."

"So she eat but you no eat?"

"No... I mean yes, she eat but I no eat."

He says something in Korean to the nurse and she leaves. Then he turns to me again.

"Maybe bad food. Too much time pass. We try help her."

The nurse returns with a black tube, a funnel and a plastic jug of some white liquid. While I hold her, he takes the tube, puts it into her mouth and runs about two feet of it down her throat. Then he takes the funnel and pours most of the white liquid down the tube until she begins to retch. Quickly pulling the tube out, he turns Young's head to the side as the white liquid comes back up along with the contents of her stomach. After that, he gives her a shot and pats me on the hand.

"Very sick. If she alive in morning, then she live."

The nurse then motions for me to pick up Young as she leads us to a little room where we stay for the night. It's pitch dark with no light from the small window. There's only a little threadbare blanket, so I lay Young on the floor and double it over her, then lay her head on my lap and stroke her hair.

In the dark with Young, I'm oblivious of time. This is probably the longest night of my life yet I'm stuck with only me and my thoughts. For a while I talk to her, then finally speak in desperation. "You'd better not die on me, you hear? I'm talking to you. Are you listening to me? You be strong. You live! You've got to live!"

The nurse comes in to check on us every so often as the darkness drags on and on. I'm relegated to talking to the only one that may hear as I lower my head and pray. Suddenly I wake up to light streaming into the window. I must have dozed off and... Wait a minute! There's no weight on my leg. Young is gone! Before I can react, the door slides aside and she crawls into the tiny room. She flops down with her head on my lap.

"I had to pee," she mumbles, then falls back asleep.

Closing my eyes, I breathe a sigh of relief and cover her with the little blanket. Looks like we made it.

Black Marketing is big business in Korea with people who

take advantage of every opportunity to turn a quick dollar, no matter what the risk. The military ships in American goods which are not available on the local Korean market. These items are sold only to military personnel for personal use at a PX or Commissary. The Commissary is similar to a large grocery store and the PX is more like a Walgreens or a CVS. Attempts to prevent American military personnel from selling those items to the local economy include rationing cards and sting operations.

Rationing cards allow troops to purchase only so much of an item per month. One bottle of shampoo, two cases of beer, three cartons of cigarettes, etc. All of these items, and more, can be purchased on base and then sold to the local economy for anywhere from twice to six times their cost. But this is strictly illegal. However, that doesn't stop people from trying to turn a quick buck — which brings us to the second prevention method: sting operations.

Plain clothes investigators watch for suspected black market trafficking and investigate troops who take their fresh purchases into an alley or other hidden places, then come out with nothing but cash. Undercover officers arrest the suspects and take them in.

One particular day, I make the long bus ride down to the Commissary in Seoul to pick up groceries. The easiest way is to take along my large duffle bag, throw everything into it at the Commissary, check out, then heft it back to our village on the bus. On my return trip, I decide to get off at another village where Young is taking art lessons. I figure we'll go back home together.

I head down an alleyway toward the building where Young's art lesson is held, but unfortunately, it's a wasted trip. She's already gone. As I come out of the alleyway with my heavy duffle full of groceries, an MP approaches me. "Hey, what do you think you're doing there? Let's see what you have in that bag."

Some of the groceries are frozen and now thawing, so I'm in a hurry to get home. As I unclip and open the bag, I notice the MP's rank is a private. I know most of the MP's around here, but haven't seen this guy before. He reaches in the duffle bag and throws my food down on the dusty street.

Shocked by his behavior, I say, "Hold on there just a second, what are you doing?"

He picks up my duffle bag and shakes the last of the contents into the street, then throws the bag down as well. Grabbing my arm, he forces me over to his MP jeep, parked on the other side of the road and smirks, "Thought you could do a little black market, huh?"

I jerk my arm out of his grasp and face him. "Black market? If I wanted to sell this stuff, why would I come out of an alleyway with a full bag of groceries? Wouldn't I be walking into the alleyway or walking out with an empty bag? Do you think I'm doing a reverse Black Market scheme where I walk in with an empty bag and walk out with groceries?"

Passersby stop and stare at us. He grabs me again and wrenches me over to his jeep, then takes out his handcuffs. "You'd better cooperate or you're going to be in a shitload of trouble."

In his defense, he's a rookie, and I'm wearing civilian clothes. He can't identify me. More people begin to gather which isn't good, because they all know me and I'm embarrassed. So I turn around and put my hands behind my back. "Oh, for crying out loud! This is ridiculous, Private. You're going to end up sorry you're doing this."

With that comment, he knocks me to the ground and steps on my head. His boot grinds my face into the dusty street as he cuffs me. Then he yanks me to my feet and slams me into the side of the jeep, causing me to fall alongside it. I don't even bother to fight back, because I know when he gets me to the closest MP station there's going to be hell to pay. He dumps me in the back seat where I listen as he calls in on the jeep radio. "I've got a criminal transport back to station."

Then he shoves the vehicle in gear and we head for a long ride to the nearest station, about fifteen miles away. When we arrive at the station, he jerks me out of the jeep and throws me on the concrete walk. By the time he drags me into the station, I have a black eye, a bruised face, abrasions on my arm, a couple of leg lacerations and a large cut above my right eye.

It's almost time for the shift change and the Post Captain stands behind the main desk. He's talking to the on-duty lieutenant. They both look up as MP Man drags me in and throws me onto a wooden bench. When they see me, the captain reacts with shock. "Sergeant Conner! What happened to you?"

Then he looks over at the MP, who answers, "Sir, I caught this guy trying to sell groceries on the black market."

The captain comes around the desk and looks incredulous. "First of all, Private, when you come into this office and see either myself or the good lieutenant here, you immediately stand at attention and salute! Is that clear?"

The MP gulps and seems to melt a few inches. "Yes, sir."

Gesturing at me, the captain says, "Take those handcuffs off of him and report to my office... Now!"

"Yes, sir."

I stand up and dangle the empty cuffs.

He gasps, "How did you...?"

"Private, you're not the only one with a key to these cuffs."

Taking the cuffs, he slinks into the captain's office.

Captain Sonofagun turns to me as the lieutenant goes to get the first aid kit. "Is this accusation true, Sergeant Conner?"

"Not exactly, sir." Then I explain the events to him in detail. "And, by the way, he left my duffle bag full of groceries lying in the street which I'm sure the local villagers had a field day with."

The captain listens to me, then goes into his office and slams the door behind him. I hear his muffled voice and make out some of the words. "...Kind of cockamamie, halfwit, ...about the stupidest, idiotic, ...better come up with all the money to replace, ...I don't care what you thought, ...damn lucky that Sergeant Conner didn't..."

After a minute of silence, the thoroughly browbeaten private creaks open the door and slinks out of the office. His face almost drags on the floor. Looking down, he walks over to the bench where I'm sitting and salutes. He shouldn't salute enlisted men; only officers. But I let it pass, figuring he's in enough trouble already.

With his voice at a low murmur and his head still down, he starts to apologize, "Sergeant Conner. I want to apologize for arresting you on false charges..."

He swallows hard. I know he still doesn't think he did anything wrong.

"...I apologize for causing you injury, and I would be happy to drive you back to your village immediately. Additionally, I will pay for all the groceries you lost and any additional damages."

After he finishes, the captain pipes up. I glance over to see him leaning against the doorframe.

"Sergeant Conner, would you like to press charges against this sorry sack?"

The private can't see him, so the captain winks.

I turn to the duty lieutenant who can barely keep from laughing. "What do you think, LT? Do you have any room in the pokey tonight for this guy?" We always refer to lieutenants as LT, pronounced "ell tee."

"Oh, I dunno, Sarge. We could probably drum up some room with the guy that got into a knife fight and beat another guy to a pulp with his bare hands."

By this time, the private starts to sniffle, and I can't help but laugh out loud. He's really taking us seriously. But I suppose as a newbie, he doesn't know any better. I stand up and smack him on the arm, then walk toward the door. "Come on my cabbie, let's get a move on. My wife will be worried."

A couple of other MP's enter the office and everybody laughs as the private says, "Yes, sir, Sergeant, sir." He follows me out the door.

We motor along in silence for most of the trip. Finally, as we begin to approach my village, he clears his throat and speaks. "Sergeant, sir..."

I cut him off. "First of all, Private, you've been watching too much TV. You don't salute an enlisted person, only an officer. Second, I'm not a sir. That's also reserved for officers."

"Sergeant, I just wanted to say..."

"Frankly, Private, I'm not all that interested in what you have to say. But I will give you some advice that you don't really deserve but are badly in need of. I don't know your motive in arresting me for supposed black marketing, so I can't really comment on that. If you really thought that was the case, then you acted on your best judgment. But here's my advice to you. If you ignore it, you're not going to last long. When you get back to your base, you'll find out what I mean because the captain is a man of honor. He won't drop this easily."

I sit back with my feet propped up against the jeep's windshield and watch the fields and an occasional person zip past.

"When you have an encounter with someone, just because you're a big bad MP — doesn't give you the right to throw someone around and treat them badly. And it doesn't give you the right to talk down to anyone either. A friend of mine once told me, 'The only time you should ever look down on someone is if you are reaching out with your hand to help them up,' and that statement has stuck with me."

"This is Korea and you are here representing the United States of America and the U.S. military to the people of Korea in every word you say and every move you make. In part, you're an ambassador. Your job is to serve and protect people, not beat them up like some kind of penny-ante hoodlum. I would highly suggest that you do some intense soul searching and find a new road to take concerning the way you think and behave."

"Sergeant, why didn't you tell me you were an MP?"

I can't stand his whiney voice. I feel like responding back to him in a weasely voice, "Sergeant, why didn't you tell me you were an MP," but I resist the temptation to add insult to injury. We approach the four-way intersection in my village. "Turn left here. That's exactly what I'm talking about, Private. It shouldn't matter if I'm an MP, an officer or the president. You can't play favorites. You do your duty and leave the rest up to God."

I'm shocked at the 'God comment' that comes out of my mouth and wonder where that came from. "Pull over right up there where those people are standing. That's my place."

As he pulls the jeep over and I hop out, I notice that the 'group of people' includes my wife, several neighbors, and a couple MP's from my compound. News and gossip travel fast. Everyone else already knows more of the story than I do. Young takes one look at my face and slews out a string of Korean words I've never heard before.

Then she starts after the private who has also climbed out of the jeep like he's coming to dinner or something. I grab her and lift her off her feet as I yell at the private, "Better get yourself out of here real fast, 'cause this crowd's gettin' a might rowdy."

"He jumps back into the Jeep, pulls a U-turn and barrels back down the dusty road. I put Young back on her feet.

Then she hits me and cries out, "What happened to you, Yobo? I was so scared!"

I hold her in my arms. "Just a misunderstanding, Baby, just a misunderstanding. Everything's okay now."

Turning to the small crowd of people, I attempt to disperse them. "Nothing more to see here. Y'all go on back home."

The two MP's are Kansas City and Bay. "Thanks for coming down, guys. I'll give you the low down tomorrow. Right now, I think I need some rest, if you know what I mean."

"Right, Sarge."

They turn and make their way back to the compound.

As Young and I walk home, I'm about to get an adjustment in my own thinking. We enter our room. I stop short, gasp and point like I'm seeing a ghost. "Wha... what's that doing here?"

My duffle bag sits in the middle of the floor with some of the contents spilling out. Evidently, some of the people in the next village saw the encounter, picked up my bag, brought it by bus at their own expense, and carried it from the bus stop all the way to Young. Not one item was missing. I'm stunned. I figured both the duffle bag and the contents were long gone. I begin to realize that my own attitude toward people is also unfair. I figured they would take my stuff without a second thought. But instead, they went to a lot of trouble to return it to us and never stuck around for a thank you.

The next morning as I walk onto the compound, I hear the captain's been in a tizzy all morning. Now he has everyone out of the barracks, in formation, on the basketball court. The orderly waits in my office and advises me that the captain wants me on the court, pronto. He stands in front of the formation as I jog up and salute.

"Sergeant Conner reporting, sir."

"Sergeant Conner, get your MP's and do a complete and thorough search of the barracks right now."

"What, exactly, are we looking for, sir?"

"Illegal drugs, Sergeant. I want you to do a drug sweep and report back to me A.S.A.P."

As I hesitate, the captain reinforces his request. "I said, 'Now'. Is there a problem with that, Sergeant Conner?"

"Yes, sir, right away, sir."

Making a smart about-face, I jog off toward our quonset hut living quarters to dredge up anyone available. This is not a good situation. The captain has never asked us to do such a thing and if we had been alone in his office, I would have told him so and refused. As MP's we have to live and work with these guys on a daily basis, and it's never good to whack a hornet's nest with a stick. We don't intentionally go looking to make trouble for anyone.

Our main mission is to secure and protect the compound, tactical site and surrounding areas. It is not our primary duty to go around and perform drug busts on fellow soldiers that we have to live with. That should be done by personnel outside our unit, and we MP's should be inspected along with everyone else. This has the potential to set up a real rift between the MP's and the other personnel here.

I shake my head and push through the door to our quonset hut where four people are present. Na and Kansas City sit on their beds, eating rice and beans. A couple of new guys are in the back. "Let's go, guys. Captain wants a drug sweep of the barracks right now." They stare at me, incredulous.

"I know, it isn't my idea. But he has everyone in formation on the basketball court, and he wants us to do a drug sweep right now." Raising my hands helplessly, I mutter, "What can we do?"

We work out a quick process. We can't just start going through someone's belongings and throw everything around. Well, I guess we could, but there's no sense making it worse than it already is. So we take five people at a time, one for each MP, go to their rooms and search through stuff. Then we take those people back out to the formation and grab five more.

We are working on our second five. I search through this guy's room and his stuff while he stands at attention at the doorway. He's real nervous and keeps talking, which I ignore. Sure enough, I open a drawer and find a big bag of marijuana hiding under a towel. I inwardly groan, because this is enough to get him in serious trouble.

As I turn around, he's right in my face. "Sarge, please help me out here. I'll do anything; I'll give you whatever you want, just don't turn me in. I can't afford to be busted again. Please... help me just this once!" The guy is practically crying, but he's keeping his voice real soft so no one else will hear.

After finish with all the sweeps, I report back to the commander. "Sergeant Conner reporting, sir."

Shoving some papers aside, he looks up and nods. "What have you got for me, Sergeant?"

I toss the forms on his desk and report the findings. "Several personnel had joints or other minor amounts of marijuana. A couple had some amphetamines from the village pharmacy. Also, one soldier had about a one pound bag of marijuana. Everything is listed in the reports.

"Very good. Where is the evidence?"

"We locked it in a container in the arms room, sir."

"I want you to bring it all over to me."

"Pardon me?" I'm taken off guard by his request. He has the reports, what can he possibly want by looking at the evidence. "Sir, the arms room sergeant is off duty and..."

"Sergeant Conner, I want the evidence on my desk right now. Work it out. Dismissed."

"Yes, sir." Turning, I exit his office. This is certainly not standard and a bit bizarre. I just hope the arms room sergeant hasn't left the compound yet. After a while I find him sitting in the NCO club with a beer in hand. It takes about ten minutes to convince him to open the arms room and sign out the evidence to me. I then take it back to the captain. "Sergeant Conner again, sir. Here's the evidence."

"Ah, Sergeant Conner, very good. You can go now."

"Actually, sir, I'll need you to sign the evidence cards showing you have received this."

"Not necessary, I'll return it myself. You can go."

As much as I hate standing up to someone, I'm not about to agree to this. I don't know if he's trying to test me or what's going on here, but I'm not leaving the office without either a signature on those cards or the evidence. "Sir, I appreciate your willingness to take custody of this evidence. But I need either a signature or the evidence before I leave your office."

He stares at me with his head cocked to one side and seems about to say something when he thinks better of it, signs the cards, and tosses them at me across the desk. "Alright then, no problem. Here are your cards, Sergeant."

Then he starts writing on a report. Assuming he is done with me, I turn and walk out. Jogging across the parking area to the arms area, I hand the signature cards back to the sergeant and go home. But the trouble has only just begun.

Two days later, I work the night shift. When I come home in the morning, Young is crying. It takes me a while to calm her down. Between her sniffles she manages to say, "Last night, some guy from compound broke into our room. He had a knife and he said he was going to kill me. But I screamed and kicked him real hard and he ran out. Then Mamasan next door came over and stayed with me 'till this morning. I was scared all night."

More tears and shaking. I go into MP mode. "Tell me what he looked like."

"Tall and skinny, short brown hair, camouflage pants and a white tee shirt." Talking helps calm her. Then she adds, "And he had a scar over his eye. He said he would come back again!"

Sitting on the floor I hold her till she stops sobbing. I know exactly who this is. The question is, what to do about it. I can't sit here with her all the time to protect her.

The next day I go to see Top in his office and explain what's happened. Top looks grim as I tell him the situation. He advises me to see the captain. I tell Corporal Snidely, the orderly, to get me in to see the captain, then I sit down to wait. A couple of hours pass. The captain's door opens and he comes out as if he's leaving. Standing up, I salute. "Captain Quigley, I need to talk to you about a critical issue."

"Oh, Sergeant Conner. I didn't know you were waiting. I'm on my way to a meeting off compound. Make an appointment to see me another time. Maybe tomorrow."

"Sir, this is important. I need to speak with you about an issue."

"Sorry, Sergeant. It will have to wait"

With a whoosh he's out the door, leaving me standing there. Turning to the orderly, I narrow my eyes and frown. "I thought you told him I needed to see him?"

Snidely's face is red as a beet and he won't look at me. "I did, but you can see how busy he is."

"When is he available this afternoon?"

Snidely doesn't even glance at the appointment book. "Not."

"Tomorrow morning?"

This time he flips open the book and pretends to study it. "He's pretty booked all week."

Grabbing the book out of his hand, I turn it around and see no appointments written in. Flipping back a page, I see no appointments today either. "Hey, what's going on here? His schedule's blank as a..."

Corporal Snidely grabs the book out of my hand and tosses it in his drawer. Then he looks at me with irritation. His voice is terse and low. "Look, Sergeant. The captain isn't available to talk to you. Not today, not tomorrow, not ever. Got it? Go see Top if you have a problem, okay? By the way, you're on the night duty roster tonight."

Backing up a couple of steps so it isn't as easy to punch him, my hands ball into fists. "What? I just pulled night duty last night."

Night duty consists of sitting in the Command Building in case any emergency calls come in or situations require attention, such as drunken brawls. It's supposed to be a rotating position, and the MP's are usually exempt since we pull other night duty stations. But suddenly I've been yanked into the pool and now, for some reason, two nights in a row. Or for no good reason. I'm starting to get steamed, especially as I see the orderly seems to be enjoying this. Better to exit his desk area and ask Top what's going on.

Back in Top's office, I don't fare much better. "Sergeant Conner, I can't help you out here. You're on the duty roster and you'll have to pull your duty or suffer the consequences. I can't make the captain give you an audience."

"First Sergeant, this soldier that I busted for drugs the other day threatened my wife, broke into our house with a knife last night and says he'll be back. That's first. Second, if I have to pull duty tonight, he's going to go back and try to finish the job. Can't you at least keep him on the compound tonight or relieve me of pulling duty two nights in a row? I'm sure someone else can be on the roster since we have over sixty personnel on this compound. If you can't help me, I'm going to find someone who will and it won't be at this command level."

I hate talking like this to Top, but I'm getting stonewalled for some reason and I can't figure out why.

"Do what you have to do, Sergeant. My hands are tied."

As he makes it clear our meeting is over, I storm out of his office but resist slamming the door. Some kind of collusion is going on here and I have no idea what or why. But my main mission right now is to protect Young.

At the gate, I tell Kansas City I will be off compound the rest of the day 'till my duty at eighteen hundred hours (six p.m.) and to send Big Joe to my place as soon as possible. I find a crowd gathered round our door and quickly push my way through. Young lies on the bed while our neighbor, Mamasan, holds a wet towel on her face.

"What happened?"

Young sits up, and the towel falls off. She has a black eye, a gash on her neck, and she's all bruised up.

"Oh my God, Young! What happened to you?" Rushing over, I make her lie back down. "How did this happen?"

Although she can't talk well through her swollen lips, she manages to mumble out the story. "I was walking down the street to the market and somebody came up behind me and grabbed me. I twisted around and kicked him, but he cut me on the neck with a long knife. Then I punch him in the nose and start to kick him again but he grabs my foot and throws me on ground, then jumps on me and punching and choking me. Two GI's pulled him off me, and he ran down the street. They ask me if I'm okay, and I ran back here and Mamasan helps me. Then you came."

Tears slide down her cheeks and I know she's hurting badly. Kneeling down by the side of the bed, I don't try to hold her because she's so bruised up. Instead, I put my head against the edge of the bed and hold her hand while lifting up a silent prayer. *Oh God, you know me, don't you? Will you help me please? It seems like everyone is against me and I don't know what to do here.*

Big Joe comes through the crowded doorway where everyone murmurs like the background noise of a movie. "Mitch, what's going on?" Then he sees Young. "What happened? How did she get hurt like that?"

I motion him outside with a nod of my head. Before we step out I turn back to Young. "It's okay, Baby. This isn't going to happen again."

Once outside, I explain the situation to Joe, who gets a grim look on his face. "I figured when we did that drug sweep, no good was going to come out of it."

Even though Joe didn't actually participate in the sweep, if one MP was involved, we were all involved. That was the spirit of our team. We stuck together for better or worse.

"Do we take this guy out?" Joe asks.

"What?" I have to look at his face to see if he's serious, but he isn't smiling. "No, of course we don't take him out! You've got to be joking; you can't be serious. What are we going to do, put a hit on him or something like the Godfather?"

"You remember what happened in the next village over, don't you?"

"No, what happened?"

Joe sits down on a concrete block and I drag one over and join him. "The whole base was out in the field on training and when they got back, this guy sneaked off base with his M16 rifle. He had some girlfriend in the village and she broke up with him for a friend of his. So somehow he got a hold of some live ammo and he went down and shot her..."

"No way!"

"Way. So he's going to get busted for murder but suddenly no one can seem to find him on base. Two days later they find him hanging on a barbed wire fence in one of the fields, beaten to death."

"Really?"

"Yep, and rumor has it that a local Korean mafia gang was responsible for the retribution."

"I didn't even know there was a mafia gang around here. These are just villagers and farmers."

"Yeah, they take care of each other. Anyway, I'm just sayin'. What should we do?"

"Well, I need your help. I'm going to the brigade level which is a good day's trip. If I talk to the command sergeant major, maybe I can get a hardship transfer 'cause they've got me over a barrel here. I've got enough leave saved up, but something tells me I won't get any time off even if I put in for it. So I need you guys to cover for me a couple of days. I'll put myself on the duty roster for Tac site and that way they can't double me on their roster. I've got to pull duty tonight 'cause I'm already listed, but they can't list me tomorrow. I'm taking Young to another village to stay tonight for safety. Soon as I get back, I'll let you know what's up."

Joe stands and we shake hands. "Consider it done, Conner. We'll take care of it, and no one will even know you're gone."

After pulling the all-night duty, I come back to our room to find it in a shambles. The door is torn off, the bed is cut up, everything is thrown around. Good thing I took Young to a first aid station a couple of villages away. No one knows she is there except the two of us, and Big Joe, of course. I don't even trust anyone else on my team with this information; it's too easy to get a loose mouth and spill it. That guy will continue to look for her. I can't fathom why in the world he's being protected, but it sure seems that's the case.

It's still early in the morning, so I don't bother waking Mamasan to pay for the damages. Instead, I hoof it down to catch an early bus to our brigade. It's a grueling ride, the bus connections are late so I end up on base after hours and have to spend the night. Next morning, I'm up and waiting in the command sergeant major's office at zero seven hundred hours. His orderly opens the door and I'm right behind him.

The brigade headquarters is as high as I can go with the military in Korea, and the command sergeant major is basically the top of the line. If he can't help me, well... I haven't thought beyond that. The orderly is basically there to protect the command sergeant major from unnecessary interruptions and to make sure he stays on schedule. I didn't make an appointment, so I'm taking a chance that he'll see me at all. The orderly shuffles some papers, then looks at me and shrugs.

"Look, Sergeant... what's your name? Conner. Yeah, look Sergeant Conner, Sergeant Major's booked all day. You'll have to make an appointment. Sorry, there's nothing I can do about it. He doesn't have time to see you today."

Turning in defeat, I run smack into a towering dark-skinned man.

"What don't I have time for?" he asks.

I'm taken off guard. "Uhhh, I, uhhh..."

The orderly rescues my bumbling.

"The sergeant here... where are you from? He says it's of utmost importance that he talks to you."

Looking down at my nametag, the sergeant major grins and sticks his hand out. "Sergeant Conner, nice to meet you. Come on into my office and tell me what's on your mind."

Quickly, in respect for his time, I outline the situation and my request for transfer to somewhere... anywhere.

He listens intently then, leans back in his leather chair. As I wait for a response, I notice his desk and office are fairly spartan except for a single picture of him with his family.

Then he leans forward and clasps his hands on his desk. "I believe you, Sergeant Conner, and that's the first big hurdle. I'll do what I can to help you. But before you get all happy about that, you need to know this is going to take some time. More than a couple of weeks, and I'm not sure I can ram it through at all. I may be the command sergeant major, but I'm stuck in the system just like you are. I will tell you that we have ongoing investigations which support what you are telling me. But you need to keep that between you and me."

Standing up, he puts out his hand again and we shake. "I'll do what I can, but there are no promises. You need to get your wife out of there. This guy is obviously a coward or he would have come after you instead of your wife. I admire your restraint and the way you handled this. It's a difficult circumstance. Good luck."

There's plenty of time to think on the way back. I've come up with a solution, but I'm not real keen on it. But every other idea is a dead end. Young could go home but, as much as she hates living on her parents' farm, I know she won't do it. There just aren't any other options. No matter where I move her to, this guy can eventually find her... except in one place.

Young looks healthier as I sit across from her at a little cafe/bar which is next door to the first aid station.

"Oh, Yobo," she says. "I don't know if I can do that. I'm scared. I've never been that far away before."

Taking her hand, I squeeze it gently. "You're pretty tough when you want to be. It's not going to be easy for you or for me, staying behind. But I know you'll be safe for sure."

She finally nods. "Okay, I'll do it. Let's get ready."

To get her out of the country only requires that we apply and receive her visa to travel to the United States. Since we are married, the process only takes a week, with the required extra 'tip' money. I go back to work on and off and the guys continue to cover for my occasional absences. She stays in a small place in Seoul to be close to the process and take care of the paperwork. Then she travels home for a few days to say goodbye to her family. A few days later we meet at the airport and sit on a bench together.

All she carries is a little bag with some of her clothes and makeup and stuff. She clutches her passport and visa in one hand while holding my hand tight in her other as if she's going to die. This will be her first experience on an airplane. Then she has to make the transfer in Los Angeles for the flight to St. Louis where my family will meet her at the gate. She has never seen them, but she has a picture of Mom and Dad and they have a picture of her. Fortunately, I called them shortly after we were married and let them know that they had acquired a daughter-in-law. Now Young is stepping out of her country all alone, and I feel terrible. I know we won't see each other for six months.

"Conner, I guess I take chance on you, huh?" Her voice trembles and tears course down her face.

I take out my handkerchief and try to fight back my own tears, but they soon drip off my face. We look at each other and then laugh as we wipe each other's face at the same time.

"Young, you write to me and make cassette recordings and send them to me, okay? I'll do the same. I'll think about you every day."

She looks down at the small suitcase. "I hope you don't get involved with some other girl."

"Oh, Young... you're the best wife I've ever had. My heart only belongs to you."

That perks her up and she looks up, smiling. "I better be the only wife you've ever had."

It's time for her flight and I can only watch as she walks through the door of the restricted area where I can't accompany her. She turns to give me a brave little wave, and then she's gone. I stand there for a long time until my legs start to grow tired. Finally, turning and walking out of the terminal, I begin what is starting to be a familiar conversation. "Well, God. This didn't turn out like I thought it would. I guess you do know about it. I'm really hoping that you'll help her along the way to get safely to her destination. I can't go with her, you know. Like I said, I guess you do know. Anyway, you've somehow helped us out before, so I thought I'd ask again. Please, please help her."

Wiping away a stray tear, I run to catch the bus that is just pulling away. Banging on the side of it, I jump in as it slows and start my lonely journey back home.

Chapter Seventeen
Going Home

Sergeant Conner! Hey, Sergeant Conner!

I duck inside the compound gate guardhouse, but I'm not fast enough. The orderly sees me. After telling Young goodbye this morning, I really don't want to talk to anyone. Especially the captain's orderly. Unfortunately, I wasn't fast enough and he saw me.

He sticks his head into the small gate shack. "Sergeant Conner, Top wants to see you right away."

I wave him off and am tempted to go straight out to the village, to avoid whatever is coming. But, being a good troop, I decide against that tactic. As I walk up toward the command office, I wonder if the orderly has ever told anyone that the Captain or Top wants to see them but 'just take your time, no hurry.'

I imagine Captain Quigley and Top on the battlefield. While the battle rages around them, they relax on beach chairs under a couple of large colorful umbrellas. Nearby metal beach tables are stacked with battle plans and a frosty piña colada with a little paper umbrella teeters dangerously close to the edge. Suddenly a large tank approaches. Just before the table is crushed under the treads, the captain snatches the drink off the table and takes a long sip. Then he sets it in the sand, stretches and says, "Well, I guess that's the end of that. Snidely, when you get a chance I'll need more paperwork. Until then, everyone can take a break."

As I laugh at the thought, Bay runs up from behind and slaps my arm. "Hey, I've been calling you since you walked out of the gate."

"Oh, sorry, I was lost in thought."

"You're the only one I know that gets so lost in his own thoughts that you know nothing around you. You even make yourself laugh."

Then he turns more serious. "Did you hear the latest?"

"No, what?"

"Well, first of all Captain Quigley resigned his command and is in a psych ward in Oakland."

"What? No way!"

"Yep, and you'll really freak over this next piece. That guy you busted that was attacking your wife? Well, someone found him lying out in one of the fields, dead as a doornail. Beat to death."

I stop in my tracks and turn to face him. "No! Bay, what happened?"

"Not hard to figure out, I guess. He bothered one too many of the wrong people. Rumor has it that he had a lot of big gambling debts, too, so your guess is as good as mine. But I reckon you won't have to worry about your wife anymore."

No one knows she is gone. I have to laugh and shake my head at the irony of it all. She isn't even gone a few hours, still in flight, and presto; everything seems to have resolved itself. It's almost as if the whole thing was a setup just to get her out of the country. Amazing. It is almost unbelievable.

Seeing my reaction, Bay looks at me strangely. "You okay?"

Breathing out a long sigh, I close my eyes and continue to slowly shake my head. "Yeah, it's just a funny thing how everything happens." It doesn't really matter now if Bay knows the situation.

"Young is on her way to the States."

"Huh? You're kidding me."

Giving him a pat on the shoulder, I leave him standing and continue walking to my meeting with Top. "No, not kidding. I'll explain later, I have to see Top. The real kicker would be if I was transferred out of here, huh?"

"Sergeant Conner. Sit down."

Top never invites me to sit down. After I'm seated, he leans back and looks at me. "I'll tell you what, Sergeant; you definitely have a friend in high places." He points to the ceiling then grabs a paper off his desk and slides it across to me.

As I pick up the paper and turn it to read, he continues. "No matter what happens, you seem to just keep coming out on top of it all. It's uncanny."

He drones on, but I'm too absorbed in reading my transfer papers which order me to report to the brigade level command headquarters for duty as... the chief inspector for all brigade K-9 units throughout Korea? I look up in astonishment as Top continues to move his mouth and shake his head about the whole thing.

After a few moments, Top stands and dismisses me. "Bay will take over your position here. I'll leave it to you to inform him. Also, please tell him to see me right away. You're officially off duty to prepare for your transfer."

As I turn to leave, he speaks again just as I reach the doorway.

"Sergeant Conner, you wouldn't happen to have any knowledge concerning Private Sledger's recent demise, would you?"

I stop, but don't turn. "None whatsoever, First Sergeant."

"I figured. But don't leave the country any time soon, huh?"

"No, First Sergeant."

"Good luck, Sergeant Conner. I'm proud to have had you serve under me."

"Thank you, First Sergeant."

I quickly leave, so he won't notice a tear in my eye. As I walk to the quonset hut to find Bay, I feel as though a great load has been lifted from my shoulders. A few tears leak through anyway. Dag nab it anyway. My dad always told me I wear my heart on my sleeve.

As I enter the old quonset hut, Na and Kansas City are eating some noodles. The rest of the guys sit around talking about the recent murder and the Captain's check in at the psych facility. Amazingly, everyone is here.

"Gather round, gentlemen. I have an announcement for you."

With a brief overview and little detail, I tell them about my transfer and also announce that Bay will be my successor. They seem stunned into complete silence for the first time. As Bay heads out to see Top, they all gather round to congratulate me and plan for a party in the village to properly see me off. I'm not a big partier, but I don't want to disappoint them, so party it is.

After I gather a few belongings from my locker, I take the Scotch tape off a picture of Young and me when we first met. In the more populated villages where GI's hang out, a few Korean guys take pictures every night to sell to the GI's. That first night, one of them saw us through the window. He made us sit together on one side of the booth, then snapped off a Polaroid picture and sold it to me for a dollar. It has been taped to my locker all this time. I put it in my laundry bag with everything else, then I head off this little compound for the last time.

I have only a few days to wrap up things in the village where I've spent the last nineteen months. We have a freestanding wardrobe closet in our room and a small variety of other things that I can't take with me since I will be living in the barracks for the rest of my time. The bed and other stuff I give away, but the wardrobe is beautiful mother of pearl. Young brought it with her from the cafe and my heart aches to have to sell it. In the end, I just give it to Mamasan. In the States I could sell it for hundreds of dollars, but not over here.

A few days later, I wait at the bus stop with my stuffed duffle bag containing my uniforms and fewer belongings than I came here with. A couple of our Korean neighbors walk down to see me off. Then a few more, and then more, until most of the village gathers. I had no idea some of them even knew me. As I climb on the bus and turn to wave, some of them bow and others wave back. The bus pulls away and tears fall. I rub at my heart on my sleeve but it does no good as I watch through the window. The villagers grow smaller and finally disappear as the bus rounds a bend.

The next six months involve a tremendous amount of work as I travel throughout Korea to inspect the K-9 units. I'm fairly certain the Command Sergeant Major created this position for me. A few times I go back to my old stomping grounds at the Tac site and inspect that facility, but I can't stay long.

The weeks and months fly past as Young and I trade letters and record cassette tapes for each other. Then, as suddenly as it began, it's all over. I'm back in the States to process out of the service. Some of the guys kiss the ground when they get back, but I'm going to miss Korea, that land of amazing people and diverse customs.

One of the first things I do is to indulge in a cheeseburger and fries at McDonalds. Having satiated my appetite, all I can do is hang out and wait until the paperwork is finished. A couple of days later I wing my way toward St. Louis. The exhaustion from jet lag sets in. Lack of sleep, along with my nervousness about seeing Young again, sets me on edge. I don't want to break down and cry in front of my parents and my brother who will most certainly be there to greet me. I haven't seen them for two years. I'm not sure what will happen. No doubt, Mom will shed a few tears.

As we circle Lambert field, I look down and wonder how I'm going to make a living. I'm fresh out of the military, don't have a job, and we're going to be living with my parents and brother. That's going to be quite a challenge in itself.

The wheels touch, bounce, then settle down for the short ride to the gate. Standing, I grab my onboard bag and wait for an eternity as the door finally opens and people begin to stream out. I walk down the flight ramp to the seating area. Through the door at the end of the ramp I see people jumping and waving.

As I get close enough to see a wider angle, I search and then see Dad. He's waving at me like crazy, and then Mom and Curtis a ways back… and… she stands there, close to the door. A red rose blazes on the side of her long black hair, and she wears a beautiful blue dress.

She doesn't run toward me but waits until I get through the door. Then she bows low at the waist. Dropping my bag, I'm caught in a slow-motion dream. All the shrieks of people greeting each other become muffled in another world.

I stop in front of her, and the tears begin to slide down her face. Then we are in each other's arms. She pulls me across to where the rest of my family wait and then it's Mom's turn for hugs. I catch a glimpse of my dad actually wiping a tear from his eye. But for him and my brother, it's just a shake of the hand. We don't really do hugs.

Later that night, I sit on the edge of my bed in my old room in the house I grew up in. I'm in shock like I've been dumped here from a time machine, right back where I started four years ago. It doesn't feel real. If Young weren't sitting next to me on the bed, I would wonder if it really happened at all or if it was only a dream. The trouble with reality is that it's real. It can't be manipulated with the mind or rewritten if you don't like the script.

Somehow, I drift off into a deep sleep. Images of Korea flit by like smoke from a campfire. We sit around the fire, telling stories. Are they true? We've both been through a lot over the past two years. No one can begin to understand the trials we've been through nor the trials we are about to face.

* * *

I watch Conner as he lies back on the bed. He's asleep within five seconds. It's amazing how fast he can go to sleep, no matter what the circumstance. Sometimes on a bus trip, sometimes sitting on the floor against the wall, reading a book.

One thing that's hard to get used to in America is the height at which we live. In Korea, we sleep on the floor and sit on the floor to eat or just talk to each other. Over here, we sit on chairs and couches and high beds. I've never seen Conner's Mom or Dad sit on the floor.

I'm lonely. I thought when he came back, I wouldn't be lonely any more. But somehow, I feel lonelier than ever. I miss my family. I miss our farm. Will I ever see my family again? As much as I resented growing up on our farm with all the work and hardships, I now miss it.

No one sees my tears spill out, so I let them flood down my face. Conner thinks I am strong. I cry when he sleeps, so he can't see that I'm not strong. I pretend to be something that I am not, hiding and running so no one can hurt me.

Keeping Young

Chapter Eighteen
Young in America

Dear diary, I'm writing once again
Please hear me, I really need a friend
I woke up today in a strange new land
It seems to me, my life is all unplanned
I'm writing, please hear me, dear diary
> *Young's diary entry - June 1980*

A new day dawns for me. I wake with a start and look around, momentarily startled and confused.

"Where am I?"

Slowly, the events of the past several days start to sink in.

Several days earlier Conner and I stood together in the Kimpo airport in Seoul, South Korea. I'm trying to make the best of it. I really don't want to cry in public and embarrass myself. I don't want to hug him in public either, but there's no getting around it and I really am going to dearly miss him.

He puts his arms around me and, with ticket in one hand and passport in the other, I abandon all propriety and throw my arms around his neck, pulling his head down to mine. Neither of us hide the tears.

As I reach up to wipe his tears with the back of my hand, he does the same and we laugh for a moment. I know him. He will keep holding me until I miss the plane, so I have to be the one to end this. Picking up my onboard bag, I look down and grimace. "You'd better not get involved with another girl."

His response is typical. "Oh Young, you know you're the best wife I ever had…."

I give him a smack on the arm. He's always trying to be funny, but I can't laugh. I can only push back a new stream of tears. Looking up, I give him my best smile. "I'd better be the only wife you have."

Wrenching myself away from him, I turn and walk toward my destiny. Then turning one last time, I give a little wave and push through the door.

This is my first time in an airplane and I don't know what to expect. The jet begins to roll and my heart feels like it will leap out of my chest and run back home where it yearns to be. Even though I hate living on the farm, something keeps tugging me back, back to the mountains I long for.

Suddenly we are airborne, tilting this way, then that way. Glancing out the window, I see Korea grow smaller and soon there is only water. I'm gone. After a while my heart feels better, but my stomach flip-flops. I'm so sick. I try to sleep, then I'm awake. I walk around this tiny prison. Where can I go? I feel trapped. How far is America? I want to get out of here.

Los Angeles

In America! My heart joins my stomach, but they don't celebrate well. I walk out of the plane as if in a dream. Some people in front of me talk about a flight to St. Louis, so I follow them. We walk a long way, then take a bus ride, then walk again. I panic. This could lead me to the wrong place, but I'm too ashamed to ask for directions. Finally I see the gate. It's my flight to St. Louis!

St. Louis

America is so big! Four hours in another prison and I want to jump out the window. I can't stand feeling trapped! Finally we land. My heart and stomach are worn out. Where is my picture of Conner's family so I can recognize them? In my purse. Good — Americans all look the same to me; except Conner, I would know him with my eyes closed.

My heart is beating out of my chest as I walk down the entry with everyone. Will I recognize them? Will they recognize me. What if no one came? No need to worry. Conner's mom, dad and brother are right in front, waiting to meet me. They hold my picture and a big sign that says 'YOUNG', and seem to know right away that it is me. When I see them, I start to bow but they surround me and hug me so fast, I can't give them an honorable greeting. America is so strange.

It quickly grows even stranger. It has been twenty two hours since I left Conner at Kimpo Airport in Seoul. I haven't slept much. We walk to the baggage collection, but all I have is my little bag.

Conner's dad looks for more. "Young, where is the rest of your luggage?"

They are all surprised that I came over here with almost nothing except a few clothes.

When we walk out to the parking garage... oh my! It's like walking into a furnace; the heat is so hot. This is my first time to ride in a private car as we begin the trip to my new home. In Korea, we walk or take a bus. Taxis are too expensive.

Everything here is amazing. Cars are everywhere as if everyone owns one. Highways are everywhere, too. Everything is amazing!

When we finally arrive home it is after seven that night, but I'm still on Korean time. It's nine in the morning for me. But I'm so, so tired. After Conner's mom shows me my room (which is really Conner's room), I plop down on the bed and fall asleep before I can even get under the covers.

I think this is Wednesday.

My head feels like I have a hangover. It rolls around on top of my shoulders and I'd like nothing better than to oblige it and sink back into the pillow. A clock goes "tick... tick... tick" on a little table by the bed.

A sudden mountain of fear hits me as my heart surges. It's after ten o'clock in the morning! I need to help with the food and cleaning! What are they going to think when I slept this late and didn't come down to help? Shame burns my face red as I quickly throw on some clean clothes, then stop by the bathroom to splash water on my face. I've heard about American toilets, but I've never seen one like this. It isn't hard to figure out.

The stairs creak as I sneak down as fast as I can, then peak into the kitchen. No one is there. The dining room and living room are empty as well.

Suddenly I hear someone coming up the stairs from the basement, and my heart leaps into my throat. I try to think of something to say, some way to apologize. I hurry into the kitchen as Mom comes up from the stairs.

She smiles really big. "Young, you're up. I hope you slept well. Can I get you something to eat?"

"Oh no, Mom. I'm sorry I slept so long. I should have helped you with breakfast and work."

She cuts me off with a wave of her hand. "Nonsense. Just help yourself to whatever we have. There's cereal in the cabinet and milk and fruit in the fridge."

Then she walks out, leaving me standing in the kitchen, stunned.

Once she is out of sight, I go back up to Conner's room as fast as possible and sit on the bed. She has to be mad at me because I did not help her. But of course, she wouldn't show that. She didn't even wake me up to eat with them. Maybe they really don't want me here. But where am I going to go? I'm really on my own here. I can't call Conner or anyone I know. I wouldn't anyway, because that would show weakness. Somehow I've got to be a better daughter-in-law and prove I'm not lazy and worthless.

Asian life is all about relationships. We eat together as a family and live in close proximity. No one would think of eating without the rest of us. When married, the daughter-in-law is subservient to her mother-in-law and the relationship is often very rough as the mother-in-law asserts her position and power. So I am puzzled by Conner's mom's behavior.

The first couple of weeks are difficult. I don't like the food here. I long for rice and kimchee. Kimchee is a dish made from fermented cabbage. Mom doesn't know what it is. So I survive by eating bananas… lots of bananas, which Mom dutifully brings home every day after work.

Dad complains that it costs too much money but mom tells him, "What do you think she's going to eat?" and he shuts up.

Mom is kind to me and talks to me so I don't feel so lonely. The other day she took me to the grocery store. Wow! I've never seen so much food in one place. One entire part of the store was just vegetables and fruits, then a whole row of breads and other things.

In Korea, we walk to a little open-air market to buy food for that day. At our home in the village, we have no refrigerators or ice. Everything is fresh. On the farm, we grow most of the food we need and sell the rest.

When I was young, I couldn't eat any kind of meat because it made me break out all over in bumps and itched like crazy. I could only eat fish or chicken. With ten people in our family; my parents, my grandma, my six brothers and sisters, and me, we could only afford a fish or a chicken a couple of times a year. The rest of the time, we ate vegetables and the rice we grew on our land.

Those were hard times. We were very poor. Grandma was my mother's mom. She had two sons and three daughters. Both sons were trapped on the North Korean side when they called a cease-fire during the Korean war in 1953. She never saw them again. Many nights she cried and longed to see them just one more time.

I never heard anything about Grandma's husband; my grandfather. He was a mystery. Usually the oldest son cared for the parents. My mom was the second oldest daughter, but somehow she ended up caring for grandma and helped her work the farm. A hired hand helped with everything, and he eventually married my mom and became the father of their seven children. Nobody ever heard of birth control, and it was better to have a lot of children who would help with the work. Children often died at a young age.

Grandma loved us more than she loved her own daughter. She was the boss of everything and maintained that status until she passed away. Shortly before her death, she signed all of her land and the house over to Dad and Mom.

Conner's dad fixed ribs today. I really like that food; something to eat with my banana diet. The other day I tried to make kimchee with some Asian cabbage from the store. Yuk, it tasted terrible. After all the years of trying to get out of cooking, now I wish I had paid more attention to how my grandma used to make kimchee.

As the oldest girl, I spent a lot of my life cooking for everyone. From as small as I can remember, I got up about four in the morning and started cooking breakfast: a big kettle of rice, kimchee that needed to be cut up and fresh lettuce. Our house had two rooms, one for my parents and grandma and one for the kids.

The open-air kitchen was between the two rooms and the wind blew through during the winter months. Early in the morning I walked to the mountain and gathered sticks and wood to cook with. The heat from the kitchen funneled under the floors of the two rooms to give some warmth.

At night we put blankets on the floor to sleep and in the summer, we used mosquito netting to keep the bugs off. In the morning everyone was up early to work in the fields. The blankets were put away, the floor wiped down and short-legged folding tables put out for the food. No chairs. We sat on the floor to eat, to talk, to study or anything else.

When I was about six years old, my mom drew a line in the dirt. "When the shadow of the roof gets here…" She pointed at the line with her stick. "…then you start to make lunch and bring it to us. When it gets here…" She scraped another line. "…you start dinner."

So that's how I knew when to cook. No clocks. Lunch was easier but I have to carry it to the field. Metal rice bowls with lids. Some pickled leaves and, of course, kimchee. First I smoothed out the cloth on the table, put the containers on it and tied it all up, then carefully stooped down, jerked it onto my head and carried it two kilometers to our fields where everyone was hard at work.

One time, when I was about seven years old, the food pack was so heavy I could hardly make it. Everyone was famished and waiting for lunch, but the trip to the fields seemed longer than usual. Finally, they saw me coming. Right before I got to them, I teetered. My head couldn't hold the weight anymore.

Mom called out. "Just a little bit more, come on, come on!"

She ran toward me, seemingly in slow motion, with my grandma right behind her. Everybody else stared at me with their mouths hanging open. Then they started running toward me, waving their arms and yelling, "Young Su Ga… don't drop the food!"

I tried to grab it, to ease it safely to the ground. When my mom was ten feet away with her hands out, all the food crashed off my head and was ruined.

Everybody yelled. Workers in the other fields stared at us. I fell to the ground and cried with the mess of food all around me. After working seven or eight hours in the field, no one was happy, but Grandma made them too ashamed to punish me or say anything since I was so young. In a rare moment of compassion, everyone came over and comforted me. "It was too heavy for you. It's okay."

Mom had to walk all the way back to the house and cook again; all the side dishes and rice and everything. I always tried to do more than I was capable of. Sometimes it worked out and sometimes it was a disaster.

On another occasion, I helped Mom clean up some of our metal bowls. She was in labor with my youngest brother and it was customary to clean everything in preparation for the new baby. As I reached up to a high shelf for the cleaning powder, my hand accidentally knocked a bottle of lye. It tilted, then spilled down into my face and eyes, immediately blinding me. I screamed. Mom grabbed me but didn't know what to do.

During late 1960's, there was no medical care in the village — only a gypsy man with a syringe who gave inoculations. Leading me by the hand, mom looked for him but to no avail. Finally, after about an hour of searching, a neighbor offered to help us. She raised ducks. She pokes one of the ducks in the neck with a needle, the neighbor woman dripped blood into my eyes. Whether it was a chemical property of the fresh blood or something else, my eyes immediately cleared. I could see again.

But the next few months were difficult because I had to wear a patch over one eye. Other children gathered around me. They pointed, laughed and shouted, "BLIND GIRL! BLIND GIRL!"

I was a tomboy, and my oldest brother hated me because I didn't act like a sweet little Korean girl. I wouldn't wait on him like a servant. One time I carried a bucket of water into the room to pour into the kettle to make rice. My brother tripped me. Water splashed all over the floor, and my father yelled at me for being clumsy.

So I ran away to my friend's house and didn't come back for a week. My friend was an only child and had a room to herself. Her two brothers and sister had died from sickness. Every time I heard my father calling me, I hid under the blankets in her room.

But that didn't stop the sound of my father's voice as it echoed in the valley between the mountains.

"YOUNG SU GA... BOLLY EDI WA...."

That meant: you'd better get home right now.' But I was stubborn and only went back home when I found out he wasn't mad any more. Finally, my sister came to see me. "Dad says he isn't angry anymore and if you come home, he won't punish you."

I always win, no matter what. I have to win. No one is going to punish or hurt me if I can help it.

Back to my cooking: for dinner I made noodles. First I made the dough, then rolled it out really thin, over and over until it stretched like pizza dough. Then I cut it into thin strips. This process took several hours. A big kettle in the yard hung over a fire. The water had to boil a while before I threw in the noodles or they would clump together in a big mess. One time I threw them in too early and had to throw the whole thing away and start over. Dinner was late that day.

Maybe once a month Dad would get a fish or some rock oysters from the ocean. With the farm work, he rarely had time for that. Even when we did have some kind of meat, Mom added it to a big pot of water with rice and made soup out of it. Everyone then ate a little piece of meat in a lot of soup.

For some reason, I can eat these delicious ribs that Conner's dad barbecues. I don't break out at all. How about that? Conner's dad frequently barbecues ribs now that he found something I like. He's kind of a strange person. On the one hand he seems to take special pleasure in finding something I like and fixing it for me. On the other, he complains about silly things like the cost of bananas.

Conner is coming back from Korea soon so I'm teaching myself to play a song on Mom's organ. I want him to be proud of me, so I practice a lot. Mom found a little Asian market that has real Korean cabbage, and they told me how to make kimchee. I made some last week, but when dad came home and smelled it, he held his nose and made a bad face. "Oh yuck, what's that smell? That really stinks."

He kept complaining about it over and over and it made me feel really bad. I hurried upstairs and cried. Mom came up, sat on the bed and comforted me.

"Young, that's just how Dad is. You can't let it bother you. I've lived with his little fits for a long time. You just have to ignore it. You make your kimchee and enjoy eating it, no matter what anyone says."

Mom doesn't understand me at all. How can I ignore my father-in-law? I'm supposed to honor him and her. I never heard my mom ever say anything against my dad. He would slap her or beat her if she dared to say something that would bring dishonor to him.

My grandma was a different story. I guess since she owned the entire farm and was older, she could tell my dad anything she wanted. But even then, she was careful of her words and didn't make him feel like a fool. We never talked bad about people older than us behind their backs and surely not to their faces.

Unlike Conner's mom and dad. They say whatever they want to each other and many nights I hear them argue. Sometimes I wake up at three in the morning and they're still arguing with each other.

I do remember times when my dad drank too much and my mom yelled at him. But he told her to shut her mouth and then she cried for a while. It was grandma, though, who held the power. If she told my dad to do something, he stepped to it. So when he came home after a night of drinking and made her daughter cry, she told him off. "Go to sleep and shut up."

And he did. Maybe people aren't so different after all.

Finally, Conner is coming home! I can't sleep. I spend a long time getting ready, and I place a special red rose in my hair. This is my first time back to the airport and I feel just as nervous as when I arrived.

We get to the airport early, find the gate then sit and wait. Dad reads a newspaper. Mom reads some magazine and almost everyone smokes. Curtis walks here and there, looks out the window at planes landing and taking off, then walks over to the magazine stand. He's full of energy.

I sit and think about Conner coming home. Finally we can start our life together as husband and wife. I've been so bored and lonely here. Now things will be much better.

Curtis announces that the plane is pulling up to the gate. Soon people stream out like water. I stand near the gate exit looking, looking, while Dad, Curtis, and Mom stand a little farther back. Suddenly I see him, and I run through the oncoming rush of people, then stop to bow.

Before I can even bow, he's wrapped his arms around me and lifts me off the ground. He starts to kiss me, but I turn away as my face burns red. I'm embarrassed to kiss in public. Instead, I grab his hand and pull him over to the family. Mom gives him a big hug and kiss, but he just shakes hands with Dad and Curtis. I thought Americans all hugged each other, but I guess not.

When we get home, I'm all excited because I want to show Conner the song I learned to play on the organ. It's for him, to welcome him home. Everyone stands around the organ as I start to play. But Conner listens for a minute, then walks into the kitchen. He doesn't even hear me. It's hard to finish because tears of disappointment push at my eyes. I worked so hard to learn to play this, and he doesn't even care to listen. Later, I hear mom talk to him in the kitchen.

"Mitch, Young practiced for weeks to learn how to play that song for you. Now you've hurt her feelings."

"Mom, I just got home after being away four years. Give me a break, will you?"

"Son, let me tell you something, and you'd better not forget it. Do not be like your dad and let that girl feel like she's all alone in this world. She came over here for you, and she's putting all her trust in you. Don't let her down, Mitch."

Then she walks out and I sneak up the stairs, feeling torn. On the one hand, I feel good that Mom is trying to protect me. But I feel bad for Conner. This used to be his home. Now everything has changed for him, too.

Later, Conner comes up and lies on the bed where I sit. "How come you're up here all by yourself?"

We talk for a little bit and he starts to fall asleep, so I let him drift off. Then I start to write in my diary. He can go to sleep so fast anywhere. Looking around the bedroom I realize it is about the size of our home in Korea yet only three people live in this house. Plus, they have a lot of other rooms and a basement and garage. So much stuff sits on shelves and in closets — everywhere. In Korea, anybody who owned a house like this would be so rich.

My family's farm was located in a valley between mountains and the ocean. I never thought much about it until now, but it was a beautiful place with the village homes grouped together and the rice and vegetable fields surrounding it all. Our water came from a well in the front of our house. I don't know how we survived because many times we fished some dead animal out of the water.

Our house had two rooms about twelve by ten each, separated by the open-air kitchen. The house and walls of our home were made from a special mud that hardened like concrete. The roof was made up of branches and leaves or clay tile, if you had the money for it.

To take a bath we went in the back of the house and scooped water out of a big tub to rinse off, or sometimes we walked down to a little stream. Surrounding each house was a tall stone wall with a gate for privacy. At the stream, we also washed our clothes by scrubbing them with a bar of soap. Then we put that item of clothing on a rock and beat it with a stick until it was clean and white.

We used a certain kind of rock, probably pumice, to clean our teeth when they turned black. After my brother made fun of my black teeth, my girlfriend and I crushed some of that rock, then used our fingers to rub it against our teeth. It made them really white and clean. Even today, I don't have any cavities.

When I went to school, we couldn't afford to buy paper or a pencil. So I used up the pencil until it was just a tiny piece. It was hard to write. I took notes on my paper and then erased it so I could use it over again. When the paper started getting too many holes in it, my mom gave me something from our garden to trade at the market for another sheet of paper or a pencil.

Girls only recently went to school, at least in the small villages. I heard that city girls always attended school but in the village we were expected to cook, wash clothes and farm, so there wasn't any reason to go to school. But I didn't want to stay on this farm. I wanted to go to school and live in the city. I hated working in the fields.

We worked all day under the hot sun. Without even a hat to wear, it felt so good when a cloud passed over and shaded us. We crouched down in a kind of duck walk, as we planted or pulled weeds for hours and hours. When I stood up, I couldn't fully straighten because my back was frozen and it took a while to stretch out.

This wasn't the life I wanted, married to some farmer and working that hard all my life, subservient to some man who thought he was the sky and I was only the earth, lower than a servant. Korean Men think that the woman is there to serve and bow down to them. I'm not that kind of typical Korean woman.

Chapter Nineteen
Running Young

I'm glad to be here with Conner. In comparison, it's better than working in the fields, but I'm bored and lonely. There's nothing for me to do. Conner has a hard time finding a job. In the early 1980's many people are out of work and very few jobs are available.

After several months of making contacts, Conner finally manages to get a security job. He works at night and sleeps most of the day. On the weekends we never do anything fun. I want to go dancing and party like we did in Korea. We had a lot of friends and would take a bus to the next village and hang out together. Now when Conner is off, he just reads a book or watches TV. BORING.

In Korea, we went to other nearby villages. We danced and had fun with some of our friends. No friends here. When I tell Conner I want to go out and do something fun he gets mad and says we don't have money to do that. I want to get a job or something, but Conner doesn't want me to go to work.

The other day we had a big fight. I told him I wanted to go back to Korea to visit and he was angry. Even though he doesn't make much money, we have enough in our savings account for me to go. When he got out of the Army, he got money for his unused vacations. We put it in a savings and loan account because we get sixteen percent interest on it. Now he doesn't want to use it for me to go to Korea. But I want to go. He doesn't understand me at all.

He works and I stay home and feel useless. The house can only be cleaned so much. I crochet and knit and make my own clothes, but after a while I get tired of it. Then when Conner is home and awake, he goes about his life like I'm not even there. I thought we would be a family, but I feel like an orphan.

Mom doesn't like me helping her. She always says, "Oh, you don't have to do that, Young." Mom helps me learn grammar, but then Dad gets jealous at her for spending too much time with me. "You're always helping Young do something and you never have time for me," he says, which is a lie. She waits on him hand and foot like a servant. I wouldn't do that for anyone.

"Jo, get me the paper. What are we having for dinner? Jo get me a drink. Jo, come and sit and watch TV. Jo this; Jo that." I wouldn't do that. She acts like an Oriental wife, doing whatever he tells her to except she talks back to him.

Sometimes Dad gets mad at me. The other day I washed some of my white clothes. Before I could put them in the dryer, Curtis came down and put some jeans in the washer and ruined some of my white pants. When I said something about it to Mom, Dad heard me and got mad at me. "You don't know if Curtis put those in the washer or not. Stop trying to accuse him of everything."

I told Conner about what happened. He got really mad and told his dad what he said was wrong and not to upset me like that. In a way I felt glad that Conner stood up for me, but he shouldn't talk to his dad with disrespect.

Conner is mad almost every day this month since he agreed to send me to Korea. I feel so trapped, I can't wait to leave, like a caged bird that can't fly. Conner tries to make me stay which makes me feel guilty. But when I make up my mind; that's it! He thinks I'm coming back, but I don't have the heart to hurt him.

I'm on my way back to Korea and airsick. I forgot how bad I feel when I fly. In my dreams, I never get airsick. I soar above the mountains of my village where no one can catch me or hurt me. I love that dream. In another dream as a little girl, an old man in my village grabbed me and put me on his back. He spun me around and around until I was so dizzy I couldn't think or see. Totally out of control. Like my life feels now. Horrible.

As I sit back and close my eyes, I remember how my grandma would comfort me. She always loved me. I remember her kind face and the way she held me and soothed me when I cried. I never remember my mom or dad touch me or say they loved me. Not once. Grandma's was the only comfort I remember. She told me the story of when I was born. My parents were farmers and it was a hard life. I was the oldest girl and third in the birth order with two older brothers. When I was born, the cow got sick.

In an Oriental farmer's mind, everything is related with many superstitions. The day I was born my mom was upset, because the cow got sick. Mom had been in labor for a while when my dad took his homemade wooden hammer and pounded a stake in the ground to rope the cow to.

Grandma started yelling at my dad. "Why are you pounding that stake in the ground? My daughter is in labor with your child. If you put a stake in the ground the same day the baby is born, it will cause misfortune to come on us. You can see her labor is already too long. Dig up that stake right now!"

Grandma was the boss of the family. Even though women of that day were thought to be of less value than men, no one messed with Grandma. Besides, she owned the land, and the house, and the cow. Father just worked for her. Although she never really said it, everyone knew she was in charge.

Father dug up the stake, grumbling the whole time under his breath, but not daring to let Grandma hear. But the damage was already done. That day a storm blew in and I was born in a chilly room. Rain cascaded a steady sheet against the thin rice paper covered sliding door.

It was common practice to put straw on the floor during childbirth and that's where I was delivered. There were no hospitals near our village and babies were born at home. When I was born, my hand grabbed some of the straw. The next morning, the cow was sick. This was a bad omen. My mom wished I was dead, so the cow could live. They already had two sons, and I was a girl — kind of useless to the family. They owned only one cow that pulled the plow, cleared the fields and gave milk.

The cow was critical to the farm work. It was used for milk, for plowing the fields and many other important tasks. A baby girl was only a detriment. But Mom would not admit that the sick cow had anything to do with her husband putting that stake in the ground. Instead, it was the fault of her newborn daughter. She wished I would die, so that the cow could live. That's just the way things worked.

Grandma stuck up for me. "Don't even say those things. Didn't you see her grab that straw? She has a tight grip. You can tell this girl is going to have a rich life, because she grabbed that straw right away." Then grandma told Mom she was a silly superstitious girl. Hmm, that was like 'The pot calling the kettle black.' Anyway, that's the story my grandma told me: I was going to have a rich life, because I grabbed some straw.

My birth wasn't reported until a year after I was born. After the Korean War, a lot of babies don't survive, so they wait a year to apply for a birth certificate. No sense paying to report a birth if the baby doesn't live. So my birth certificate reported me as a year younger than I really was. I liked that.

As I write in my diary, a Ping-Pong ball flies through the air and bings me in the forehead. I reach down to pick it up and bang my head on the edge of the counter. Ouch, that's going to leave a mark. Two months in Korea; working at an electronics company, which barely pays my expenses and as an au pair for a lady in Seoul. She owns a Ping-Pong business, and it's always crowded with lots of people.

I take care of the her kids and watch the counter at night. But I'm not happy. When I came back to Korea, I thought I could go to the clubs like Conner and I used to do. But it isn't any fun, especially when I work twelve hours at the electronics factory, then come and work at the Ping-Pong place. It's not as bad as the farm, but I work a lot yet barely survive.

On the farm, just the simple task of getting water was a chore. Our water came from a stone well in front of the house. The rope was slippery as I struggled to pull the heavy bucketful to the top. Sometimes a rat or some other animal got stuck in the well, and we had to fish it out.

Once the bucket was at the top, I dragged it to the top of the stones and balanced it there. Then I stooped down to get it on top of my head because it was too heavy to carry by hand. Balancing it on my head, I carried it to kitchen, which was about fifty feet away. Squatting down, I brought the bucket to my knees, then to the ground and poured the water into a big pot. On the farm there wasn't a lot of time for a childhood. I had to grow up fast.

When I was young, it seems like whenever I did something wrong, it turned into a huge mess. This pattern plagued me throughout life. My messes could never be hidden. I couldn't pretend they didn't happen. Like that bucket of water I dropped in the kitchen; mud, muck and water spread everywhere. I feel as if my return to Korea is disaster on top of disaster.

When I'm with Conner, I feel trapped and can't wait to get away. I thought it was a mistake to marry him in the first place, so I left. Now that I'm away, I miss him and realize it was probably a halfbaked idea to come back to Korea: disaster on top of disaster. I should have stayed in America and submitted to it all.

But I'm just not a typical Korean woman who can bow down to her husband: the sky. I'm as good as any man and can probably win in a fair fight — maybe because I don't always fight fair. With two older brothers and younger sisters and brothers, I've learned to be tough and stick up for myself, even if I'm only a girl.

I started life as a fighter. When I was just under three years old, I was sick with the measles or chicken pox — something like that. We rarely took any medication. Since I was running a high fever, Dad brought some expensive medicine. It was a white powder with an awful taste. I had no appreciation of its value.

Buying the medicine and forcing me to swallow it were two different things. After trying several tactics, we had an all-out fight. I twisted and jerked. Even Grandma couldn't force me to take that medicine.

Finally, they pinned me to the ground. Mom and Dad held me down while Grandma squeezed my mouth open and poured in the powder. Then she squirted some water in, and forced me to swallow. I'm not sure why it didn't occur to them to mix the powder with water first and then pour it in my mouth. When they let go of me, I vomited everything out. At that point, they decided no one was going to force me to do anything.

I fought with my mom and dad for the right to go to school. Girls usually didn't attend school in those days and it cost a lot of money. But I was determined and made life so miserable for so long, they finally relented.

I fought with my brothers and sisters but was scared of my older brother. He was a black belt in Tae Kwon Do and didn't like me because I was a tomboy. I didn't act like a girl and I didn't do what he told me to do. He tormented me daily, waiting until my parents and grandma weren't around. Then he practiced his martial arts on me like I was a punching bag.

One time I told my dad about it, and the next day my brother almost killed me. If I hadn't run to my friend's house, he probably would have finished me. I got in trouble because I didn't fix dinner until late, but I didn't dare say anything to my dad or mom again.

When I was in school, I always told the teacher when the other students did something wrong. When they got into trouble, they didn't like me. The teacher made them put their hands on the desk. Then he smacked them really hard with a heavy ruler. Sometimes he also used a heavy stick and beat them on the head or the back.

I didn't need my teacher to intervene, because I was plenty tough. One time, my girlfriend was mad. She took poison ivy and rubbed it on my arm, then she ran off. I ran her down and rubbed it all over her face. My arm broke out with the poison ivy, but her face swelled up about three times bigger. All the girls and boys knew that if they messed with me, I would punch them in a second and always win — even if they were bigger. It seemed everyone was against me so I learned to strike first and run fast.

Last night I had a strange dream. I'm so scared because I think I died, or almost died. I watch myself sleep and think this is strange; standing here and watching myself sleep. Shouldn't I be sleeping instead of watching myself sleep? Then I wake up. My eyes open and I can see the ceiling, but I can't move. I try to move my hands, my arms, feet, legs, anything: but I can't. My heart stops beating and I feel myself pulled down into blackness. Terror overtakes me, and I try to cry out but I can't. Suddenly a bright light shines all around me and someone speaks, "What are you doing here?"

All my guilt and pain wash over me, but I cannot respond.

"Why are you here?"

Somehow, my mind cries out, "I want to go home. Please let me go home and I will go; I promise."

Just as suddenly, I'm back in the bed and I gasp, pulling precious air into my lungs. I can move, but just barely. The world spins to a stop. Maybe I will try to call Conner today.

I remember that today is Conner's birthday. He no longer lives with his parents. Before I left, we moved into a little apartment. Conner's job only paid three dollars and fifty cents an hour, but it was enough for a tiny apartment and food. We had to be frugal. We bought powdered milk to save money. At first, Conner didn't like it but I found out if I shook it like crazy, skimmed the foam off, and let it get it cold, it didn't taste half bad.

I was always accustomed to living with little money. Conner's mom and dad helped us get started with dishes, pots and pans and other household goods. I washed our clothes by hand in the bathtub and hung them out to dry. At least it was better than hauling them down to the village stream like I did in Korea. I wonder how he is doing without me.

I really hate to call Conner because it makes me feel weak. It is almost midnight there and he has to work early but once I make up my mind to do something, there's no changing it. On the other side of the line I hear the phone ring. My heart flutters. What am I going to say? What can I say?

Ring. Maybe he found somebody else and he's forgotten me.

Ring. He could have moved back with his parents or something could have happened to him.

"Hello." His groggy voice tells me he just woke up. I can't find my voice anywhere.

"Hello? This is Mitch. Hello?"

I manage to say, "Conner, this is Young in Korea."

"Whaaa?" Silence. Then, "Young, is it really you?"

"Yes, Conner."

More silence.

"Young, what happened to you? I tried to call your parent's village phone, but no one could understand me. Then I wrote letters, but you never wrote back. What happened? Where are you? Are you okay?"

"I'm okay."

I try to form the words, "I want to come home," but tears choke my voice. I hate to cry and sound weak. Fortunately, Conner blabbers on about how much he misses me and it gives me a minute to breathe and get control. "I'm thinking about coming back."

Silence.

"Are you there?" I ask him.

"Yes, I'm here. Are you coming back or just thinking about it?"

I hear the frustration in his voice. Everything in me wants to blurt out, "I'm coming back as soon as possible," but I can't because I'll start to cry. Then I answer, "I'm thinking about it."

More silence. Why doesn't he beg me to come back? But then I wouldn't like that either, because I can't stand weakness. I need someone strong to lean against, not a piece of foam that will break in a second.

"Young, you have to let me know for sure so I can pick you up at the airport."

Always the practical one. I'm indicating that I may come back and what does he think about? Picking me up at the airport. I feel like crying again, but this time from disappointment. Can't he encourage me just a little? "Okay, Conner, I'll let you know."

I can't keep the knife-edge out of my voice. We haven't seen each other for more than three months, and he's already starting to aggravate me within a few minutes on the phone.

"Did I say something wrong?" he asks.

There's no hiding my feelings. He knows my voice. I feel exposed and more upset. We need to end this. "No. I'll call you when I know."

I quickly hang up. Tears of disappointment and frustration flow and this time I let them run freely down my face. They drip onto the yellowed linoleum floor. How can men be so stupid? Can't he show a little excitement that I may come back? We speak a few sentences and we're instantly locked in some kind of battle. Why can't we talk to each other like normal people? Why can't I be happy? I want to die, but I can't. When I dream I am dying, I plead to live. Somehow I mourn myself to sleep.

Conner meets me at the airport, this time alone. He tries to hug me but my arms hang limp at my sides and I pull away. I'm not trying to be cold toward him, but I'm embarrassed to hug in public. Later, in the car, we fight about it. Not even together an hour and we're fighting.

"Conner, you know I hate people watching us hug or kiss. We don't do that in Korea."

"This isn't Korea, this is America."

Then he goes on and on until I'm sorry I came back. The truth is, after our phone call in August, I almost didn't. But when I felt like I was dying in my dream, I asked to come back here and I was afraid to not do it. So here I am. We spend the next three years fighting until I can't stand it anymore.

Then the most amazing thing happens.

Chapter Twenty
Young Life

I've felt sick for a couple of weeks. I hate going to doctors, but I wasn't getting any better. Finally, Mom took me to the doctor and guess what? I'm pregnant! Can you believe it? Conner and I have been together for six years, and we never tried to not have a baby. I really didn't think I could have a baby. Now I'm pregnant! I never would have believed how wonderful it feels. Actually my mood has been great for the past two weeks, even though I've felt nauseated every day. Usually I feel depressed every day. Every spring I want to run away or die. But now I feel so good. Wait till I tell Conner! I'm so excited! This baby is going to save us!

Conner wasn't excited like I hoped. He's worried about our finances and the cost of raising a child, but I don't care. I feel great and I love this; I finally feel useful.

Tonight we went to see the fireworks. Conner was upset because I kept asking him to feel the baby kick in the middle of the fireworks show. Men are so dense! Isn't our baby more important than some stupid fireworks? But I made sure Conner didn't start a fight.

Dr. Ahrens says it will be a boy. I can't wait, in more ways than one. I'm huge. I've gone from one hundred and two pounds to a hundred and forty five, and I'm still gaining. Oh, my gosh, I feel like a tank! I can hardly lie down and sleep because I'm so big. But Dr. Ahrens says everything is good. He thinks August tenth is the day.

It's the ninth. Conner was at work so Mom stayed with me since I was so close to the due date. Did I mention how big I am? The other day I breached a hundred and fifty pounds! I started out at barely one oh five, so that's a lot of weight. Oh my God! I can't survive like this much longer. Fortunately, I don't have to.

My water broke at two o'clock this afternoon. Mom took me to the hospital right away and they admitted me. I called Conner at work about three o'clock and told him I was at the hospital. Now it's five, and he's still not here. I'm in labor and the on and off pain is excruciating. Mom holds my hand through a particularly painful episode. Then Conner finally walks through the door, but I'm really pissed off because he didn't get here sooner. Doesn't he even care? I called him over two hours ago.

"Where were you? I've been in labor for hours and you're just now showing up?" A tear or two escapes and I turn my face towards the window. I really hate being vulnerable.

"You said your water broke, but you weren't in labor. So I finished work, changed clothes, then came right over here."

I can hear the always present defensiveness in his voice and words. I just can't take an argument now so I say nothing. Then he starts going on about how it's my fault because I didn't say anything, blah da blah, blah, blah. Finally Mom stops him and instructs him to help me with my labor and breathing. But I can't stand him hovering over me with his, "Breathe in, breathe out, make shallow breaths."

"Stop it! I'm breathing the best I can. You're not helping me!"

I see the hurt in his eyes, but I really just want him out of here.

"Go sit over there and let me get through this."

We spent a couple hours a week for eight weeks in Baby Class learning how to breathe and get through a natural childbirth with no painkillers or chemicals. We were adamant about it; we were absolutely going to have a natural childbirth. No painkillers like an epidural or C-section for me. I'm tough.

By seven that evening, I had been in labor on and off for about four hours and I begged for an epidural or painkiller. "I need an epidural! Can I get an epidural? When can I get an epidural?"

The nurse comes in. "We can't do that right now, honey, because you're not dilated and it would slow down your dilation."

At nine thirty someone talks about a C-section. The doctor comes in, as I'm hit with another series of contractions. I manage to gasp out, "Oh yes… let's do a C-section right now!" So much for natural childbirth.

After about eight hours of labor, I'm not dilated, the baby hasn't dropped an inch and is in distress. I'm wheeled into an operating room where I'm draped off from my chest down. Conner gets to be with me, and for once I'm glad he's there. I'm scared and really need a friend.

Up to this point, everyone has said we will have a boy. A girl hasn't been born in the Conner family for generations. So we secretly hoped for a girl, but we will be happy with a healthy baby of either sex. The OB/GYN's office did a couple of ultrasound tests along the way that seemed to indicate a boy. So we go ahead and pick out a boy's name; Howard Jonathan.

The epidural allows me to stay awake while they cut me open like a piece of meat. The extraction of the baby feels like they are scooping out a chicken; a lot of tugging and pulling. Even though there is no pain, I can feel the pressure and the tearing.

The pressure stops and Dr. Ahrens says, "Oh, you have a beautiful boy" while the other doctor says, "girl."

Then they look at each other and reverse; Dr. Ahrens says, 'girl' and the other doctor says 'boy.' Docs and nurses laugh and then he says, "You have a girl, honey," then adds, "I was joking, Young."

Dr. Ahrens is a personal friend of the family and can get away with it. He never even sends us a bill. It is a great gift, because we are fairly poor since I'm not working and Conner makes a meager wage. Even with the doctor's gift, we owe seven thousand dollars.

Dr. Ahrens hands off the baby to one of the nurses who takes her to a nearby table where they begin to frantically work on her. The baby isn't pink; she's kind of a gray color and limp.

"Why isn't the baby crying?" I manage to squeak out.

Conner holds my hand and another nurse, also a dear friend of the family, holds my other hand. No one seems to hear me. A timer bell dings. I feel tugging as they stitch me up. Squeezing Conner's hand, I barely whisper, "Is there something wrong?"

A timer bell dings again and I hear a suction machine in the background. More tugging. Behind the sheet that drapes me, I hear the nurses count down in unison.

"Ten, nine, eight, seven…"

They count instruments to make sure nothing is left inside of me.

"Four, three, two…"

Conner and the friend nurse look down at me strangely. He mumbles something. "I think we should pray."

His lips move but I don't hear. Stars begin to roll around the room and Conner and the nurse fly away. A bell dings dimly in the background, and a nurse rushes out of the room holding our baby.

As I wonder where she is going, I'm swept back to Korea, to the bright green farm fields and the dull brown house surrounded by a dirty gray stone fence and a green gate. A burst of pain explodes in my stomach and I'm lying on the ground while my oldest brother kicks me in the stomach. Everyone is in the field and there's no one to rescue me from his punishment.

"You're an embarrassment to the family! You'll never be anything but a tomboy girl! No one will ever want you!"

He kicks me over and over and over until I retch and throw up, then he beats me and throws me across the dirt against the side of our stone well. My head hits hard and something cracks as the kindness of darkness swallows me. The last thing I hear is my father calling me from the distant mountain. I can't tell if it's his voice or maybe the mountain itself is calling to me.

"YOUNNGSUUGAAAAAA… EEDIIIIWAAAA."

Come home, come home to stay.

My eyes snap open. Conner sits next to my hospital bed, holding a football and grinning. Suddenly he throws it at me and it hits me hard in the face. As my face burns, he laughs.

Suddenly I wake up and he's sitting next to my hospital bed, reading a book. There is no sign of the football.

"Dawr… wha yow fil me foollba." My mouth seems full of dry noodles, and it's hard to talk. "Wa..Wa…"

He seems to understand and pours some water from a tan-colored container. "Welcome back to life."

He smiles and strokes my hair, but I push his hand away. "Why did you hit me with a football?"

"What?"

"You threw a football at me and hit me in the face." I can still feel my face burning.

"Young, I'm sitting here reading a book. There's no football..."

With a wave of my hand, I cut him off. Here we go again. I don't know why he has to get so defensive. He's just banged me in the head and then denied it. "Just leave me alone, I'm beat up." What am I doing here anyway? Suddenly, the truth floods in! My baby! "What happened? Where is…?"

Before I can finish, a nurse wheels in a little cart and lifts up… my baby! Oh my God, she's alive! Tears course down my face.

"No, no, honey! You can't try to get up yet. You've had a C-section. Just lie back or you'll injure yourself."

She lifts the baby and brings her over to me. "Here you go."

Oh wow! My baby lived. She's really alive. I gently rock her and touch her face and her hands and feet and her head. Wow! She's heavy too. Ten pounds and one ounce at birth.

I'm in the hospital for almost two weeks with narcotic painkillers which apparently affect my mind. When I fall asleep, Conner keeps slamming me in the face with a football. I finally admit, there really isn't a football. Still...

We have to come up with a girl's name since we had only chosen Jonathan. She will be Allia Hyon. Allia because I like it and Hyon which means wisdom.

Conner works most of the time, so Mom stays with me and helps with the baby. I try to regain my strength, walk, and move.

I'm alone.

Conner comes up after work but spends most of his time with the baby. It would be nice if he would pay some attention to me — at least a little bit. Curtis and Dad visit as do a number of our friends but they're more interested in the baby, too.

One day, right before I'm discharged, Mom sits down on the bed next to me. "How are you feeling, Hon?"

"I'm lonely, Mom."

Mom puts her arm around me and draws me close, careful of my tummy. "You know, Young, when I had Mitch and Curtis, Dad wasn't even there. It was a weekend both times, and he went hunting with his friends. All my sisters and family were in Memphis and I didn't have any friends up here. Nobody came to visit me except Grandpa Conner, who sneaked away once and brought me some flowers and a card. I was so alone and depressed. You don't have to go through that. I'm here. Mitch is here every day after work. Your friends from church care about you. You're a lucky girl."

"Mom, I feel so bad. When I was pregnant, I felt great." I hate to whine, but I'm into it now so I might as well get it all out.

"It's not unusual to feel empty and depressed after childbirth. You'll get through it and feel better after a while."

That was three years ago. I didn't get through it: the depression that is. It just got worse and worse along with caring for the baby and Conner making me so miserable about everything. He tries to make me go to church. If I don't go, then he goes without me and leaves me by myself. He's always helping everyone else but us. If I didn't have a heart for him I would have left a long time ago and never even tried. After Allia was born, I told him I wanted to leave. But then, just three months after Allia was born, he had an accident at work.

About 11 a.m., the phone rings.

"Is this Mrs. Conner?"

Nobody calls me that. "Who is this?"

"This is Matty up at the Bakery. Your husband was just in an accident, and he's on the way to the hospital."

Gasping, my heart leaps out of my chest. "How bad? What hospital? Is he alive?"

It turns out his arm got caught in one of the machines and almost torn off. Later, at the hospital, I let Conner know I'll take care of things until he gets better. I can't just leave him like this. His arm, hand, and elbow is broken in multiple places and they don't know if they can save it.

After several surgeries and nine months of recovery and therapy, he is finally able to go back to work. It's a good thing because while he was home, he drove me crazy. I felt like I was suffocating. Plus, workers compensation only paid seventy five percent of his five dollar an hour salary.

An amazing thing happens during the time he is disabled. At least once or twice a week, the doorbell rings and when I open the door, no one is there. Bags of groceries and disposable diapers lie on the porch. But no one is around, and they couldn't have disappeared that fast. Nine months later, a week before Conner goes back to work, the secret deliveries stop. When I tell people at our church about it, they think I'm a little crazy so I'm not sure it's them doing it. But someone is. Isn't that too weird?

I came back to Korea when Allia was almost three. Actually, I stayed with Conner longer than I said I would. I've been here for almost six months trying to find a job. Conner thinks I came to visit and I didn't have the heart to tell him anything different. He's too controlling. When he doesn't get his way, he mopes around and makes life miserable. He argues incessantly to make his point; it's just too wearing on me.

Yesterday, my mom made rice cake for Allia's third birthday, and I gave her a couple of toys. She keeps asking for her dad.

"Where is Dad? I want to see Dad."

As I sit outside the door and pull on my shoes, my mom sits down beside me. "Where are you going? Since you got here, you haven't stayed home for two days in a row. Your daughter needs her mother, you know."

Without looking up, I yank to set the knot. "Mom, I have to find a job in Seoul. You can keep Allia and take care of her. I'll be back in a week or so."

Hopping off of the wooden porch I call Allia. "Allia, come and give me a hug."

"Mommy, I want to go home."

"You are home, Baby."

"No, Mommy. I want to go to my real home with Abba."

Abba means daddy in Korean. She has only been here a short time yet speaks fluent Korean. Looking down at her, I smile. "You'll be fine. I'll be back soon."

As I walk through the gate to catch the village bus, I hear Allia crying and my mom upbraiding me. I can't stand this village for too long, but this is the place I'm most comfortable leaving Allia. I'll be back soon.

When I return a week later, I walk through the gate and…gasp! Conner stands there holding Allia and he's not looking happy. How did he possibly get here? My village is on the very Southern coast, and isn't easily accessible.

Covering my surprise, I stoop down and call Allia over to me. Then I look up at Conner. "How did you manage to find us?"

My meaning was; it's a difficult trip, but after I say it, I realize it sounds like we were hiding.

"I'm pretty resourceful. I missed you both."

Before he comes over to hug me, I pick up Allia and walk to one of the rooms. "Come on, let's talk."

Conner convinced me to come back to the states to finalize a divorce. When we were in Korea I remembered the day we left my home to go to the airport. Mom sniffled back her tears. Dad came out and put his shoes on so he could go play cards with his friends. They argued, because Mom thought he should at least be respectful and wait until we left. He apologized, then took off, leaving the three of us standing there with angry Mom.

The arguing… the fighting… was that the best a marriage could be? I knew then that this was the end. Conner was hoping to reconcile. After we returned it was no different. I wanted to get a job but Conner didn't want me to. I wanted to go dancing or go to the movies but he didn't want to. All he did was work or sit around the house studying the Bible. Boring! I felt as if I was wasting my life, like being stuck on the farm.

Finally, I decide that if I treat him poorly, he'll give up on me and let me go. He thinks I'm just being mean but I'm trying to make it easier for him. He just doesn't get it. We've been at this almost ten years and I'm tired of going through it; I just want to make it on my own. To feel I am useful and not just some useless tomboy girl. Life has to be better than this. I know he will take good care of Allia, so there's really nothing holding me anymore. When I make up my mind, there is no turning back.

* * *

I look across at Young but she avoids me. The judge bangs his wooden gavel down on my last shred of hope and crushes it to ashes. I feel the storm clouds of an impending doom.

"Divorce granted, next case."

Today is May eighteenth. Tomorrow we would have celebrated our tenth anniversary. Can one man who wears a robe seemingly more fit for a choir, really tear us apart in those few words? Who gave him the right to do this? My vision blurs the brown wooden courtroom benches and chairs as my mind spins back in time.

Things My Daughter Taught Me

Chapter Twenty-One
Life on the Rocks

Much as I had hoped for some normalcy of life, it didn't seem to be in the stars for me. The past ten years flipped by, and I can't even keep track of them. We break up, get back together, and start again. But it's the same beginning, middle, and end; over and over and over. I can't seem to understand what we are doing wrong. I remember some of my older and longer-married friends trying to give me advice.

The sky is a brilliant blue with a few puffy clouds. It's a toasty July day and ice-cold tea goes perfectly with the wonderful smell of hamburgers and hot dogs grilling on the pit. Young is in the house helping to prepare some of the food. As I sit out under a tree with a couple of the guys, the conversation turns to relationships.

"How about you, Mitch, how are things with you and Young?"

"Oh, okay I guess. You know how it goes. We have our days."

"Yeah, we all do, don't we? Everyone does but, overall, do you think she's happy?

"Probably not but I suppose I never really thought about it. Is that the goal in life? To make her happy? What about me?

"Well, you know what they say, don't you? If mama's not happy ain't nobody happy.

"To tell you the truth, I wouldn't even know where to start."

Did you ever think about letting her be your partner?"

"Like what do you mean?"

"For instance, what's the last thing you bought recently?"

"Uh…well, I was down at the Leader and they had motor oil on sale so I bought a case for future use."

"What did Young say about it?"

"When I got home she asked why I bought it without asking her. I told her it was on sale so I got it. I don't know what the big deal is over a little oil. It was only about twenty dollars"

"Mitch, it's not about the oil or any other thing you buy."

"What is it then?"

"You're married to Young on your terms. What about her terms?"

"Her terms? I didn't know she had any terms."

"That's my point."

Waving my tea at them I respond, "What is this? Get Mitch Day?"

"We really care about you and Young and see some of the struggles you have. We're just giving you some advice, born from a few more years of experience."

"I don't get what you're trying to tell me."

I'm kind of feeling defensive, but I really do want to understand this.

"When you buy something without consulting Young, she feels as if she doesn't have a voice about things that happen in your relationship. She wants to be an equal part of it, not a bystander while you do it all."

I nod slowly like I understand…but I really don't. The only thing I can draw out of it is that I need to consult Young before I make a purchase. So when I try to do that and she still isn't happy, I'm at a loss. I'm so self-centered and focused on me, it never occurs to me that she has needs I am not aware of. All I know is that I work very hard to make a little bit of money so we can live. When I have time off, I usually do something that I want to do like work on the house or read a book. Sometimes I help her out with laundry or something but I don't think to ask her what she would like to do. I'm trapped in my vat of self-centered soup and imagine she's the one turning up the heat. Yet it rarely occurs to me to climb out of that pot and look around. Instead I think, "What's her problem anyway? Why can't she just be happy?"

These thoughts of regret go through my mind as we make our way out of the courthouse. As much as I love her, I can't seem to overcome my bad attitude and behavior. My heart is as heavy as the wooden exit doors. Outside in the bright sun, she stops and turns to face me. Still looking down, she bows slightly and murmurs, "Goodbye, Conner."

Then turning, she walks away and disappears into the crowd, leaving me clutching some legal papers that finalize the ruins of our relationship. There's nothing more to do than go home and cry it off. I think about five years should do it.

Regrets will kill you and I've had more than a few. When we reach the edge of the cliff and teeter on the edge, what do we do? How can I continue on? Not only continue, but press ahead with gusto and joy, if nothing else then for the sake of my young daughter? As I sit on a step of the courthouse, I remember some wise advice.

About six months ago, desperate, out of options, and down on my luck, I went to the place of last recourse: church. I still had hopes of saving our marriage.

The pastor politely listened to my plight, then he spoke, "Mitch, I don't have a magic pill for you to fix this, but I can give you a bit of advice if you like?"

"Anything you can do…."

"Go home and love your wife the best you possibly know how, with everything that lies within you. No matter how you are treated, be kind. Don't turn your offense into a weapon against her. Keep your mouth quiet. It will probably not change the outcome in any way. But when it is all said and done, you will know in your heart that you gave it your best shot and you won't have as many regrets."

That was probably the wisest advice I've had to this point and I wish I'd heard it long ago. But that was as good a time as any I guess. I can't undo the past and bring her back. But I can live forward into the future with a better attitude and maybe even some happiness. As I climb into my car and slam the door, I take a moment to bow my head and ask a favor.

"God, I hate to bother you here but if it's okay, I'd like you to help me out…again. I guess there's no sense telling you what's going n because if you don't know by now then you aren't God. I want to be a good daddy to my daughter, and I really don't know how to do that. My dad never really taught me much about that, or maybe I'm afraid he taught me more than I would have liked. Anyway, I don't want to take up a lot of your time here, but if you could help me have peace it would be awful nice because I'm not feeling too good right now. There's just one more thing, before I sign off with you. I still really love that Korean girl. If you don't mind and if there's any way possible…could you please put our marriage back together somehow? I know I haven't been the best husband and I've sure made a lot of mistakes. I'm not sayin' I deserve to have you hear me. I'm just sayin'."

Wiping the back of my hand across my eyes, I start the car and drive, unwillingly, into a brand new life.

After picking up Allia at Mom and Dad's, we head home in silence. At four and a half years old, she knows her mom and I aren't married anymore but what does she really understand of all this? What can I say? It's hard for me to bear. How can I possibly help her?

At home, she runs up the few steps to the concrete front

porch, then blocks my way. Since she is on the porch and I am standing on the sidewalk, she can look me in the eye. She points to the top step.

"Sit down, Daddy."

Bewildered, I comply. Then I watch as she puts her hands on her hips and looks at me sternly. "I have a question."

"Okay, Baby. What do you want to ask me?"

She walks a few steps as if in contemplation, then turns again to face me. "Will you leave me, too?"

A car passes by in what seems like slow motion and a cool May breeze blows at her long black hair. I look at her in amazement, stunned by her insight and ability to process her feelings and ask this question. Calling her over, I wrap my arms around her and press my head against her little chest.

"Allia, Mom hasn't left you and neither will I. You will still see both of us. Even though things will be different, we will always be your mommy and daddy."

I know there are circumstances beyond our control, and what happens if one of us dies or we can't keep that promise for some reason? But as much as lies within us, this is a promise both Young and I will do everything in our power to keep.

Chapter Twenty-Two
Up Close and Distant

Apart from each other, Young and I manage to muddle through and raise our daughter. Between work, being a dad, and a little play thrown in, the years seem to fly by. Struggling to capture awe-inspiring moments, I jot down some of the more memorable events as they blast past me like a high performance racecar at the Indy 500.

"Mom, you've got to be kidding!"

I'm kind of stunned. Mom is in the kitchen making a cake for my birthday. The oven light is on, and I can see the cake turning a nice golden color accompanied by the sweet smell of baking.

She looks up from her place at the sink. "Don't stomp around, or the cake will fall."

"What do you mean Young is coming over for my birthday?"

"She's just as much a part of our family as she was before you divorced. She's like our own daughter."

"Allia's birthday I can understand, but my birthday?"

Allia's birthday falls right before mine. I can understand Young being there of course, but I think it's a little much to invite her for my birthday. It's like they're trying to get us back together again.

Allia runs into the kitchen and begins to dance around. She's just turned five and can get away with dancing in the kitchen. "Mom is coming over today? Hooray!"

My Mom starts making some icing for the cake. "Allia, no stomping or the cake will fall."

Retiring to the living room, I fall into the couch and grab a pillow. Some golf tournament crawls by on the TV while Dad runs a cleaning rod down one of his favorite rifles.

"Dad, did you know Young is coming over for my birthday?"

He looks up and gives a rare smile. "Hey, that's great."

Then he returns to the task at hand.

"I'm really glad you two get along so well. You know she's like our daughter."

I'm in the minority on this subject, so I stretch out on the couch with the pillow over my head in hopes of sudden suffocation or at least the muffling of my screams. Somehow, I can't suppress a smile at the absurdity of it all.

Young arrives like the queen of the ball, and dinner is served. In spite of my earlier feelings, I can't help but enjoy the occasion. There is nothing quite like the friendly banter which occurs across the dinner table. In our family, everyone likes to try to out-do the other, a habit my five year-old daughter has quickly picked up. Allia finds any excuse to become the center of attention and I can't imagine who she got that trait from. In this particular case, however, I think my daughter's grandfather manages to get in the last word.

As I blow out the candles on the cake and begin to dutifully hand out large pieces with icing and whipped cream, my brother turns to my daughter who is holding a particularly large plate of cake. "Allia, you'd better not eat any cake or you'll get fat."

Allia drops her plate on the table, puts both hands on her hips, cocks her head and looks at her uncle. "I take that as a regret!"

Grandma pipes up to correct her misuse of language. "My dear, I think you meant to say 'insult', not 'regret.'"

Allia, not missing a beat, grabs the saltshaker off of the table. "Oh, yeah? I'll show you some in-salt!"

She begins to dance wildly around the table, saltshaker in hand like a tambourine. Salt flies through the air onto the table and floor. "Grandpa! Grandpa! How do you like my dancing?"

I imagine my dad would act upset and say something, what with the salt flying all over the table and the floor. I could never have gotten away with something like that at five or, for that matter, at any age. However, Dad sits there, calmly eating his cake, completely unperturbed. He replies without even looking up or missing a bite.

"That's dancing? I thought you were having a seizure."

Thanksgiving Day arrives with a cold, blustery wind, scudding clouds, and a hint of early snow. Allia and I step into the warm house to the aroma of cooked turkey and pies baking in the oven. The oven light reveals a golden apple and dark brown pumpkin pie. Mom stands at the sink. "No stomping or the pie will fall."

"Mom, I don't think pies can fall."

"Oh yes, the pumpkin pie can fall. Is Young here yet?"

"Mom is coming over today? Hooray!" Allia retires to the living room to dance around Granpappy's recliner.

I shake my head and have to grin. Let's see. The day after we were divorced, we celebrated Young's birthday. On the 4th of July holiday, Young spent the day with us and then we went to the fireworks display. Allia's birthday came after that, then my birthday, then Labor Day, then my brother's birthday. Young is not only dutifully invited to these events, but expected with great joy.

"Why did we even get a divorce?" I ask myself.

Mom responds, "That's a good question. I really don't know why."

Looking up quickly I see my brother standing in the doorway in conversation with Mom. He must have asked her something. I sneak by them and hide on the couch until dinner is called.

During dinner, we enjoy this maverick incident. The table is set with the best china and silverware gleams from each place setting. But the star of the show isn't the turkey... or is it? The cast consists of my brother, mom and dad, Allia, myself, and, of course, Young. Sitting next to my just turned five year-old daughter in her lace pink and white dress, I decide to use this as a teaching time for how to eat in a more formal manner than 'let's just shove it in.'

The plates are full of food and a cut baked potato lies on each plate. As my dad carves the turkey, I notice that a piece of my daughter's potato has fallen off onto the tablecloth in front of her plate. Leaning over, I say to her in a low voice, "Allia, I see you dropped some of your potato on the table."

My thought is that she will pick it up and put it back on her plate; my error in judgment, soon to be revealed. Allia cranes her head to look over the top of the plate where the offending potato piece lies. Then daintily picking up her fork and holding it like an expensive pen, she carefully moves the dropped potato piece to the side of the plate where I can't see it. By this time everyone has stopped talking and all attention has turned to see the results of my correction. Replacing her fork in perfect position, she smoothes the napkin in her lap, puts her arm on the table, and then tilts her head up to look me in the eye. "Do you see it now?"

Everyone at the table dissolves in genuine, hearty laughter as I have to admit I do not.

As a result of the divorce, we sell our home. I made the mistake of letting the real estate agent talk me into buying a house before we had a contract to sell the one we have. With two house payments I'm going underwater financially. It is during this time that Mom and Dad make an interesting decision.

Dad retired a few years ago and Mom will retire next month. Their plans have always been to move up to the country house that Nona sold to them. Dad has been looking forward to this for as long as I remember and they have just been waiting for Mom to retire. I've never heard of any different plans and assumed they would put their house on the market pretty soon.

On a weekend that Allia is with her mom, my Mom and Dad invite me over for a private dinner. After we eat and clear the table, I sit in the living room and watch TV with Dad. Mom finishes up the dishes then joins us. Dad mutes the television.

"Mom and I have been thinking about something and we wanted to run it by you."

This is unusual, as they don't often ask for my opinion.

"You know we've thought about moving up to the country. On the one hand it would be great but we hate to be that far away from our granddaughter and miss out on her as she grows up. The problem is that this house is too big for us now that you and Young aren't living here. So, we would like to know if you would sell your house to us so we could downsize to something more manageable."

I'm stunned and stare at Dad, speechless. After all the plans to move to the country where he could hunt and fish to his hearts desire, how could he just give that up? Is this really a joint decision or more of an edict from Mom? "What about Curtis?" My brother still lives with them.

"Actually, we have already talked to Curtis and we would sell this house to him."

I shake my head in astonishment. "I don't know what to say."

Mom smiles, "Just say yes. It would help us all."

So we all trade houses. They move into our old house and Curtis buys their house. Within a month I'm back on the road to financial solvency and have only one house payment, a great relief. But I still wonder whose idea this was.

In spite of the occasional joy, I feel overshadowed by bitterness and sorrow. It feels like I live in a dark basement where a tiny bit of light filters in through a small dirty window. The only peace seems to come from prayer. One day, after some intense soul searching, I realize I don't have to stay stuck in the darkness. The person I am fighting against is not Young or God. It's me. One day, after my weekly house cleaning, I pen this poem:

The Imaginary Martyr
On a lonely, gravel, dusty road, he came to his senses one day. Looking back to the city from whence he'd come: destruction, smoke, and decay.

A tear ran down that dusty cheek as he gazed at the distant smoke. Even though mind and memory were kind of light, he knew there was no going home. No going home or turning back or anything of such sort. How he'd come this far was anybody's guess, he didn't much care anymore. Nothing to do but plod along with an ache in the head and heart. Wondering desperate, "Where to now?" "Where to go? Where to end? Where to start?"

So picking up a simple bag, the simple bag of a bum. I started off in a half-dazed state just wondering from whence I'd come. Trudging mile after mile with nary any style and thinking how far I'd come, left me sick and sore looking straight down the bore of a .44 mag or some other gun. But the thing misfired, I was on my way too late to catch a flight. Of ducks and geese as I sat by the lake, to reflect on another life.

A breeze rolled past and it scattered my thoughts too far to ever collect. Tried to pick one up of being a bum or a priest of some other sect. Then I thought I would really like being a monk, or maybe a cow or a pig. It's a game I play in my mind, you see, kind of like telling a fib. To become a martyr of the nth degree requires some sorrow and a lot of pain. So I walk on searching, it's kind of slow when you're wearing a ball and chain.

Tried to love a girl once but she left me to cry and drown in a ton of tears. Guess I'm over her now but as you can see I can still dilute a beer (or my tea), I just can't get away from here. I took her aside (but not too far) and whispered sweet things so dear. Then she stamped on my feet and punched out my lights… she laughed as she bit off my ear.

Although you may balk and disagree it's the price of a martyr of the nth degree. It didn't come cheap that year. But it did help me face my fear. To be left alone like a carving in stone was a silence I couldn't ignore. So I packed her up and trundled her off and changed all the locks on the door. If this sounds familiar it could well be you've seen a tear or two… or three. It's the price and cost of a friend now lost, it's the payment on the martyrdom of nth degree.

For it's me on that road and it's sometimes you. Trudging a dusty mile or two. Sometimes three or four or more, wondering to God what we're put here for. Having come a long way I can tell you this: That life ain't always a pile of bliss. Yet I've come far enough I can also say, I know my God will provide a way. Not the easy one or the one I like. It's many times a rough and tumble hike. Yet the cost, as I'm sure that you know by now, never pays for the nth degree martyr scow.

I'm only a martyr to me it seems. In my heart, in my mind, and within my dreams. The price of imaginary martyrs.

Chapter Twenty-Three
Sandbox Love

The holidays come and go and by mid-January, the snow flies. An afternoon of sledding leaves both Allia and me tired. As I carefully guide the car onto the dark driveway, the car slides on the slick concrete and finally comes to a stop. I peer over my shoulder into the back seat where my daughter is now sound asleep in her car seat. I don't have the heart to wake her up, so I get out of the car and carefully hoist her up against my chest. Her legs hang askew. She's almost too big to hold with one arm.

Gripping Allia with my right arm, I shut the door with my left arm. As it closes with a muffled thud, my shoes start to slip on the icy pavement. In a microsecond, I know I can't regain my footing and I'll fall backwards. I have a choice; let go of my daughter and catch myself, or wrap my arms around her and take the fall.

Children are an amazing gift. I never realized how much my mom and dad loved me until I became a father. I love my daughter, but do I really love her more than I care about myself?

I wrap my arms around her and hold on for the ride. With her added weight, the impact of hitting my back and head on the pavement brings a fireworks display. But somehow, I'm not hurt and my daughter never even wakes up. Some events in life can't be explained. I step off a ladder and wrench my back. Yet I fall backwards full force to the icy concrete with my back, neck, and head taking the brunt of it, and have no ill effects.

Mid-March and the blustery wind swirls winter away with the promise of warmer spring days. Tonight a missionary from Africa is speaking at our church. I'm not really excited about going but for some reason my daughter is, so I'm going to take her.

But then she makes this impossible request. "Can the little girl next door come with us?" The reason it's impossible is because the 'little girl' really is little. She's three. I don't know the parents very well. But my daughter's faith is strong.

"I'm sure God will let her go. Can I go ask her mom and dad about it?"

What do you say in the face of child-like faith? I watch out the window as Allia trots across our front yard. A few minutes later she runs back across the yard and into the house. I'm wondering what to say to comfort her disappointment. However, Allia isn't disappointed at all. In fact she is bursting with smiles.

"She can go!"

I'm a bit stunned. "What happened?"

"Her dad came to the door. I asked if she could go to church with us to see a missionary and her dad said 'No,' then closed the door."

Now I'm really confused but she continues, "I went down the steps and asked God to change her dad's mind. Then he suddenly opened the door again and said he had changed his mind! Isn't that great, Dad?"

In shock, I have no response. Needless to say, we all go to church to see the missionary and have a great time. I learn something about a child's heart and faith.

It seems I stay so busy that the years become a blur. But sometimes things happen and life comes to a screeching halt. Last week my computer crashed, effectively disabling my personal and business life. I should have made a backup but didn't have time. My fingers pounded the keyboard, recreating my files, as I dreamed of fifty or one hundred hour days instead of a measly twenty four.

Late Saturday afternoon, I am still busy. I had planned to take my daughter to the park. At six years old, she does not understand my busyness. She wants to play with me now, not later. After several interruptions, I roll back my chair in frustration.

"Allia!" I pull at what little hair I have left. "This is really important! Now go play or something."

Returning to my work, I am troubled. I can't shake off the feeling that I have somehow just communicated something to my daughter. Is this computer and all it stands for really more important than my daughter? When I look back on my life will I rejoice in the fond memories of all the time I spent with my computer and my work? I complain out loud to no one in particular. "But I really don't have time."

Before the words are out of my lips, I know I am lying. I always make time for important things. Sighing, I slide back my expensive desk chair which is made for long periods of sitting.

My daughter is in her room playing. I peek in. "How about we go to the park?"

She is up in a split second. "Yes! Alright! " she exclaims.

As we drive to the park, I turn on a radio talk show so I do not feel I am wasting any time. It is an interesting show and before I know it we are at the park.

Allia hops out of the car. "Come on, Dad!"

"Go on, I want to hear this show."

She joins a bunch of other kids who run and play. The radio show begins to irritate me like fingernails on a blackboard and with a click of the switch, I sit in relative silence.

The sounds of laughter and crying seem remote as I drift to another place and another time. It seems only yesterday a younger daddy pushed a tiny girl on a swing as she squealed,

"Not so high, Daddy! Push me low!"

Looking over the park through my windshield, I see her swing up, up, up, so high and back down again. It seems like my work as I pump so hard to get just a little higher. Unlike me, Allia would like it if someone pushed her. Grudgingly I step out of the car and make my way through the crowd of children to reach my daughter. As I push her ever so high, she squeals, "Stop pushing, Daddy! Don't push any more!"

The other swinging youngsters look on with jealousy. Suddenly something happens which burns into my memory like a forged brand. A small boy wanders into the path of a swinging youngster. Before I can speak, the swinging child's feet impact the little boy and throw him several feet away. He jumps up, runs a short distance like a wounded animal, then collapses to the ground, crying.

Kids continue to swing as though nothing has just happened. A few parents look at the boy, but no one moves to help. Shaking off my lethargy, I go over to him. As he looks up at me, I see blood streaming from his mouth. It drips off his chin and makes bright red pools on the sand. I hesitate. This is not my child. What should I do with him?

Where is his mom or dad, I wonder as I look around and desperately search the small playground for a clue. Still, no one moves toward us or appears concerned. Pulling out my handkerchief, I kneel down and wipe away some blood from his face. "Do you know where your mommy or daddy is?"

Sobbing, he points to a car parked next to mine. I am familiar with the car. Two women sit in it, supposedly watching their children from a distance... just like I did. They talk to each other, obviously not watching the children.

Picking up the small lad in my arms, I carry him toward the car. As we approach, the woman looks up and sees us but simply stares, maybe in shock. Finally she gets out of the car and I turn her child over to her, handkerchief and all.

Returning to the sandbox, I sit and watch my daughter and

another girl her age dig in the sand. She doesn't need my assistance, so I ponder many things. How long would the little boy have lain on the ground bleeding before someone went to help him? How is it that not one child stopped swinging or playing to help? The boy who actually hit him never missed a beat. Surely it wasn't intentional. Is this how we bring up our children today? Don't get involved with it; it's too dangerous.

I was hesitant to help as well. What if the parents sued me or thought I hurt their child? As I pondered what I teach my daughter, I trusted that in this case she saw an example which will stay with her for life. But what about all the other days? Those busy days I don't have time to play or help. Fast Lane Days when we rush here, then there, then another place, and still end up late without accomplishing anything. Times when my tension and aggravation spill over on a little girl like a shaken can of beer suddenly opened.

The child-rearing books remind us to be consistent. I am consistent all right. But I am not sure I like what I am consistent about. No answers pop into my mind. I know we live in a high-powered world with too much to do and too little time to do it. Our knowledge and the complications of life have increased almost more than we can bear.

It is so easy to rush down life's road. Then suddenly years roll by and we miss the simple pleasures of life: taking a walk after dinner, taking time to ride our bikes to the park instead of rushing there in a car, looking at the stars with someone I love, sharing the beauty and secrets of God's great creation. What could be more important?

For today, I am glad I took time to tear myself away from a computer that I won't remember in the future. I took the time to build some memories with my daughter that will shape our lives, and that both she and I will remember for many years.

Seasons stream by as the years melt into a blurred puddle and quickly evaporate into the air. As I pull up to the curb at my daughter's fifth grade school, she hops out and slams the car door with a force that belies a girl of her age. Before I can object she is already halfway to the school door, melting into the river of children on their way to first hour class.

Silence settles over me like a wet blanket. Through the car window I watch as she momentarily reappears, climbs the stairs, and disappears into the building without a backward glance. After a while, the sidewalks empty and are silent. Long after Allia is out of sight, I sit as though frozen in time. Ghosts from a long past day rise on the sidewalk like steam after a hot summer rain and my mind thinks back.

A multitude of children fill the sidewalk, milling around in their brightly-colored clothes. Huge yellow monsters discharging fumes squeal to a stop and spew out these small ones, rumbling off in a belch of smoke to reside in their nests before returning to gobble them up again. The sweet noise of a multitude of voices swirls out of the past to dissolve in the silence around me.

This child did not cry. I could feel the fear as she tightly gripped my hand. A quick hug, a peeling away of the fingers and I let go; watching as my five year-old daughter, holding the hand of a stranger, walked into the strange new world of school.

That day another door slammed shut with the resounding thud of finality. I wasn't ready to send her spinning off into the future. I wanted more time. Time to watch her as she struggled to take those first unsteady steps, speak those first simple words. Time to push her on a swing which engulfed her, listening as she squealed, "Not so high, Daddy! Stop pushing me!"

More time to study her and watch her grow. In the halls of a gallery containing the greatest and most beautiful art I have ever witnessed, time pushes much too quickly. I want to stop and gaze in fascination. Yet no matter how hard I dig in my heels, the relentless surge of the crowd drives me unwillingly on. Many times I neglect to see the beauty until I am far, far past it. Those are the times I want to revisit, to look upon the missed beauty and thank God for the gift of memory. A tear tickles my cheek, snapping me back to reality Embarrassed, I glance around and am relieved to find myself alone.

Memoir of a Man

As I drive slowly away, I promise myself a gift; to take time to enjoy this art while it is still before me.

As time continues to push me on a forced march, one day a mail ad catches my eye. The advertisement seems to leap out of the page: "Be noticed with the new Gold Card. This special card is only awarded to those with an above average credit rating." The accompanying letter congratulates me for spending more money than I can pay back and offers me more credit. Feeling a bit depressed one day, I decided to get myself a gold card and be someone special. My first use is underwhelming. The exasperated store clerk announces the total for my new tennis shoes that light up in the dark.

"That will be $175.59."

I proudly pull out my new gold card and snapped it smartly down on the counter. "That's a gold card," I say with an air of authority.

"I don't care if it's a pink polka dot card as long as you have credit left on it."

The tired clerk runs my card through the sensor and I leave feeling oddly deflated. The next time I attempt to use my card is at a local restaurant. This time I am humble and simply hand over my card without comment. The manager does have a comment.

"We don't take this credit card."

"Well, what credit card do you take, I have several." Reaching into my wallet I extract a pile of plastic cards.

The manager eyes them curiously. "We don't take any credit cards. We don't take checks. We take cash."

I feel my face turn red. "I, uh... I think I'll have to run over to the ATM machine and get some cash if you don't mind.

"No, I don't mind. You can just leave your credit card here until you come back."

"I thought you didn't take credit cards."

The manager grins. "Oh, I'll take it all right. You just can't use it to pay the bill. We got some dishes in the back that need washing..."

I paid the bill with money obtained from an ATM machine

with yet another plastic card. Having been thoroughly humiliated I murmur, "touché" to my gold card as I stuffed it into my wallet. That night after everyone is asleep I cut it into little pieces and feel avenged. Years later when the last payment was made I felt truly free of the bondage that little piece of plastic had lured me into.

The early evening sun pierces through the windows of my office like the knives of Ali Baba. Many years have passed and I don't have to run home any more to take care of Allia. She's graduating from high school in a few weeks and has grown into a responsible young lady. As the sunlight runs across my desk I pause from my work to look up at a faded Father's Day card pinned to the cubical wall.

"Happy late Father's Day!"

Things are not always as they appear. Some things in life burn into the memory, never forgotten. There are parts of life I long to forget. Others I want to hang on to as precious memories. This counted as one of those, 'I want to remember' times. So to remind myself, I kept that little 'Late Father's Day' card pinned on my wall.

I dislike all the holidays we have and the pressure to come up with gifts and cards, but I do like to be remembered on those days. My daughter was sixteen at the time this occurred. I suppose no one reminded her it was Father's Day; I know I didn't. I figured she was old enough to remember it herself.

That Father's Day past I waited for the card or gift that never came, some comment acknowledging my fatherliness. Finally it was time for bed but still nothing. No 'Happy Father's Day,' no notes; no nothing. So I went to sleep angry; determined to bring up the issue the next day.

The next morning I rolled out of bed at five. Usually, I grabbed some cereal and a piece of toast, but my favorite breakfast was eggs with cheese, bacon, pancakes — The Works.

I padded sleepily down the stairs and flipped on the dining room light. The first thing I saw were dishes on the table. Immediately I stopped and thought, *Oh great, my daughter not only forgot me on Father's Day but now she's left dishes on the table from last night and thinks I'm going to clean them up!*

Anger burned in my heart, partly because she left dishes for me to clean up but more from my feeling rejected on Father's Day. Grimacing, I turned to go back up the stairs, wake her up, and yell at her to get everything cleaned up, but something stopped me. Something about the whole scene was not quite right.

As my sleep-fogged brain began to take it in, I noticed little things that were out of place; things that didn't make sense. A cup of coffee with steam spiraling out of it. How could that happen if it sat there all night? Saran Wrap over the plate. Silverware and napkin laid out perfectly and untouched.

My sleep-clouded mind couldn't make the connection. As I rubbed my eyes and walked over to the table for a closer look, I noticed a handmade card and the plate full of food. Hot food! I still didn't get it. Who put all of this here? As I picked up the card and flipped it over, I read the words in Allia's typical fashion:

> *"Happy late Father's Day! I know this is kinda' late,*
> *but hey? Let's face it, you weren't expecting it were you?"*

I sat down and in tears, ate the best breakfast of my life; the works! I keep that card in my office so I can see it every day and be reminded that things aren't always the way I think they are and neither are people. It keeps me tender and helps me stop and think before I charge into a situation like a bull in a china shop. When I remember that infamous non-Father's Day, I still shed a tear or two.

Over the years, my daughter has given me many Father's Day gifts and I really couldn't tell you what they were or where they are now. But that year, she gave me a gift I would treasure for the rest of my life.

Chapter Twenty-Four
The Move

Pulling tape across the last box, I sit down heavily on the floor. I've carted about fifty boxes out to the trailer and I'm bushed. It's moving day and time to embark on a new journey, stranger than ever. I gaze across the empty room. Life can be unbelievable.

As I stand, a single sheet of paper on the floor of the closet catches my eye. Stooping over I snatch it up, crumble it, and then jumping like a star basketball player, toss it across the room for a fantastic, complete miss of the trashcan. I stoop once again to scoop it up, but something makes me pause to unfold it. The writing is scratchy on the yellowing paper and almost twenty years old:

Echoes
The tears and fears of my little girl's world, the laughter,
joy and happy songs still ring within my ears.
From early morn to setting sun and then till late at dark.
She tippy toes through in and out the chambers of my heart.

Echoes of her proper words like 'mommy' all day long. And all the words that pierce my heart, her lilted singing song.
Tipping round the house she goes and reaches out to know. Yes if we make you say it nice or otherwise it's "No!"
Songs are sometimes sung along with Daddy and with Mom. This I know, and Strong, and So, but please don't suck that thumb.
Days on days skim quickly by. Oh how you grow as time does fly. Building memories in my little girl's mind as she echoes within this heart of mine.

Somehow my little girl grew up into a young woman. I still look at her in confusion and wonder, "Where did my daughter go?" It's the way of generations to gain and lose in happiness and sorrow while standing with one foot in the light and the other in the shadow. She isn't mine anymore and I feel a deep sadness at the realization, but also a great hope and joy for her as well.

As I carry the last box out into the sunlight and stuff it in the trailer, I'm momentarily blinded and squint against the brightness. Turning to look at the home we've lived in for the past fourteen years, I feel a bit of sadness at leaving it behind, yet happiness for the future. It's never easy in this world, but I've learned that in all aspects of life, there is much to learn and always an opportunity to pass something good on to someone else. As I take one last look around, I think back on events of the past few years.

Along the way, Mom and Dad grew old. Dad survived lung cancer, and Mom survived colon cancer. At some point he couldn't walk in the woods any more or hunt or fish, and I think that was the day his spirit died. A few years prior, he had a hard time getting around but had the opportunity to go over to Africa on a Big Game Hunters' trip. I remember Mom's conversation in the kitchen.

"Mom, you've got to be kidding! Why wouldn't you and Dad take this once in a lifetime chance to go on this trip?"

Mom doesn't look up from washing some dishes in the sink. "We just don't want to spend what would eventually be part of your brother's and your inheritance on an expensive trip."

Looking back, I wonder how much of that was really my mom's edict. On the one hand she seemed so reserved and subservient; just wanting to please people and do for them. She was a real old-style southern belle. But I learned that when she made up her mind, that was the end of the conversation.

I talk to Dad about the Africa trip and he has the same story as Mom plus he adds that he has trouble walking too far. But there would be assistance there and they could do it. After a conversation with my brother, I sit mom and dad down in the living room and turn off the television. Our roles are curiously reversed as I speak to them.

"Curtis and I have talked about it, and we want you to take this trip. It's probably your last chance for something like this, and you have a short window of time to do this. We really want you to go, no matter what the cost. If you need help, then we'll help you."

They wouldn't allow us to help bear the cost, but they did go. Dad managed to bag a big kudu and had it mounted and shipped back to hang on the wall. The horns were so long it had to be mounted half way down the wall, but he was so proud of bagging that kudu. It was their first time out of the country, and they both had a great time. We were all glad they gave in and did it.

Dad surprised me now and then as well. Like the time he waited while we fished so Allia could catch her first fish. The time he reprimanded me about being rude to one of his hunting buddies. He never allowed me to back talk Mom although he always let me have my say. I just had to be respectful.

Young fell on difficult times with a business she opened so she ends up living at, where else, my mom and dad's home while she gets back on her feet. After 14 years, we begin to talk to each other again. At first we talk about her business and then gradually the talk dissolves into conversation about us. Relationships that seem to go nowhere, the emptiness of a party life, loneliness at the end of it all. One particular evening we finish talking and I start to leave.

"Conner, wait. There's something I want to say to you."

We're in Young's room. She sits Asian-style on a blanket on the floor with a pillow on her lap — a tradition she hasn't overcome in spite of a multitude of chairs.

Turning from the door, I cock my head in a questioning manner.

"This probably isn't the greatest time to ask you this because of my situation, but I think you know me well enough that I wouldn't suggest this just because of my circumstances."

I'm truly baffled at where she is going with this. Young is definitely a woman of few words. She rarely talks about her feelings and explains herself even less, so this is unusual.

"You know, it's taken me a long time to come to this point to understand how much I really love you. I know that I've hurt you more than you can ever say, and I really don't deserve for you to forgive me."

My thoughts begin to reel. What is she saying? I look at her face but she's looking down; her now short-cropped hair covering her cheeks. A tear drops and stains the pillow in her lap.

Slowly, she raises her head to look me straight in the eyes, another uncommon action as Korean custom considers it rude to look another person in the eye. "The first time you asked me, but now I'm asking you. Conner, will you marry me?"

The earth and heavens seem to move, and the floor shifts beneath my feet. Questions run through my mind in a split second: Marry her? Can I trust her? Will she leave again? Will we end up divorced a second time? Am I willing to take a chance? What will people think? What will my parents say? What will Allia say?

I'm stunned by the immediacy of it all. How I would have longed for something like this twelve or fourteen years ago. But now? Allia is all grown up and capable of sustaining herself. She needed us together when she was five, not at nineteen. For that matter, I needed us together during the last fourteen years. It has been a difficult and tiring journey, and now I'm in my mid forties.

Uncertainty and fear wash over me like the waves of a stormy sea. "Young, why now after all these years, after Allia's all grown up and ready to go out on her own? You want to get back together now?"

She squares her shoulders and brushes her tears with a stroke of her hand. "Wall…"

She always pronounces the word 'well' as 'wall'. It's one of the endearing things l love about her. I also know that when she squares her shoulders and starts off with, 'Wall,' that she's about to launch into a well thought out defense. Young never makes casual decisions; they are forged in the fire of careful thought and planning. She didn't just say this on the spur of the moment.

"Wall, neither of us is getting younger. Plus, Mom and Dad are getting to the point where they need more care and help. It's better for us all if we marry again. They made me part of this family the moment I came over here, and they've never taken it back. I owe them everything. It's better to grow old with someone you love than be alone by yourself."

She looks down at her hands and gives a wry smile. "You know I never say sorry. I make a decision and stick with it to the bitter end. I'm still not convinced it was a mistake that we divorced. I needed time to get my head on straight. I think you needed it, too. But I am sorry for hurting you and for hurting Allia, and Mom and Dad for that matter. I really respect that you did everything possible to be a good Dad to Allia and to stabilize her life. Plus, you never put me down or tried to get back at me. I don't know what you said to your friends but at least to me, you never put me down."

She puts out a hand so that I can help her to her feet. When I reach down to grasp her, she remains sitting but doesn't let go. "If you just feel sorry for me or something, then say 'No.' I won't hold it against you. But if you still love me like I love you, then marry me again."

The truth is: I don't know. This is so out of the blue, I can't process the risk versus the gain. My mind goes back to a day fourteen years ago.

It was about three months after the divorce. As I fixed dinner, I heard a knock at the door. I opened it and in came Young. It was the middle of the week so she couldn't be here to pick up Allia.

Allia heard her mom's voice and came running in. "Hooray! Mom came for dinner."

I thought, *Oh great, now what do I do?* But I needn't have worried about it.

Young gave Allia a big hug. "Allia, I can't stay for dinner but can you give Dad and me a few minutes to talk?"

As Allia ran into her room to play, I looked at Young, puzzled. This was somewhat out of character for her to want to engage me in a serious conversation.

Suddenly she collapsed to her knees in front of me, bowed down and grabbed me by the feet. I was taken completely off guard.

"Conner, please let me come back home. I miss Allia. Please let me come back home."

Stunned, I could only stand there with my mouth hanging open. What I didn't realize at the time is that this gesture was a Korean expression of surrender.

I've often thought back on that day. What would have happened if we had tried again? Would we have continued to go through the same struggles only to end up in the same situation, eventually divorced? Would it simply have prolonged the agony?

"Conner? Did you hear me?"

I guess somewhere in my heart I half expected this day to come, because I hear myself reply, "Yes," without hesitation; well, a little hesitation. It's a chance, a risk, but one I am apparently willing to take. "So what do we tell Mom and Dad?"

In her typical style, she takes me by the hand, drags me out to the living room where my dad and mom are watching a football game on the tube. My heart beats like I'm a teenager again.

Young interrupts the game and gestures to me. "Mom. Dad. Mitch has something to say."

My mouth falls open. Me? I look at her but she's looking at Mom and Dad with a big smile on her face. They look at me. Dad grabs the remote and mutes the sound. Mom's favorite clock on the wood shelf by the fireplace ticks like a metronome.

"Ahh, well. It's ahh…"

Dad's looking at me like I'm an alien and he can't quite figure out if I'm there peaceably. Mom glances from Young to me then gestures as if to say, "Well?"

Dad finally breaks the ice. "Come on, Mitch. Spit it out and say whatever it is."

"Ahh, well, Young and I are going to get married." Then, not knowing what else to say I add, "Again."

Dad claps his hands and jumps to his feet faster than I've seen him move in years. "Well, congratulations. It's about time!"

He goes over to hug Young with Mom right behind. Then he grabs me and, for the first time I can ever remember, gives me a big hug and says, "I'm really proud of you, Son, and I love you."

Mom's right behind with, "I'm so happy for you both."

I'm flabbergasted, and now it's my turn to stare at both Mom and Dad, with my mouth hanging open. I shake my head as my brain tries to process what I just heard.

Did he just say, "It's about time?" You mean all these years he figured we would get back together and he never said anything to me? Not one word of encouragement or suggestion? For fourteen years? Then suddenly he hugs me, tells me he's proud of me and he loves me? I've never heard him say such a thing, much less hug me. Now I feel as if *he's* the alien that suddenly dropped into the living room, sucked the life out of me and left me gasping for breath.

A little later Allia arrives after visiting a friend. We invite her into her mom's temporary bed-quarters and break the news to her, too. She looks at her mom in astonishment, then at me and I'm surprised to see a deep hurt in her face and eyes. Big tears roll down her face and she cries in big gasping breaths, but not for joy. Once again I'm stunned. After a few minutes, she manages to catch her breath.

"I can't believe you guys! All these years I needed you together and you stayed apart. Then when I'm grown and don't need you, you get back together. It isn't fair."

What a night! I feel exhausted. I thought my parents would be reserved and cautious, but they are thrilled. I thought Allia would be thrilled, and she's hurt. My mind and emotions feel as if I've been poured out of a blender on high-speed puree.

Allia doesn't say much on the drive home and immediately goes to her room. Over the years I've learned to give people space to mull over things, and so I let her alone to process the thoughts of her heart.

As I sit on the floor of the living room, I laugh myself to tears. Then I can't tell if I'm laughing or crying and somewhere in between. Finally, I fall asleep and wonder if it all was just a long, long dream.

That was a few weeks ago. Now, as I stand by the trailer, I smile again at the thought of it all. With the house all packed up, Young and I are ready to embark on a new journey. I'm not sure where we will end up but I don't doubt it will be the ride of my life.

Chapter Twenty-Five
Legacy of the Rose

The phone rings me awake from a dead sleep and my heart is pounding. The events of yesterday have mixed with my dreams and I'm confused as to where I am. The phone keeps ringing and I can't find it.

There is sudden silence. I pause to determine the location of the last ring. In a moment it starts again. Finally I find it in the sofa cushion. My thumb hits the green lighted Answer button and I mumble, "Yeah?"

"Mitch, this is mom. I'm sorry to bother you so late but Dad fell in the bathroom and I couldn't help him get back up. The ambulance just came and they are going to take him to the hospital. Can you meet us at St. John's? We are leaving in a minute."

"Okay, Mom. Let me get some clothes on, and Young and I will meet you there."

Dad's been having a hard time getting around lately. He's fallen before and bruised himself, but nothing that required a trip to the hospital. I wish I had asked for more information but we need to get there as soon as possible.

Time drags by in the Emergency Room as Dad goes through different scans and tests. After several hours of waiting, the staff announces he has a slight concussion and high levels of ammonia. Luckily nothing is broken and they discharge him. At home we manage to get him up the steps and into bed, but its clear that the tables have turned and Mom is going to need additional help.

That was four years ago. After that incident, Dad acted strangely. Although he had a concussion from the fall, there was supposed to be nothing wrong. He started complaining about everything Mom did, yelled at her, called her names, and even accused her of trying to poison him. The last straw was when he tried to run her down with his handicap scooter.

Mom can't take care of him any longer. He's in the hospital again and we all gather for a family meeting with one of the hospital eldercare workers. She talks frankly to Mom, but addresses all of us. "You have to make a choice as to whether Mr. Conner is going to go home this time or transfer to a higher care facility."

Mom pipes up, not mincing words. "You mean put him in an 'old folks' home."

The eldercare worker is used to resistance. "I mean a skilled nursing facility where your husband can regain his strength and get the therapy he needs to go back home."

When mom gets something in her mind, she doesn't back down. "I'm not sending him off to the farm. I can still take care of him just fine."

Dad puts in his two cents worth of humor, "The Farm? I'll be glad to go to the farm. Let's all go to the farm." He starts to sing "Old McDonald Had a Farm" under his breath as if he's just as happy as can be.

Mom gives him a tense look, with a definite edge to her voice as if she's clinging to the face of a cliff. "Don't have to worry about me,

I'm fine, I'm just fine."

This is the fifth hospital visit in the last three months. We cajole, we reason, we explain — all to no avail. After the next bad fall, both Mom and Dad finally agree to move into my brother's house so at least they have some help. It only lasts a few months until Dad takes a particularly bad fall and is delirious and uncontrollable. This time the social worker is less accommodating.

"Here is a list of skilled nursing facilities. We can only discharge him to skilled nursing."

Dad is relegated to the "old folks factory," a term he explains as being a factory in reverse. Instead of creating old folks, it eats them up. His days there are chaotic. Sometimes, he's as nice as can be and others, he is a handful for the staff. On my daily late afternoon visit the social worker gives me the news.

"Mr. Conner is just about at the cutoff of his Medicare coverage. We can transfer him to the Medicaid facility, but it's a step down from where he is now. However, it does cost quite a bit less."

I go to Dad's room where he's taking a nap. It's a nice semi-private room, but pricey. With Medicare footing most of the bill, it's affordable. Without Medicare, he has to move to the other facility which is more of a hospital room setting and not as nice. He had asked me to prepare a power of attorney.

"Hi, Dad."

He looks up and nods his head.

"I brought the power of attorney for you to sign."

He suddenly sits up and shakes his head vigorously. "No way! What kind of trick are you trying to pull? I'm not signing that."

No amount of explanation pierces through the fog, so I put the paper on his nightstand. I can't help my frustration. "Look, Dad. You asked me to do this and it took a lot of time to get it done. Now you act like I'm trying to do something wrong. Here it is. Sign it if you want."

Then I turned and went home. The next afternoon, I'm in the middle of a meeting when I get a call from the nursing home staff.

"Excuse me, I need to take this call. Conner here."

I listen as the nurse describes the latest fiasco. "He's been sitting in his wheelchair all day at the nurses' station, demanding that we call him a taxi to take him up to his place in the country. So we put him in one of our transportation vans and drove him to the other entrance and he was okay for a while. But he didn't sleep last night and hasn't eaten or taken anything orally all day. Now he's trying to throw things through one of the glass windows and won't go back to his room. He's dehydrated and we really need to get him to the hospital, but he refused to go in the ambulance and they couldn't calm him down enough to restrain him."

Closing my eyes to clear my thoughts, I shake my head. The meeting will have to wait. Fortunately the facility is only minutes from where I work.

"Ok, I'll be right over."

When I arrive, Young, Allia, and Mom are already there Every time someone tries to move Dad, he plants his feet and hands against the doorway like a cat. We can't budge him. Then he tries to grab something and throw it through the window.

We make the mistake of turning away to discuss options. He removes the footrest from his wheelchair and hurls it at the window. Fortunately, the window doesn't break but enough is enough.

There's no reasoning with him, and I grudgingly agree to distract him while they give him a shot to calm him down. It works, but he looks at me like I stabbed him with a sword. He snarls, "How could you do this to me?"

In spite of the injection, he still manages to fight the ambulance team for a while. By the time we get to the hospital, he is pretty well out of it. Turns out he has a bladder infection and high ammonia levels which account for some of the confusion and fighting. The kind staff admit him again.

Later that night, after a day's infusion of fluids and antibiotics, Young is able to feed him a bit. He even jokes with the nurses, seemingly oblivious to the just past events. I get the call about five o'clock in the morning.

"Mr. Conner, this is one of the nurses from St. Johns. Last night your father suffered a major event, and we don't think he's going to survive. We can take him to critical care and put him on life support, but your mom indicated yesterday that wasn't his desire. You should come quickly and bring the family."

We're there within the hour, standing around Dad's bed. Curtis, Mom, Allia, myself, and, of course, Young. He's intubated with oxygen and can't talk. I try to speak in his ear but he just turns away, perhaps still angry with me.

The nurse assigned to us comes into the room. "Last night about one thirty a.m. he suffered either a blood clot in his lung or a heart attack and possibly a stroke. We have him on a high rate of oxygen, because he was struggling to breathe. We think he can hear and understand what we are saying, but he can't respond. We'll give you a few minutes to say whatever you need to, then we'll start giving him morphine to ease his struggle to breathe. Within the next few hours, his heart rate and blood pressure will decrease until it reaches a critical state. I'll be right outside the door if you need me."

What do you say? What can you say? Whatever we wanted to say, should have been said years ago. I whisper in his ear that I love him and kiss him on the head like I kissed his father so many years before. Then we wait. An hour, two hours, four.

Mom and Curtis stand in the hall and talk about going downstairs for a smoke. I'm watching the machine that's tracking Dad's life. The heart rate has been around sixty for a while. It dips to fifty, then forty. "Mom! I think you'd better come in here."

The alarm sounds and the machine flat-lines.

Mom cries.

> Eras pass and no one sees.
> A flower blooms, a bird flies.
> The wind blows, and someone dies.

Stepping up to the podium, I look out on the small chapel. Mom didn't think even three people would show up, but there are over fifty. Looking at her now, I take my notes and fold them twice, stuff them in my pocket and begin to speak.

"My dad never held a political office. He was never famous. He never sought out any recognition for himself. I've never seen him do anything dishonest to another person or cheat in any way, even on his taxes. Dad really cared about people. He inherited a natural sales ability from his dad and he could easily talk people into doing whatever he wanted, and even make them like it. But he never used that against people. His ability was well used in the field of investigation, and most of his working career was as an insurance investigator. He went around and made sure people were really as disabled as they stated.

"He and my mom were and are unbelievably generous, even when they had little themselves. They would never kick someone who was down, but they wouldn't just walk away either. My dad always held out a helping hand to those in need.

"After he retired, he worked as a salesman at Best Buy. Electronics was something he liked to play around with, and he was a great salesman because he liked people. After that, his health started to decline. Yet again, he took it in stride, and never really complained.

"When I left the Army, I brought a very special girl home with me. And you know, after you bring up two rough and tumble boys, you wonder what it might have been like to have a daughter. Well, Dad got his daughter because for both him and my mom, they never treated Young like anything other than their own daughter — to this very day. It's a little odd being married to a girl that my mom and dad treat like my sister.

"In the Conner family, no girl had been born in many generations. But my daughter would break that mold as my mom and dad became Granpappy and Gramcracker. So they had the great joy of helping to raise a daughter: their granddaughter. Again my dad came out smelling like a rose. He was just crazy about his granddaughter and her mom.

"My dad was a man of honor. He voluntarily served in the military during World War II. But more than that, he taught my brother and me to live honorably in everything we do, and in his own words, to be lovable, kind, patient, peaceable, good, faithful, gentle, and self-controlled.

"In the end, I can't really honor my dad without honoring my mom. They were married for sixty four years, and that's really something in these days when divorce is so prevalent. I can truly say they both lived their lives for my brother, my daughter, Young and me. They gave up a lot of their own life so that we could have a great life.

"The greatest legacy that a person can leave to the next generation isn't money or property. Instead it is the values that live on in our children; those great and lasting values that ultimately make us great men and women. And now you know that the rest of the story lies within us. It lies within you and me to carry on the values that have been entrusted to us, and to successfully pass those values to the next generation. This is the Legacy of the Rose.

"At a football game, when the chips are down and your team makes it across the goal for a touchdown, people generally stand up and cheer. Both my dad and my mom have scored the winning goal, and I would like to invite you to give my dad and my mom a standing ovation, just as if you were at a football game."

Since we were in a chapel, I wasn't quite sure what to expect. But I will never forget what happened next. As I turned to my mom and began to applaud, everyone in that little chapel stood as one and gave her a thunderous ovation that lasted for several minutes.

Mom made it two more years. She moved in with us before

having to move into assisted living. I remember the day we moved her into a small assisted-living apartment. I helped her put her few belongings away. Unable to walk very well she sat on the bed.

As I finished up, she looked at me with a deep sadness.

"I guess this is where I'm going to die."

I didn't know what to say so I just held her while she wept.

Six months later, on a cold November day, my brother called me.

"Mitch, this is Curtis. Mom fell this morning and they took her to the hospital."

This wasn't earth shattering as she had fallen more times than I could count. "Okay, I'll come over after my meetings this morning."

"Actually, you should come now. The reason she fell was that she had an aortic rupture. Right now she's in a coma and she won't survive much longer."

We stood around the hospital bed once again. There was nothing to say that hadn't been said but we said it anyway. Then we bid farewell as she silently passed away from us.

It was a small private family funeral on a cold and blustery December morning. I felt she deserved more but I didn't have the strength to do it. I did it for my dad's funeral to honor her. My dad didn't care. But I knew she would. Now she didn't care and there was no one left to honor. As I went through her things, I found a note she had typed on the computer in the early morning hours before she died. It was dated November thirtieth at two a.m.

Dear God,
>I'm in a lot of pain these days and I'm pretty well useless. My legs are swollen, my knees and back hurt really bad. I can't get around anymore. My family put me away in this place. I don't have much left. Seems I spent my whole life taking care of others. Now there's no one left to take care of me. So if you could go ahead and let me die now, I think I'm ready.

The next morning she died. Our last phone conversation that morning had been terse. I was in a meeting and she was trying to talk about her finances and… It just wasn't a good time to talk.

I never really know when God is going to speak to me. Sometimes I pray and pray with nary a break in the frozen silence. Maybe get mad and stomp out of the room, vowing that it's useless and what good does it do because God doesn't listen anyway.

Then, when I least expect it, a still small voice pierces the darkness and I see something that was hidden all the time. And that little something changes my whole outlook. The heavy chains fall off, and it's a bit shocking because I forgot I was wearing them.

This past year, I have carried around the guilt of Dad's death. All he wanted was to go up to the country and visit his place one last time. Was that such a big deal? Couldn't I have taken a couple of days to do that for him? Then there was the argument over the power of attorney. The worst of it was providing a distraction while they hit him with a knockout shot. I'll never forget the look in his eye when he felt I betrayed him. Then there was my last conversation with mom.

A couple of month's go by and I feel guilty. We sit around the dining room table one night; Allia, her fiancé, and I. Young is in the kitchen making some food. Suddenly Allia pipes up out of the blue with a life changing statement.

"You know, it was a real miracle the way Grandpa passed away."

I look at her strangely. With no context for this statement, I feel as if the oxygen has been sucked out of the room.

"What do you mean, Allia?"

"Well, the way it happened. We were all with him when he passed. He could have died alone. Same with Grandma."

Later that night I sit alone and ponder many things. Allia's statement was just what I needed to hear to give me peace. It changed my outlook from one of guilt to one of thankfulness. Allia didn't know how I felt. What made her say that; especially so completely out of place with our conversation? Are we just lucky in life or is there something more? Everyone called Dad lucky and they even gave him an award that said, "Like a Rose Award for Kit Conner." He always seemed to come out of every situation 'smelling like a rose'. People look at my life and call me blessed. Is it simply the 'Conner Luck' — all coincidence and no purpose to life? I'm not here to argue the existence of something more than our lonely lives here on earth. But there are things that go farther than coincidence.

When I go out my front door and find a fresh-cut rose lying there, maybe the first time doesn't impress me. Could be an accident. The second time makes me wonder. The third time, I look around but no one is there. When it happens time and time again, I start to think there's something more than chance at work.

In the course of life, sometimes I face grave situations. It may seem I am alone with no rescue. When all appears dark, it helps if I stop and listen. I may hear the still, small voice of God. I may find the darkness lightens up around me. I may feel the light, comforting touch of His hand on my head...

Perhaps I will see that I stand on solid ground. I may even learn to fly.

Epilogue

The Visit

Sitting across the desk from the pastor, I'm reminded of my short encounter with the brigade command sergeant major who helped me out so many years ago. Towering height, older but still strong, tough, with short-cropped jet white hair and an imposing character. He's the kind of person you know you don't want to mess around with. But when you meet him, there's an incredible kindness and empathy. You initially expect him to speak down to you with gruffness. But he doesn't. He stopped what he was doing and took time out of his busy schedule to listen and help me.

My previous encounter with the pastor was almost 25 years ago and, amazingly, he doesn't appear to have aged even a day. I'd like to know the secret to that. Back in those days, I was desperately searching anywhere for help. My marriage and relationship with Young was falling apart and I wanted someone... anyone... to put it all back together again and make everything okay.

The pastor didn't make everything okay, but he gave me that piece of advice I've never forgotten. In fact, I think it's the only thing he said during the hour I was there.

Most of that time was spent as I tried to explain the situation and all of the things I had gone through, how Young wanted a divorce and she was doing this and that and some other thing.

He let me talk for a while then suddenly interrupted me by standing up, extending his hand, and saying, "Thanks for sharing that with me. I hope everything works out for you."

As I unwillingly stood up, I was stunned and, I suppose, a little hurt. "Aren't you going to help me?"

Looking at me with kindly patience he replied, "I can't help you, Mitch. I can only give you some advice, if you want it."

As he came around the desk to escort me out, I didn't know what to say. Without waiting for my reply, he put a fatherly arm around me, and, as he walked me to the door, he gave me that famous advice: "Go home and love your wife the best you possibly know how, or can, with everything that lies within you. No matter how you are treated, be kind, don't turn your offense into a weapon against her, curb your tongue, and love her."

Then he looked me in the eye, shook my hand and I was standing in the parking lot trying to make sense of it all. I had expected him to commiserate with me and pull a magic pill out of his desk that would make me feel better. Maybe even give me something to slip to Young to wipe all of this desire to leave right out of her mind.

But all he did was leave me with the burden of action to do something that was entirely against my human nature: love her, be kind to her, serve her. Was he crazy? How was I supposed to do that? What kind of stupid advice was that?

As I think about that first encounter with this pastor, I suddenly realize he is staring at me as if waiting for a response. My face feels hot and I stammer, "I'm sorry, what did you just say? I was thinking of something else."

Nodding slightly, he smiles and says, "I was just asking what you thought about that."

Normally I would try to cover the fact that I heard nothing of what he just said but he's given me no clue as to what he was talking about so it seems futile anyway.

"Actually I didn't hear anything you just said."

"What do you think about my advice to you the last time we met?"

How in the world could he possibly remember that from over twenty-five years ago? Maybe he has a file on me or something.

"I did what you suggested as best I could, and it did help me to feel better about the situation. I've come to appreciate that advice maybe more than anything anyone has ever said to me."

He doesn't nod with satisfaction or pander me with small talk. "What brings you back to see me today?"

So I launch into this explanation of what is bothering me now. "I guess I'm struggling to figure out how to be happy. There's so much going on with work, social events, church, our new house, resolving mom's estate and her house, writing a book. I'm really exhausted."

As I pause to take a breath, he laughs. "I'm laughing because that's a lot going on for anyone and then you're surprised at feeling exhausted and perhaps depressed? You could probably go on for an hour and still not explain it all. What is it you really want to know?"

"Why am I so frustrated with everything? I don't want to feel like this. When Young and I divorced it felt as if she had dropped my fragile glass heart on the ground and shattered it into a million pieces. Eventually, Young and I did end up back together and you would think that this is the fairy tale ending I so much wanted and we should be so happy. Why do I feel so terrible?"

The tears sneak out before I realize it. My mind wanders back home where I'm reminded of the behavior of one of our dogs. He is a big German Shepherd. A hundred and five pounds! When he was a puppy, we went to the pet store and bought a cage for him. Anticipating the end result of his size, we purchased the largest cage they made. This was where he grew up, sleeping in his cage.

Eventually, after he was trained, we left the cage door open for him to come and go as he pleased. You would think that, with the whole house at his leisure, he would lie down in open spaces on one of his nice rugs or on the cool wood floor, but no. Invariably, he finds his way back to his now cramped cage and lays down in it with a big contented sigh. He has to curl up to fit, so why? Why try to fit in a cage that's really too small? Because it is familiar and there is something about it that makes him feel at home.

Me, too. Over the years, I've been in and out of my own cage. The door is wide open. To escape, all I have to do is take a deep breath, step through the open door and I'm free of it. But in a sense, I die. No longer a helpless child, I have to grow up and take responsibility, give up my self-centered thinking, realize it's not about me anymore. Maturity requires that I make the attempt to understand other people better than myself. To hear their point of view and help them achieve their potential. It's an impossible task. Some days it really is easier to go back to my familiar cage and behave in my self-centered ways.

The pastor stands up and I'm drawn back from my thoughts to reality and his office where I realize I've been looking down at the floor. Did I say all of that or just think it in my mind? He comes around the desk; an indication that our session is over. As I stand he puts an arm around my shoulder and guides me to the door.

As I drive to Mom's house to clean it one last time before the sale, I try to clear my confusion. Our session ends and I never feel complete. I'm expecting some exposition that will magically heal my struggle. His advice today was no different now than it was those many years ago.

As we approached the door, he placed his large hand on my head like a father would a child and looked me in the eye.

"Mitch, Mitch. You are concerned about many things. You see the faults of other people, but have no compassion for them or yourself. Go home and love your wife and the people around you the best you can. Love and be kind. Don't worry about all the little irritations. Serve in every way you can without any strings attached. When everything is said and done, at least you'll know you did the best you could."

Pulling up to Mom's house I park at the curb. As I open the door, a black pickup roars by, horn blaring. It momentarily stuns me into shock as I hear the muffled screams of the driver fading into the distance as it disappears down the road. I have to laugh. I could be that driver, all up in a tizzy about nothing.

Suddenly, everything the pastor said seems to fall into place like the pieces of a puzzle. Other people aren't the problem. My attitude is causing my frustration and struggle. It's my responsibility.

The front door is sticking like it always has and is hard to push open. Suddenly, an agonizing pain grips my chest. The door opens and I half fall through it. Taking in ragged breaths, I look down to regain my step and freeze. Someone is standing there. I look up and gasp. It's a younger version of… me. But it's not me and that is confirmed as he looks at me in his typical, all knowing, way. His voice is the same as it was so many years ago.

"Mitch, there isn't much time. Follow me."

The house begins to vibrate from an oncoming train. My dad turns and walks down a hallway. When I step through the door, I see Grandma and Grandpa Conner waving like crazy as a brilliant light surrounds me and I'm filled with peace once again.

****

The Note

Young says:

I will say this about Conner and me. We have gone through a lot together and it took me a long time to get my head on straight. Both of us have said and done some really stupid things. I just want to be free of everything and everybody. Yet I could never get him out of my heart or my mind.

Having watched him over the past thirty years, I have to say that dreams really can come true. Somehow I found a guy who is so very loyal and who has stood by me and loved me even when I wasn't lovable. He is like a polished stones while I'm like the earth and rough stones, jagged and cutting. Now I finally realize that I adore him and really love him, too.

Conner says:

Life seldom works out like the fairy tale ending we dream of. After the curtain falls, life is harder still as we can cause and receive much heartache and pain. Yet it is often those fiery trials and pressure that form us into something beautiful. Young may not realize it, but those rough stones to which she compares herself are really like the facets of a brilliant and beautiful diamond. It just depends on your point of view. In spite of everything, she's found a place in my heart and I love her and greatly respect her.

Don't forget to visit us at http://MemoirofaMan.com where the story continues...

About the Authors

H M Taylor

…is an Information Technology Engineer with a Masters in Information Management and has provided technical design and implementation consulting for fortune 500 companies. H lives in the Midwestern United States with his lovely wife, two large German Shepherds, and a multitude of fish; but not for eating.

Andrea H Taylor

…is an illustrator, designer, creator, and performer. She works primarily in the field of children's book publishing, and has appeared on both stage and screen. Andrea shares her studio with her two cats, Max and Samurai, as well as her Shiba Inu, Hige.

Thank you for taking time out of your life to read and consider these things. We hope you enjoyed the story.

A Farewell Poem

My mind is thought to think at times of mom and then of dad
Of how life ends before it starts, old timers, lasses, lads.
The lives of men and ladies dance and work their lives away
And then before we know it well, the piper all do pay.

I've stood before that open door and wondered what the gain
To hunt and fish, to love and wish for more or lessor pain.
And yet I've seen the beauty of a life, or two or three
Have come to know its grave affects on others and on me

So as we part these final words, the memoirs of a friend
The lives of those around you is the garden to attend
For roses do not oft-while bloom among the weeds and trash
It takes a special care of love — a legacy to last

In Memory of
Kit & Jo Taylor
Jo Taylor 1928 - 2012
Kit Taylor 1927 – 2010

What do you think?

Visit and tell us your thoughts and share your story at
http://MemoirofaMan.com

Made in the USA
Charleston, SC
07 April 2014